P9-DDF-339

THE TENDER YEARS

Janette Oke

The Tender Years

BETHANY HOUSE PUBLISHERS
MINNEAPOLIS, MINNESOTA 55438

The Tender Years

Cover by Dan Thornberg,
Bethany House Publishers staff artist.

Published by Bethany House Publishers
A Ministry of Bethany Fellowship, Inc.
11300 Hampshire Avenue South
Minneapolis, Minnesota 55438

Printed in the United States of America.

ISBN 1-55661-952-9 (cloth)

DEDICATION

For
Thomas
of Nappanee.

I have no way of knowing if you will
ever read this dedication
or have the assurance that it was
meant for you.
The years have passed quickly and
you now have reached manhood.
Be assured that I often think of you and
remember you in prayer.

Books by Janette Oke

*Another Homecoming**
Janette Oke's Reflections on the Christmas Story
The Matchmakers
Nana's Gift
The Red Geranium
*Return to Harmony**

CANADIAN WEST

When Calls the Heart · *When Breaks the Dawn*
When Comes the Spring · *When Hope Springs New*

LOVE COMES SOFTLY

Love Comes Softly · *Love's Unending Legacy*
Love's Enduring Promise · *Love's Unfolding Dream*
Love's Long Journey · *Love Takes Wing*
Love's Abiding Joy · *Love Finds a Home*

A PRAIRIE LEGACY

The Tender Years

SEASONS OF THE HEART

Once Upon a Summer · *Winter Is Not Forever*
The Winds of Autumn · *Spring's Gentle Promise*

WOMEN OF THE WEST

The Calling of Emily Evans · *A Bride for Donnigan*
Julia's Last Hope · *Heart of the Wilderness*
Roses for Mama · *Too Long a Stranger*
A Woman Named Damaris · *The Bluebird and the Sparrow*
They Called Her Mrs. Doc · *A Gown of Spanish Lace*
The Measure of a Heart · *Drums of Change*

DEVOTIONALS

The Father Who Calls · *Father of My Heart*
The Father of Love · *Faithful Father*

JANETTE OKE was born in Champion, Alberta, during the depression years, to a Canadian prairie farmer and his wife. She is a graduate of Mountain View Bible College in Didsbury, Alberta, where she met her husband, Edward. They were married in May of 1957 and went on to pastor churches in Indiana as well as Calgary and Edmonton, Canada.

The Okes have three sons and one daughter and are enjoying the addition of grandchildren to the family. Edward and Janette have both been active in their local church, serving in various capacities as Sunday school teachers and board members. They make their home near Calgary, Alberta.

PROLOGUE

Mama? Mama, why don't you sit down and rest some? You've been on your feet all day."

"Well, with the crowd we got us here, it's gonna take every pair of hands to be feedin' them." The soft chuckle that followed the statement answered more than the words did. Mother and daughter turned to survey the kitchen of bustling women. Marty glanced out the lace-covered window toward the yard spilling over with youngsters rushing about in near-frantic explosions of energy. From the back porch where Clark and his "boys" had gathered to reminisce came loud bursts of laughter. Someone must have shared another humorous family memory.

Marty smiled and squeezed Missie's arm. It was so good to have them all gathered. All home.

No, not all. Not everyone had been able to come. Why, had they *all* been there, Marty did not know where they would have put them. The Davis family had grown until it was "most an army," Clark liked to say, and Marty always nodded in silent and thankful agreement. God had been good to them.

Her reverie was cut short as Missie gently urged, "Mama—you just sit down over here and supervise from this corner chair. You'll be worn out come sundown."

Marty allowed herself to be led to the appointed chair and lowered herself carefully onto the padded seat. She *was* tired. Flushed from the warmth of the kitchen, she withdrew a cotton hankie from her apron pocket and wiped her brow. It was an unseasonably warm fall day. She was glad that there was no rain—or snow. But the heat did make it more difficult for those laboring to prepare the family dinner.

Again her eyes passed over the laughing, chattering group who filled her kitchen with their sweeping skirts and busy hands.

They were no longer children—her girls. All home. All, that is, except Nandry, one of their adopted. They had lost Nandry four years back. Marty still grieved to think about it. Neither daughter, Mary nor Jane, had married, so Nandry's family had not expanded beyond the two offspring. The girls—actually maiden women whom Marty still thought of as girls—now cared for their father, who had become somewhat strange since losing his wife of many years. The two women sent regrets that they would not be able to join the rest of the family for the gathering.

But Clae, Nandry's sister, was with them. Clae and her retired preacher husband, though Joe's health was not good. He looked pale and thin in Marty's thinking. She longed to keep him there and see if she could put some flesh on his bones, though Clae no doubt had already tried. She supposed that ministering to people, with their many needs and the complex times, was a hard job for any man. And Clae and Joe had not been without their own woes. One child lost to whooping cough at an early age, one grandson wayward and belligerent, causing his parents and grandparents a great deal of pain. But the others, and there were now fourteen family members in Clae's family, seemed to be doing fine. One son even had received high honors in his field of medical research.

Missie, who had moved to the large black stove to stir

the pot of simmering brown beans, had already marked her sixtieth birthday. Now a grandmother a number of times over and expecting her first great-grandchild, Missie did not look her years. The West had been good to Missie and her Willie. Clark joked that they had populated one county all on their own, and it was true that many of the ranches in their area were now run by sons and grandsons. One of "the boys" had taken over the homespread. Willie maintained, with a glint in his eyes and pride in his voice, that all he was allowed to do now was boring paper work.

But most of Missie's family members, thirty-seven in number, had not been able to make the long trip east. Only Willie and Missie and their Melissa—who had traveled all the way from the West Coast where she lived with her husband involved in coastal shipping—had come.

Marty could hear her son Clare's voice from the back porch, insisting that he was enjoying the chance to "put his feet up" since retirement. He had moved with his wife, Kate, from their farm into the little town nearby, letting Dack take over. Marty smiled as she thought about it. Why, she often wondered aloud to Clark, if he liked retirement so much, did he drive back and forth from town to the farm all the time just to "check things out"? Marty guessed that Clare's real reason for leaving the farm was Kate. She was badly crippled with arthritis, and had they remained on the farm she would have continued to plant her big garden and insist on carrying her "share of the load." Marty knew that Clare worried about Kate.

Clark and Marty were used to having Clare and Kate with their sons, Dan, Davey, Dack, and Stan and their families around for family gatherings. The sons and their seventeen offspring had not scattered far from home. But their daughter, Amy Jo, was another matter. She had moved to a large city on the West Coast so she could pursue her work in art. "The most beautiful city in the world," according to Amy Jo. Her rancher husband had retired, sold his spread, and dabbled in real estate while Amy Jo dabbled in oils. They had no family, but at times Marty was almost thankful. It would be so hard to have more grandchildren that she would never be able to meet.

Son Arnie and his wife, Anne, had also always lived nearby. Arnie kidded Clare about quitting work "to loaf." He insisted that Clare would be healthier and happier if he was out pitching hay or cleaning the barn. But Marty knew that Arnie understood the difficult choice Clare had made. She wished that Arnie himself didn't have to work so hard. He was getting a definite stoop to his shoulders. Arnie's family now totaled twenty-two. Silas, John, and Abe all worked area farms. Trudy and Anne Louise had also married farmers.

Clark and Marty's daughter Ellie and husband, Lane, had shared the trip home by train with Missie and Willie. None of their offspring, and there were now twenty-nine counting in-laws and little ones, were able to make the trip with them.

Ellie was still slim and lithe, though her once-golden locks had now turned a silvery white. Premature gray, she called it. But Missie smiled and teased that Ellie was old enough to have earned her gray hair, already being a grandmother. Ellie's family included nine grandchildren.

Luke, the Davises' youngest son, was their town's very busy physician. He had just built Abbie a new house. His office was now apart from his home, a fact that Abbie declared was only about twenty years late in happening. Poor Abbie had been subject to knocks on the door at all hours of the day and night. Their son Aaron had married a local girl and settled down to run the community's funeral parlor, a fact that caused a good many smiles of amusement and made Doc Luke and his mortician son the butt of many friendly jokes. Thomas had chosen to follow his father in medicine, so he was off getting his training. Daughter Ruth Ann married the town pharmacist, making another prime target for the local wits. "If ya go see Doctor Luke, he sends ya off to his son-in-law fer medicines, an' if thet don't work, ya end up his son's client," people ribbed, always seeming to think that the little joke was original with them. Georgia was a bookkeeper at the mayor's office, still single but much pursued. Clark maintained that she so enjoyed keeping the local young men in a tizzy that she would never settle on one of them. Luke and Abbie and their family had, over the years, been frequent visitors for Sunday dinner at the Davis family farmhouse. On this special occasion, only Thomas and his new bride were missing.

Belinda, Clark and Marty's last, had married Drew Simpson and also lived in the nearby town with her lawyer husband and five children. Having made her appearance in the family when Marty was past forty, Belinda was still considered a young woman, not yet having reached her own fortieth birthday. Her children, younger than the other cousins, had not been raised with the rest of the bustling pack but were young enough to be given special pampering by all the older cousins.

Belinda's Clara already had herself a beau. Marty silently hoped that the courtship would not move too quickly. There was no reason for Clara, only eighteen, to rush into the duties of homemaker. Rodney, following closely in age, was an industrious and capable student. His father, Drew, took great pleasure in the accomplishments of his eldest son. Virginia, named after the lady that Belinda long ago had nursed and come to love as dearly as a grandmother, was thirteen, followed by Daniel, age twelve. Belinda often quipped that she had her offspring in pairs, as close together as they could be without being twins. The final pair brought heartache as well as joy. They lost baby Pearl when she was two months old. No reason for the death was ever known, even after Luke had advised them to get the baby to a large city hospital where she could be given the best of care. Little Pearl never came home to them again. The next year Francine arrived, chubby and healthy and totally endearing. Belinda dried her tears and gave herself totally to caring for her baby. Francine, now seven, was still the darling of the family. Dimple-faced and tender-hearted, she often reminded Grandmother Marty of the little Belinda whom they had welcomed as a *tag-along* to the Davis family so many years ago.

"Mama, where's the ginger?"

The question brought Marty's attention back to the activity of the large farm kitchen. She had to stop and focus on the present. The ginger? Where did she keep the ginger?

"In the pantry. On the . . . the second shelf. To the right," she eventually was able to answer.

Ellie moved with graceful steps toward the pantry.

The kitchen door opened a crack, and Clark poked his head in. His once-dark hair was streaked with gray, and wrinkle lines marked out the place where smiles and frowns had furrowed his brow over the years, but his eyes still sparkled with good humor. "How long ya be temptin' poor hungry stomachs with all them fancy smells and nothin' to fill our plates?" he joked good-naturedly. "I don't know who's findin' the wait the hardest. Me or all those younguns."

Marty smiled at him and teasingly waved him back outside. "Look out or you'll be havin' yourself a job to do," she said as he quickly withdrew. She rose from her chair and crossed again to the window. All the "younguns" she observed looked totally occupied with what they were doing. Four young men played horseshoes out by the chicken coop. Younger versions raced about in a wild tag of their own making. Three little girls were being read to by an older cousin as the lawn swing rocked gently back and forth. Another little cluster, skirts spread, sat under branches of the maple, laps filled with kittens from a barn litter. Two lads were coming from the direction of the spring, pant legs rolled up, shoes strung over shoulders by their laces. One carried a pail. Marty wondered if it held frogs or turtles, or maybe even a garter snake. Another two dashed from the direction of the haystack, an egg held in each hand. Obviously they had discovered a hidden nest.

But off to the side, alone and withdrawn from all of the activity, was a solitary figure. She leaned rather listlessly against the trunk of an old apple tree, seemingly with no interest in the fruit that was maturing above her head. Marty's grandmother-heart went out to the girl. Virginia. Virginia, her newest teenager. Virginia with her perplexity of *becoming*. The transition from childhood to adulthood seemed to be particularly puzzling and difficult for the young Virginia. Marty's brow creased in a slight frown as she breathed a silent prayer. "God be with her. Help her to make it through." She felt a lump rise in her throat as a tear came to her eye. She reached for her hankie again. She had prayed for all her children and grandchildren over the years. Now it was for Virginia.

"Mama—we're ready. Abbie has gone to ring the dinner bell."

Marty turned and swallowed away any remnants of tears. She would not weep. Not on her eightieth birthday. Oh, not actually the birthday—the family had needed to choose a day that would work for everyone's convenience—but her eightieth year. Imagine that. Eighty. Eighty and so blessed. Reasonable health. A wonderful family. And Clark. She still had Clark. So many women her age were widows now. She was so thankful to still have her Clark.

"We have your spot all reserved," Anne was saying. "We've set the tables up in the shade of the trees. We want you right in the middle—with Pa there beside you."

Marty nodded and took Anne's arm. "Virginia," she said suddenly. "I'd rather like Virginia to sit on my other side."

. . . This is Virginia's story.

CHAPTER 1

It was silly to hasten her footsteps now. She was already so late getting home from school that quickening her pace on the final half-block toward the big white house on the corner would avail nothing. Still, she could not hold back the agitation that now sent her rushing headlong toward home.

"Late again, missie?" came a raspy voice from beyond the picket fence to her right.

Her steps faltered. Her head began to nod in agreement even before her eyes picked out old Mr. Adamson in the shadows of his gnarled apple tree. Often her gaze found him rocking gently in the chair on his front porch.

She couldn't just hurry on by. That would be rude. She turned toward his fence and watched as the old gentleman brushed at his soiled pants with a dirt-stained hand and creaked to an upright position. His faded eyes peered at her from beneath his sweat-rimmed hat.

She placed two hands on the pickets and drew closer to the yard.

"Should you be out in your yard yet, Mr. Adamson?" A frown drew her feather-light brows together. "The ground is still near frozen. You'll ruin your gimpy knees for sure kneeling in the cold. Look there. Still snow where it's drifted in."

Her gentle scolding only brought a smile to the old man, showing stained teeth where teeth still remained. But a twinkle gave life to the tired eyes.

"Sound jest like yer mama," he responded good-naturedly. "Ya gonna be a nurse when you grow up, too?"

She shook her head, and brown curls tumbled over her shoulders. No. She had no plans to be a nurse. Nursing was too, too filled with bad things. Bad smells. Bad pain. Bad duties. She had no plans on being a nurse. If she was going to be anything—anything in medicine, that is—she'd rather be a doctor like her uncle Luke. A doctor got to give the nastiest jobs to the nurse. Doc Luke got to fix broken limbs and take out tonsils and give out medicines. Maybe it wouldn't be so bad to be a doctor.

But she quickly dismissed that idea as well. She didn't think she'd care to be a doctor, either.

The elderly man straightened bent shoulders as far as they could be forced and worked his mouth. She knew he was getting prepared to switch the conversation. He always worked his mouth that way before words actually came out.

"So—what you gonna tell yer mama this time?" he finally asked in a hushed, conspiratorial tone.

She hesitated. She could not help but wonder again how he knew so much about her. How he seemed to even read her inner thoughts. Trina Hughes, a schoolmate from down their street, said the old man was spooky. She also said that he was the filthiest person in town. Trina did not stop and talk to him, even if he was a neighbor. "It's disgusting," exclaimed Trina. "That's what it is. How could one go from being well-kept and proper to living like a hermit? I don't think he ever bathes or washes his clothes."

Virginia thought of Trina's words now as she looked at their old neighbor. She knew he was different since Mrs.

Adamson had died. Her mama said the poor old fellow was desperately lonely. But Trina, when presented with that argument, had stated flatly that lots of people lost mates. That didn't mean they had to turn into dirty pigs.

Virginia had to acknowledge that Mr. Adamson did not care for himself. She had seen him in the same multi-stained plaid shirt for the last several weeks, and his pants looked stiff with dirt and stains. Were they really too stiff to fall into a normal heap on the floor? Trina suggested that he had to lay them down on their side when he took them off at night—or else lean them up against a wall.

She looked at the dirty pants now. Damp spring garden soil had been layered over the dirt of the past. The old man seemed totally oblivious to it. He did not attempt further to brush it off. A glance up at his face reminded her that he was still waiting for her answer. She swallowed. The excuse she had for being late now sounded foolish. Even to her own ears. What would her mother have to say about it?

"I was . . . with Jenny," she managed, brown eyes looking down in embarrassment.

"Jenny? Thet little fire-headed gal who is always gigglin' over some fool thing?"

Virginia nodded. That was one way one might describe her friend Jenny.

"An' what were the pair of you up to this time?" he asked candidly.

"We . . . ah . . . a couple friends had nickels. We went to The Sweet Shop."

He stepped closer and placed his own hands on the pickets. His voice dropped, as though entering into a conspiracy. "Sodas?"

She nodded again. Her carefully fashioned excuse was crumbling before her very eyes. Her mama would not find sodas a good reason to be late from school. Her mama saw afternoon sodas as a destroyer of supper appetites as well as making one late for after-school chores. Chores that would still need doing. And time was quickly passing. Each moment that she lingered with the elderly man meant another minute ticked off on the large grandfather clock that stood in the hall.

"Cherry?"

"No," she said slowly. "We had chocolate, and Jenny had . . . had strawberry."

He passed a tongue over dry lips. "Vanilla's always been my favorite. Others like all them fancy flavors, but there ain't nothing like vanilla. Deep and rich and jest plain."

"I should go. Mama will—"

"Of course. Of course."

He waved a dirt-covered hand in the air and turned back to his soggy flower bed. Virginia moved away from the fence. She was really going to be in trouble. The added moments wasted in conversation had made her even later.

But before leaving she turned to the man once more. "You really shouldn't be kneeling in the cold," she cautioned gently. "You'll not be walking at all if you keep that up."

For one moment he seemed to contemplate her warning. Then he waved it aside as he would brush at a pestering fly. "Garden's the only thing I got," he told her. "Once they take that from me—won't be no reason to go on a'tall. Been waiting all winter to git back to the diggin'. See things grow. Look there. See thet little viola. Already bloomin' and the snow jest melted from off its little face. Brave little souls—violas. Some years they even beat the crocuses."

"Well, maybe you could find something to kneel on," Virginia suggested as she turned reluctantly away from the strange old man. She had to hurry home.

Fear filled her being, and in spite of her hurrying feet her heart lagged. What would her mother say? It was the latest she had ever been, and she had been scolded before, many times, for tardiness. But this. This was different. It was the first time a boy had ever invited her to share a soda. It would have been *unthinkable* to turn him down. After all, she was no longer a child. She had turned thirteen on her last birthday and was now moving, though it did seem at times slowly, toward birthday fourteen. Even her papa said that she was growing up. It was only her mama who acted as though she still needed constant parental supervision. Surely she should be able to do something on her own. Surely she didn't need to account for every waking moment.

She was almost to the gate before she thought of her old neighbor again. Her mama did not view Mr. Adamson as did the snobbish Trina. Her mama was always kind, gentle, and neighborly with the old man. If she, Virginia, forgot about the soda excuse and just said that she had been visiting with Mr. Adamson, might her mama be more forgiving? The very idea took a little of the slump from her shoulders. It would not be a lie. She *had* visited with Mr. Adamson. But it wouldn't be all of the truth, either—and her mama and papa were sticklers for the truth. What if she said she was late because she was visiting Mr. Adamson, and then someone else, like nosy Mrs. Parker, were to inform her mother that she had seen her with Freddie Crell in The Bright Side Sweet Shop sharing a soda? Then there would *really* be trouble.

No, it was best to be up-front and honest from the very beginning. Besides, even if she did get away with it with Mama, and she doubted that she would, there was still the matter of her own conscience to deal with. Virginia knew she would have a difficult time living with deceit.

As she entered the yard and swung around the walk to the back door, her shoulders slumped again and her steps lagged. Were boys really worth it, she began to wonder, when one had to pay such a price for their company and attention? But they'd had fun. They had laughed at silly jokes. Mostly, Jenny had laughed. Giggled, Mr. Adamson had called it. She, Virginia, had tried to sound a little bit like Jenny with her high-pitched, boisterous laughter.

And Freddie had said that Virginia had cute freckles. How could one have cute freckles? But that's exactly what Freddie had said. It made her face flush again just thinking about it. And they had talked about school. Even leaned close together and whispered some *unnice* things about the teacher and laughed because no one had caught them and scolded them for the comments. It had been fun. But now—she was in trouble. She knew that before she even opened the back door.

The inner door to the kitchen was open, only the screen door was snugly in place. For a moment her hand rested on the handle. She could smell the pleasing aroma of fresh-baked cookies. Likely Clara had been at it again. It seemed to Virginia that all Clara liked to do was bake. Bake and make eyes at Troy Dunworthy. She hoped with all her heart that she would not meet Clara in the kitchen. Meeting Clara would be even worse than meeting her mama. Clara could be so bossy. So nosey. For the umpteenth time she wished that Clara would just up and marry her Troy and get her own house. It was not easy living with Clara.

She peered through the screen door. The kitchen was empty. The counter was spread with cooling cookies. They smelled rich and inviting, and even though Virginia had already spoiled her supper with the soda, she was reminded that there was still plenty of room for cookies.

Slowly, noiselessly, she pulled open the screen door and eased it shut without a sound. If she could just make it down the back hall to her room, she could spread out her books on the small desk and be busily engaged with homework when she was called to set the table for supper. Who would know how long she had been there?

"Shut the door," called a voice from somewhere within the house.

Clara.

She glanced heavenward. Her whole plan had just been destroyed. It both frustrated and angered her. "I *did*," she answered, her voice agitated.

"Tight. I don't want flies getting in."

She turned and gave the door a sharp tug to set it firmly into place. The latch clicked. Clara had been right. It hadn't been fully closed.

She had taken two steps when Clara called again. "And leave the cookies alone. You'll spoil your supper."

She made a face toward the part of the house from which the voice came and started toward her bedroom.

She had barely entered the room when a new irritation surfaced.

"Where ya been? You're late."

Without even turning to give her younger sister a glance, she responded over her shoulder, "I have homework. Shut the door on your way out."

But Francine would not be dismissed so easily. She followed Virginia into her room and stood, feet planted apart, blue eyes shining with open curiosity. "Where ya been?" she asked again. "Mama said for Clara to assign you your chores. Ya didn't come. Clara had to do them herself so you wouldn't get in trouble. Where ya been?"

Virginia let her bag of books flop onto the desk and stood eying her younger sister. A bit of the anger at being caught began to seep away. She knew that much of her feeling was not justified. Clara was not really unreasonably bossy. She was just a big sister.

Still . . . still it was not an enviable position to be in the middle of a family of five. Clara was her mama's *right hand*. Her papa's oft mentioned *firstborn*. Rodney, who came next in line, was her papa's first son and her mother's pride because of his intellect and his gentle reverence toward his God. Rodney was almost too *perfect*, Virginia reasoned. How could anyone ever live up to a big sister like Clara, who was always sweet, always busy, always rushing to help Mama, and a big brother who was so smart and so good? It was an impossible position.

And then, after her, there was Daniel. Daniel with his dreamy eyes and his tender heart. Danny, who always brought home stray dogs that limped and cats with torn ears or birds with broken wings. And Mama was always right there to help with the mending, and Papa was always hammering together another coop or cage to hold the new patient while healing took place.

And if that wasn't bad enough—there was Francine. Francine with the big blue eyes that looked, innocently, right into your soul. Francine, who laughed and clowned and teased her way into her father's heart. Francine, who had arrived after the loss of another child and filled her mother's soul with renewed singing, her papa's world with laughter. Francine, who forever would be the family's baby.

It didn't seem fair to Virginia that she had been planted right in the middle. She—the only one in the family who didn't have some redeeming trait. The only one who questioned, appealed, argued for reason, and longed for some special acceptance at the same time as a right to freely choose. It wasn't fair. Not fair at all.

"Where ya been?" Francine was not going to give up. Her blue eyes were fastened on Virginia's face. They clouded. "Will Mama be cross with you again?" There was such honest concern in the spoken words, in the straightforward look, that Virginia spun away.

"Why don't you just mind your own business?" she asked crossly.

"I can't," came the wavering answer.

Virginia turned to give her younger sister a stern look. Francine's chin was quivering, large droplets were tugging at her dark lashes. "Why?" she demanded.

"I'm scared. Scared Mama will scold you again. Make you stay in your room—or do the dishes."

"Well—don't be. I can take care of myself. It's none of your business."

The teardrops fell, making shiny wet tracks down the silken cheeks.

"I don't like it when you're scolded," Francine sobbed.

"What's it to you? What—?"

"You're my sister."

"So—?"

They stood only feet apart. One staring in open defiance and anger, the other blinking back tears expressing a deep concern.

"I love you," said the younger in little more than a whisper.

Virginia came awfully close to spewing out an angry retort. But she could not. There was something about the little figure before her that assured her the simple words were true. Francine did love her. Perhaps the love was undeserved. Perhaps the affection was not always readily returned, but it was there. It was not something to be spurned. "I'll be fine," she said before turning away from the brimming blue eyes. Her voice had lost its edge of irritation. "I need to do my homework now."

Francine mopped at the tears, running the back of her hand over her cheeks and drying them on her skirts. She sniffed, mopped some more, and sniffed again. Then she was gone, leaving a troubled Virginia alone.

But Virginia did not spread out her books. Did not settle at the small desk. Instead, she crossed to the window and stood looking out at what was left of the spring day. Patches of green showed all around the fence line. Buds swelled on the corner maple tree. An early dandelion dared lift a sunny face toward the sun. It would not be long until it would be rooted from its spot and deposited with disdain in the alley garbage.

Virginia lifted narrow shoulders as a sigh escaped her lips. She could not formulate her thoughts and feelings. Would have had no idea how to express them. But she felt old. Tired. Growing up seemed to be such very hard work. Why did one have to do it all alone?

CHAPTER 2

"I think that young hawk is about ready to fly."

Her father's comment came during a brief lull in the supper conversation. Virginia had been sitting quietly, hoping not to draw any attention to herself. She lifted her head to take a quick glance at Danny. Would he be pleased or disappointed at their father's words?

Nothing had been said—yet—about her tardiness. Clara must not have reported to their parents, and Francine, who still cast nervous glances Virginia's way with big blue eyes still ready to spill over in tears if anyone spoke harshly, had also held her tongue. Virginia squirmed on her chair. The easy family conversation only heightened her agitation.

Danny lifted his eyes from the meat loaf on his plate. "You think so?"

Virginia could not see his face as he turned to their father, but she could hear the excitement in his voice.

"He has healed nicely" was the reply. "I saw him stretching and exercising that damaged wing. He looks like he would like to put it to the test."

"I'll be glad when Danny can turn lose that weasel of his," commented Clara frankly. "The critter stinks."

Danny was immediately on the defensive. "He don't

stink." Then he added truthfully, "He might smell—a little—but it's not a stink."

Virginia heard the soft chuckles that rippled around the table.

"Well, I think the weasel is almost ready to be given back to nature, too."

The comment came from her mother. Virginia shifted on her chair. When was someone going to say something to her? Get her agony over?

"It's Mother's good nursing," said Danny. "That's what makes them get better so fast."

"Good nursing? Yes, I'm sure it is. But you have a big part in that nursing, too. I'm sure those little creatures appreciate your good care." Father, who was always interested in Danny's little animals, seemed unusually so on this evening, to an impatient Virginia. She felt the frown that creased her forehead. Couldn't they get on with it? When were her father and mother going to turn their questioning eyes on her?

The evening meal was the family time for reviewing the day's activities. Her father and mother always went around the table, checking with each child on something of their personal interest. Virginia had always wondered if the conversations were planned—or just happened. She did know that by the time the meal was over, each child around the table would have been engaged in conversation, and her parents would know the highlights from the day. Eventually the conversation would get around to her. She knew. Wished that she could escape and go to her room. If she begged for extra time for her homework, would she be excused? No, likely not. She had never needed extra homework time.

"How did that test go?"

Her father was now addressing Rodney.

Rodney casually shrugged his shoulders. "Fine—I think."

"Good."

"Is Howard doing better?" This question came from their mother. Howard, a boy who was having difficulty in class, had been getting some private and volunteer tutoring from Rodney.

"He said he thought it went better. He was even grinning after the test. We'll see when the grades are back."

"Good," said her father again.

"Francine, honey—aren't you feeling well?"

The question from their mother brought all heads up, all eyes turned toward the youngest member of the family. Francine sat quietly, her supper plate almost untouched. At the words directed her way her face appeared about to crumble.

Oh, boy, thought Virginia with annoyance, *here it comes*.

But Francine bravely straightened her shoulders and blinked back the threatening tears. Without even a glance toward her errant sister she replied evenly, "I'm fine. I just . . . just am . . . amn't hungry."

Chuckles followed the unusual contraction.

"I'm not hungry," corrected Clara softly.

Francine lifted her head and looked at Clara. There had been no chiding in Clara's words, and Francine had taken no offense. "I know the right words," she said simply. "I just . . . got stuck."

"What do you mean—got stuck?" asked Danny with a grin.

"Well . . ." said the small girl, "when I said *am*, then I couldn't take it back." She lifted two small hands, palms upward. "It was too late. But I couldn't say *am* because I'm not. So I had to say *amn't*."

The ripple of laughter following the words was full of affection. Their father reached out and laid a hand lovingly on the small girl's head. "Makes perfect sense to me."

The hand went from the crown of flaxen curls to the

forehead. "You don't seem to have a fever." He looked across the table at their mother as he spoke the words.

Francine picked up her fork and began to eat her peas. Virginia knew they were her favorite vegetable. She seemed to wish to prove her point by starting with them.

"Is Troy coming over this evening?" Belinda's question was directed at Clara.

"He can't." Clara's voice held disappointment. "His father has him helping take inventory at the store."

"Then why the fancy cookies?" teased their father.

Virginia peeked up just enough to catch a glimpse of Clara's face. She was flushing slightly.

"I thought I might just . . . just take a few over to the store around nine. By then, he's always hungry. And his father. They'll both be hungry."

"Don't we get any?" asked Danny.

"You'll get your share. Don't worry. I've already got a plate of them ready to go with our supper pudding."

Oh, groaned Virginia inwardly. *My turn. They have talked to Danny, Rodney, Francine, and Clara. I'm the only one left. Here it comes.*

But it was to Danny that their father spoke. "You want to take a run out into the country on Saturday and let that hawk try his wings?"

"What do you think, Mama?" was the boy's reply.

"I think it's the weasel that should go," responded Clara flatly.

Their mother disregarded the remark. "I think your father's right. I think the bird is anxious to fly."

Virginia looked up in time to see Danny's nod. She knew that this was a struggle. He was always eager to get his little creatures back to the wild, but at the same time he was worried that they wouldn't be able to make it on their own. He nodded his agreement, but his eyes held his uncertainty.

"If he can't fly, we'll bring him back home," assured Belinda.

"But what if I can't catch him again?"

"Then I guess nothing else would catch him, either."

Danny pondered a moment, then nodded again.

Francine had finished her peas. Virginia saw her turn her attention to the mashed potatoes, take a bite, and work them around in her mouth before trying to swallow. In spite of herself, she felt sorry for her young sister. She hated to try to eat when she had no appetite. She also was quite sure that Francine's lack of appetite was due to concern that Mama and Papa would be upset when they discovered how late she had been from school. Francine, with her liquid eyes and tender heart, could not bear to see anyone get in trouble.

It's not fair, thought Virginia crossly. *It's not fair that she's so . . . so prissy and fussy that I have to sit here and feel guilty just looking at her. If she'd just mind her own business. . . .*

But Francine would not "mind her own business." Her tender heart ached for everyone who ached. Cried for everyone who cried. Felt the pain of everyone who suffered pain. That was just Francine.

But the thoughts brought no comfort to the heart of Virginia. Anger smoldered. Why was she born into a family of such goody-goodies? Clara with her cookie baking. Rodney with his tutoring. Danny and his pens of healing animals. And then Francine. Francine, who took on the whole world's woes. It wasn't fair.

Virginia cast another nervous glance toward her father. When was he going to turn those probing eyes her way? When would her mother notice that something was indeed wrong? Why did the pair of them continue to play cat and mouse with her? Did they enjoy her torment?

"Much homework tonight?"

This question was hers. She knew it without even looking up.

She nodded. Then she thought better of the unspoken response and shook her head. No. Truthfully she did not have much homework.

"Mr. Adamson said that you stopped to chat on your way home," spoke her mother. "He says he always enjoys your little visits."

Virginia could not keep her head lowered. Had Mr. Adamson also told her mother the time of day when she had stopped? But she saw no indication that the man had reported to her mother. The face before her was as serene as it had been engaged in conversation with each of her offspring.

"He also said that—"

Virginia felt the fear rise up in her throat. *Now it's coming.*

"—you kindly warned him to guard his poor old knees. He thinks you would make a good nurse."

Virginia let the air leave her lungs in a slow, relieved flow.

"I've often thought that," put in her father.

Virginia was shaking her head. She did not want to be a nurse.

"Well, we have lots of time to think about that," continued her mother.

"Lots of time," agreed her father.

They still think I'm a kid, fumed Virginia silently. *And they don't think I can make up my own mind. They think they have to decide for me. Well, I—*

"Danny, let's check on that weasel," her father was saying. Virginia knew that it was his way of dismissing the table. He laid aside his napkin, gave a nod to their mother, then turned to Clara. "Nice meal, Dumplin'."

Dumpling had been her father's pet name for Clara since she had been a little girl. He still used it on occasion. Clara smiled and flushed her pleasure in response.

They were all leaving the table. Leaving the table, and

nothing had been said about her disobedience. For one moment Virginia breathed a sigh of open relief. Then her shoulders slumped. It would have been better to have been found out. At least then she could have taken her punishment and gotten it over with. Now she would be forced to carry it with her into the evening ahead. She hated that. Hated it. And there was Francine, big eyes turned upon her, fear still making her chin quiver.

Virginia tossed down her napkin in disgust. Nothing was fair. Nothing. And it was her turn to do the supper dishes.

The remainder of the evening did not go well. Virginia broke a cup while doing the dishes. She spilled cold tea on the kitchen floor when she went to empty the teapot, then got the hem of her dress wet when she knelt down to wipe up the mess.

Her homework did not go any better. Her pencil lead broke as she worked through her arithmetic problems. When she went to her father's small office to look for the pencil sharpener, it was not in its accustomed place. She blamed Rodney. He was always taking things off to his own room, as though he were the only one in the house who ever studied.

She could hear voices in the backyard. Her father and mother were returning with Danny after having released the weasel. Francine had gone with them. Virginia was glad that the child was not following her around, looking soulful and anxious.

"I hope he doesn't go near Mr. Powell's chicken coop again, or he might get another foot in the trap," Francine was worrying.

"He should have learned his lesson," responded Danny.

"But if he gets hungry and he knows there is food there . . ."

Francine let the words hang on the evening air. Virginia flipped back her long hair with one defiant motion. Surely the weasel wasn't so stupid that he would walk right back into trouble again. Surely he now knew the traps were there.

But then, as Francine said, if he was hungry, perhaps he would be willing to take the risk. Virginia shrugged. If he was that dumb, maybe he deserved to have his leg dangling, damaged by the cruel teeth of the trap.

"I hope he can find his family again." Francine picked up a new worry. "Do you think they might have moved away while he was getting better?"

"He'll find them," their father assured her.

Virginia glanced out the window to see her father place an arm about Francine's shoulder. The other sleeve was pinned up, revealing the fact that the limb had been lost. Virginia hated to see her father without his prosthesis. It was such a grim reminder that her father was not perfect. At least not physically perfect. Then it was too easy to entertain the next thought. To realize that he actually might not be perfect in other ways as well.

There had been a time in her life when she had felt that her father was perfect in *every* way. Anyone who had a father with two arms simply had one who was different from her own. Not better. Likely not even as good. Just different.

But she had learned a great deal in the last year. Many of life's discoveries had come through her new friend Jenny. Jenny had moved to their small town from a big city, and Jenny knew all about life. Jenny's father was a newspaper man. Had served on the staff of a large city paper until he had decided that he wished to run a paper of his own. Jenny's father knew all about things. He had "seen it all," Jenny said. And along with that *seeing* had come a good deal of mistrust. Life, according to Jenny, could be pretty rough and rugged. And people—people were not really what they seemed to be. Everyone—no exceptions—presented the face they wished the public to see. Underneath they were only looking out for their own good.

Jenny should know. Her own mother had deserted them, her and her father, to run off to some island with a news reporter. But then, Jenny had shrugged, her father didn't care much for her mother, anyway. What difference did it make that her mother was no longer with them? She supposed her father might be glad she was gone. She was always complaining, he'd said. Never happy with anything. He actually had treated her rather badly in private.

When Jenny had shared all of her personal secrets with Virginia, the young girl had at first felt an unknown fear tear at her heart. Her mother would not do that. Would she? But then her father did not treat her mother badly. Did he? But what did she really know? What went on behind closed doors? Did her folks, too, put on a different face for everyone else?

Virginia had not slept well for the first several nights after Jenny's frankness. But with Jenny's assurance that they were now big enough to take care of themselves, she had tried to lay aside her fear. Jenny had even extracted Virginia's solemn promise that they would always take care of each other. That's the way it would be. The two of them. Together. Against the world, if need be.

It really hadn't put Virginia's mind at ease as it should have. There seemed to be something flawed in the plan. But to date, Virginia had never been able to sort it all out.

And now as she stewed about a broken pencil lead and listened to soft voices coming through the open window, she thought again about how topsy-turvy her world had become. Everything seemed to be spinning out of control. Everything.

Her wayward thoughts were unexpectedly brought up short with the memory of her mother's words. Mr. Adamson had told her mother about their little chat. Mr. Adamson had not told her mother that she had been dreadfully late getting home from school. That she had visited The Sweet Shop with Jenny and their two friends. Why? Why had Mr. Adamson said only nice things about her? Was he trying to protect her? To bring a good report to offset the badness? Virginia frowned.

Poor Mr. Adamson. She knew that other kids made fun of him. Held their noses while they ran by his place. Told unkind jokes when out of earshot. Even made up false stories about dead cats and rotting garbage.

Granted, he was a little dirty. Her mother had tried for many months after the death of his wife to get him to allow her to care for his laundry. He always assured her that he didn't have anything that needed washing—yet. But when he did, he'd wash it himself. Of course he never did. But her mother had at last given up. She couldn't intrude in his life, Virginia heard her mother tell Clara.

Somehow, the thoughts of the elderly man made Virginia more uncomfortable. Everything was making her uncomfortable. The broken cup, one of her mother's favorite set. The soggy hemline. The weasel that, though now healed, might not have sense enough to stay away from the traps. Her father's empty shirt sleeve, Francine's dewy-eyed face, Jenny's gloomy perspective on all of humanity, the broken pencil. Everything . . . everything made her feel more miserable. She wished she could just crawl in her bed and forget everything. *Everything*. If only . . .

The world wasn't fair. She was sure that Jenny was right about that. It wasn't fair—and for some unexplained reason, it wasn't even fun anymore. She wasn't sure what had happened over the last months to take all of the joy out of life, but she knew that something had gone and spoiled things.

She tossed the broken pencil across the room in the direction of her wastepaper basket. If she couldn't sharpen it, it was useless to her. She began to rummage around in the desk drawer in search of another.

And all the time that she muttered and fumed, she had no idea that the discontent was not because of her outer world but was coming out of her own inner conflict.

CHAPTER 3

"Mama?" Virginia stood in the doorway and watched as her mother looked up from the book in her hands.

"Virginia. I thought you were sleeping."

"I . . . I couldn't get to sleep."

Her mother laid aside the book and patted the divan beside her. "Something wrong?"

For one moment the young girl held back. She knew from her mother's tone and small gesture that she was being invited to open her heart. At the same time, she also knew that Jenny would scoff at the idea. Mothers were not to be trusted.

But her years of being raised in a loving home soon helped her overcome her hesitation. She crossed the short distance to the divan and perched herself on the edge of the seat.

"Where's Papa?" she asked for something to say.

Her mother reached out a hand and smoothed back the hair tangled from Virginia's tossing and turning. "He's in his study. He has some work to do before tomorrow's trial."

"Whose trial?"

Virginia had always been familiar with her father's occupation. He often went to court to represent one case or another. And to her mother's pride, he was usually successful. Virginia had always felt that her lawyer father was some knight on a white charger, always there to defend the right.

"A land dispute. Two different parties claim ownership."

"So how does Papa know which one really owns it?"

"He's gone back to the records. He has the legal title."

"So he'll win?"

Her mother smiled and reached for the girl's hand.

"I'm sure he will win. The law is on his side."

Virginia licked dry lips. She had been stalling for time. Her father's court case was not what was keeping her awake.

"What's really troubling you?"

The question was so straightforward that Virginia could not avoid it. Her mother knew that something else was on her mind. Her mother always knew.

"I . . . I . . . I talked to Mr. Adamson."

"Yes, he told me." The words were accompanied by a smile. "I'm pleased that you stop and chat with him when you go by. He really is very lonely."

"I . . . I was late from school."

The admission, in clipped words, hung in the air between them. Her mother waited.

"I was late from school even before . . . before I talked with Mr. Adamson."

"Yes, I know."

Virginia's head began to reel. Apparently her mother did not understand.

"I was real late."

"Yes."

"But you told me to come directly home."

Again her mother nodded. Her hand on the girl's hand

tightened. "And I was very disappointed when you disobeyed," she said quietly.

"You knew?"

"Yes, I knew."

"How?"

"I walked by The Sweet Shop while you and your friends were having your sodas."

"But how—why—?" She couldn't even finish the question.

"Why didn't I demand an explanation?"

Virginia nodded.

"Your father and I walked home together. We talked about it. We are very concerned about—about your recent attitude. We wanted some time to pray—to think—to decide what action to take. We have tried punishment. Placing restrictions. Taking away privileges. More chores. It just seems to make you angry. We aren't sure what to do next. I was planning to talk with Grandma tomorrow. To ask her advice."

Virginia's heart felt as if it were being squeezed. Not that. Not share her disobedience with Grandma. What would Grandma think? Virginia could imagine how shocked her grandmother would be to learn that she was openly defiant of family rules. Grandma loved her. Trusted her. What if her mother's disclosure destroyed all that?

"Please . . . please don't," she heard her quavering voice pleading. "I won't do it again. I promise. I'll come right home."

"Virginia." Her mother's hand left her daughter's in a tight ball on the damask divan and lifted to brush curls back from the troubled face. "We love you. We want to see you grow up without . . . without painful scars from mistakes of youth. I know that . . . that it is important to spend time with friends. To stretch your independence. To grow. But Papa and I—we worry. Worry that you might be trying to grow up too fast. That you might have chosen—well, not bad friends, but confused friends. That they might . . . encourage you to . . . to make some choices that you will later regret. Do you understand?"

Virginia thought long and hard before she slowly nodded her head. With her mother's calm voice easing away her anxious thoughts the words seemed logical—even acceptable. She nodded slowly.

"All we ask is that you obey the rules. Is that so difficult?"

Virginia shook her head. It really wasn't *that* bad. There weren't too many rules.

"We want you to report home after school. To ask permission before going off on some . . . some venture of your own."

She nodded again.

"You are to do your own chores—not pass them off on Clara."

So her mother knew about the missed chores, too.

"Your misconduct affects our entire family. Francine has worried herself sick that you might get into trouble."

Now Francine. Her mother even knew about that. Virginia swallowed hard and nodded again.

"Am I?" she asked at length.

"Are you what?"

"Going to get into trouble?" The words were difficult to force out.

"Yes. Yes, I guess you will. You have disobeyed. You know our family's rules. Disobedience has consequences—right?"

Virginia swallowed again. She had been foolish to suppose she could get away without any punishment.

"What?" she asked when her mother did not go on.

"I really don't know yet. Your father and I have not worked it through. What do you think it should be?"

Virginia frowned. She had never been invited to propose her own punishment before. She wondered for a moment if her mother was serious. A glance at her face assured Virginia that she was.

"I . . . I don't know. Maybe . . . maybe . . ." She could not think. She was very unwilling to condemn herself to a harsh punishment. But on the other hand, she should not be too lenient. The punishment must fit the crime, her lawyer father often stated. He had tried hard to practice the principle within his own household. To suggest some light penalty for what her folks saw as a serious offence would be to admit that she was not mature enough to make a reasonable judgment.

"I . . . I really don't know," she finished lamely.

"It is not easy," acknowledged her mother. "One never takes pleasure in disciplining one's children." She hesitated, then went on, "However, I am grateful, as your father will be, that you came to us with your confession. That will lessen the punishment, though not erase it."

Virginia nodded. She wanted to cry, but she really was too old for that. Still, it would feel so much better if she could throw herself into her mother's arms and weep against her shoulder.

She still had to face punishment. Should she have just kept quiet and pretended that nothing had happened? No—her folks already knew. They already were talking, praying about which direction to take, and her mother was even planning to talk with Grandma. Oh, she hoped with all her heart that she had avoided that.

"You won't talk to Grandma now, will you?" She had to ask.

"You don't wish for me to speak with Grandma?"

Virginia shook her head. Her mother seemed to think about it for some time before she responded with a nod. "Very well. I will not talk with Grandma about it—this time."

Virginia felt relief.

"You'd best get to bed. It's late. Do you think you can sleep now?" There was concern in her mother's voice.

Virginia nodded silently. She thought that maybe now she could sleep. At least she would try.

Her mother's hand rested lightly on her shoulder, and she leaned over to place a kiss on Virginia's forehead. "Good night, then," she said, and Virginia knew that she was dismissed.

At the door she turned back and spoke once more.

"Mama." She hesitated. She could feel the tears again threatening to spill and thought of Francine and her unusual ability to cry. She willed the tears away and lifted her chin slightly.

Her mother's head had lifted from the book she had picked up again. She waited.

"I'm sorry." Virginia's voice faltered.

A look of intense relief washed over her mother's face. Then a smile followed, illuminated by the light of the parlor lamp. "Oh, I'm glad to hear you say that. I feared those words would never come."

As Virginia turned away, she wondered if her mother's hand was brushing away tears of her own.

"The boys are going to the creek after school."

The message had been slipped to Virginia on a small scrap of paper and smuggled across the aisle under cover of a passed eraser. Virginia read the words and then scrunched the note up into a little ball that she let fall into her sweater pocket. She pretended to use the eraser before passing it back across the aisle to its owner. But she avoided Jenny's eyes. She knew what the note meant. Jenny was asking her to join the boys at the creek. There wouldn't be time to run home first and get her mother's permission. Even if there was, Virginia was rather sure that her mother would not okay such an outing. The local public soda shop was one thing, the wooded creek bank quite another.

Yet she longed to go. She knew it would be fun. The small creek that passed near the town would be brimming with spring runoff. Most of the ice would be gone. There might even be pussy willows along the banks. And frogs, fresh up from their long winter's sleep.

There would most surely be daring. Fun and frolic as one boy tried to outdo another. Virginia could almost visualize it. Feats of log-walking, good-natured pushing, dares to challenge patches of remaining ice. Maybe even chases with squawking frogs or slimy garden snakes. Yes, it would be such fun.

She knew without even looking up that Jenny was waiting for her answer. All she had to do was to lift her head and give a brief nod. That would assure Jenny that she was *in*.

But she couldn't lift her head—nor nod. A funny little sick feeling curled itself into the pit of her stomach, twisting up as in a tight fist, making her squirm with the discomfort. She couldn't go. Jenny would be angry. They would all think her a sissy. But she couldn't go. No amount of fun was worth what she had been through when she had disobeyed last week. She was still assigned every other night of supper dishes and the Saturday duty of sweeping the walks. She hated sweeping the walks. Especially in the spring when so many people clumped along the wooden boards with boots cluttered with spring mud and clinging with last fall's leaves.

She continued to work at the sums that had been their assignment. Her face felt strangely hot, her concentration zero.

She felt her elbow nudged. Jenny was again passing her eraser. If she kept it up, she'd be getting them both in trouble.

With eyes still on the page before her, Virginia accepted the eraser, making sure that her fingers fully supported the note she knew would be hidden underneath. With one glance toward the front of the room to make sure the teacher's back was turned, she slipped out the small paper. Jenny's writing was so small that Virginia's brow puckered as she tried to sort out the words.

"What's wrong? Are you coming or not?" The paper almost seemed to burn her fingers.

She knew she had to answer then, but she hated to face Jenny's eyes. She knew they would be filled with anger. Jenny could be nasty when she was put off.

Virginia shook her head with one quick, little sideways motion as she handed the eraser back across the aisle. For just one moment she looked at Jenny. The green eyes flashed back their reply. Jenny was not at all pleased. Virginia turned back to her work, her stomach in even more knots.

Another nudge on the elbow. The eraser was coming back again. Virginia was tempted to ignore it, but she was afraid Jenny would make a scene that would attract the attention of the teacher. Without looking Jenny's way she held out her hand, palm up. Jenny placed the eraser and the note in the center of Virginia's hand and gave her little finger a sharp pinch. Virginia almost gasped.

"Maybe I need to get a new friend" read the terse note.

Virginia's inner turmoil made her feel physically sick. The last thing she wanted was to lose Jenny. Jenny with her flaming hair, her dancing eyes, and her infectious giggle. Jenny with her commanding ways and know-it-all looks. Jenny with her anger when crossed and strong rules of rightful leadership. Virginia had felt so smug about being chosen as Jenny's friend. It had given her status at her school that she had not enjoyed before. If she lost Jenny, she would be right back where she had started. Just another one of the class. Just a nobody. A nothing.

But if she went along with the scheme? What then? She would be in trouble at home again. Her mama would most surely have that talk with her grandma. Maybe even her grandpa would be brought into it. She could not face that. Couldn't stand to see disappointment shadow the love in their eyes.

It was a difficult decision. A tough one to make in the middle of arithmetic class. She did wish that Jenny had left the matter until after school when she could talk it through without the worry of getting caught. But she knew Jenny wanted her answer now.

Throwing caution to the wind, she flipped over the small scrap of paper and wrote in equally small letters, "I can't tonight. Ask me another time." She pressed the note tightly up against the eraser, checked the front of the room for the teacher, and handed them both back across the aisle. Jenny was no more pleased with this message than she had been with the shake of the head. She frowned, then gave a slight shrug of her shoulders, as though to inform Virginia that she was the loser. And she would be sorry.

The day was definitely spoiled for Virginia. She knew that no matter what happened for the rest of it, nothing would make things right. She was going to miss out on a lot of fun. Jenny was mad at her. The boys would think she was stuffy. Nothing was going right. Nothing.

"Virginia?"

The teacher's voice interrupted her distracted reverie, and her head jerked up sharply. She was being called upon in class, and she had not even heard the question. She felt her face flush as snickers began to pass around the room.

"I'm sorry," she managed to stutter. "I . . . I didn't hear the question."

The snickers turned to loud guffaws. Miss Crook thumped the end of the pointer on the floor to summon attention.

"If the rest of you had been as intent upon finishing your arithmetic assignment as Virginia was, you would have no cause for your merriment," the teacher reprimanded.

Virginia's face flushed an even deeper crimson. It was not her arithmetic that had her full attention.

"I asked for the solution to question number seven," the teacher went on. The titters among class members had stopped. Only silence filled the chalk-smelling air.

Virginia let her glance fall to her page. With deep relief she saw that she had completed number seven. She lifted her book, slid to the side of her desk, and stood to her feet. With careful concentration she worked her way orally through the arithmetic problem. When she reached the end, she lifted her eyes briefly to observe the teacher's response. She fervently hoped that she had completed the question correctly.

"Well done, Virginia," the teacher stated with a satisfied little thump of the pointer end on the wooden floor. "William—problem eight."

Virginia sank into her desk. She felt as if she had just faced one of her father's juries and been found "not guilty." Relief flooded her whole frame. Until she cast a quick glance Jenny's way. Her friend was still glowering. There was no ready commendation there.

CHAPTER 4

Jenny did not give up easily. She was waiting on the school steps when Virginia left the building. Virginia's step lagged as she spotted her friend among the little cluster that lounged together. There were three boys, along with Jenny and Ruth Riant. Virginia felt her heart sink. Had Jenny already picked a new friend to replace her?

When Jenny looked up and called, Virginia forced a smile and started forward again.

"I thought you had already gone," she offered lamely.

"Thought you might change your mind," responded Jenny.

Virginia frowned. Jenny was really making it hard for her. All three of the boys lifted their heads and studied Virginia's face. She took the stares as a challenge. Was she, or wasn't she, one of the group?

It was so tempting to just go along with them. Take the consequences when she got home. But Virginia held back. It was the vision of her grandmother's face, with disappointment darkening her eyes, that held Virginia in check. "I can't," she managed. "I already told you."

"Well, you're gonna miss a lot of fun," Jenny thrust at her with a toss of her red hair. She threw in a shocking curse to emphasize her point. Virginia could only stare.

With a howl of laughter, Jenny led her little entourage down the steps to the street that led out of town toward the woods and Carson Creek. Virginia stood and watched them go. Already they were teasing and laughing and calling out comments to one another.

Her heart ached. With all her being she longed to be a part of the crowd. She was tempted to call, "Hey, wait!" and hurry off down the street to join them. But her voice choked up and her feet refused to move. She stood until they disappeared around the corner, her face hot with emotion, her angry thoughts whirling round and round. It wasn't fair. It wasn't fair that her folks were so . . . so stuffy. They didn't let her have any fun. She couldn't even get out of their sight. They thought she was still a child.

Virginia started the slow walk home, her mood anything but light. All the way along the board sidewalk she fumed, kicking at small stones, deliberately scuffing the toes of her new black boots. She took pleasure in telling herself all the unreasonableness of her parents. All the privileges that each of her siblings enjoyed. All the unfairness of life. By the time she reached her own street, she was convinced that she had the hardest lot of any person in town. Probably the whole county. Maybe even the entire world.

"What's got yer tail in a knot?"

Virginia jumped at the sound of the voice. Mr. Adamson was leaning on his picket fence peering over at her. His dirty shirt had a distinct new stain. Virginia wondered if he had spilled his morning coffee.

"I didn't see you," she responded.

"No—reckon ya didn't. Thet heavy cloud hangin' over yer head likely kept ya from seein' anythin' else."

Without thinking, Virginia looked upward. The elderly man began to chuckle. Her face flushed when she realized that he had been teasing her.

"Somethin' go wrong?"

How could she tell the old neighbor man that just about everything was wrong? Here she was on her way home when her friends were all down at the creek having fun. *Their* parents trusted them. They were allowed to grow up. It wasn't fair.

"Well—?"

Virginia tossed her head. "It's just—well, my folks—"

"Ah . . ." said the old gent with a nod of his head in understanding. "Folks. They can be a real burden all right."

Virginia watched as the old man took off his beat-up hat and scratched his balding head. His silvery locks were now darkened. Virginia supposed that the hair was not washed any oftener than the shirt.

"I remember when I was a lad," the man went on. "Had me the most disagreeable father. We never did see eye to eye—until I got in my twenties. Suddenly the old fella got smarter about things. By the time I hit forty he'd really learned him a lot." The words were followed by a chuckle, but Virginia did not find the comment amusing. She knew exactly what the elderly man was trying to say.

"I don't expect my mama and papa to improve much," she said abruptly.

"Don't ya now? Well . . ." He flipped off the hat and scratched his head again. Virginia watched as the garden dirt from his fingers liberally deposited itself on the thinning hair. No wonder the silver had turned dull.

"Give 'em time. Jest give 'em a little time," the old man advised. "Even old dogs can learn new tricks—iffen they have a good teacher."

"Well, they sure don't learn from me," Virginia grumbled.

"From you? No. I expect maybe they don't. Ya see, thet ain't really the role of younguns, as I've got it sorted out."

His words were not condemning, and Virginia found

it hard to take offense. She was on the verge of asking what he thought the role of youngsters was when he abruptly changed the subject.

"Got some tulips blooming."

He looked so pleased that she could not help but respond. "The pretty striped ones?"

"No, they come a little later. It's the bright reds. A few yellowers are just ready to pop as well. Another day or two of sun and I'll have a bouquet for ya. Stop by on Friday. They oughta be ready by then."

Virginia nodded. She liked the bright tulips. They were a wonderful reminder that winter's snows were finally gone.

With a nod the elderly man turned away. He picked up his hand trowel and turned back to the flower beds. Virginia could tell that he regarded their little discussion over for the day. With slow steps she moved off toward home.

But even though she was still upset, she could not work up the same sense of injustice. Something had derailed her line of thought. It wasn't that she didn't still wish to be with the others having fun down at the creek. But she just couldn't get quite so angry over the fact that she was not.

She entered the house to the smell of fresh-baked bread. Her mother was there. Francine and Danny were already seated at the kitchen table, tall glasses of cold milk set before them and slices of fresh bread liberally covered with strawberry preserves disappearing quickly. Her mother smiled. "Welcome home." With a nod of her head she indicated the spot where Virginia's milk and bread were already waiting for her.

For one moment Virginia was tempted to say, "No thanks," and head on to her bedroom to sulk. But the bread smelled so good and she was suddenly so hungry that she checked herself. As she lowered her books to the corner of the table and slid into the chair, Francine spoke up excitedly.

"Uncle Luke is coming for supper."

Virginia adored her uncle Luke. It was hard to suppress her own enthusiasm. She flicked a look in her mother's direction to verify Francine's statement, even though she knew that Francine would not be telling a lie.

"Just Uncle Luke," her mother explained. "Aunt Abbie and Georgia have gone to see their folks at Fowler Creek. I happened to see Luke at the post office and invited him to have supper with us."

Virginia almost grinned. It no longer mattered so much that all of the others were down at the creek chasing frogs and sliding over moist logs. They didn't have an Uncle Luke. An Uncle Luke who was a doctor.

The next morning Jenny was full of exaggerated reports about the trip to the creek. Most of the comments were not directed to Virginia but spoken in her hearing. Virginia knew they were intended to be little rubs to inform her of just how much she had missed. She could have made comments of her own. Tales about her uncle Luke and his joining them for supper. She could have told of the interesting accounts of his medical adventures. About his deep laughter as he shared little family jokes with her mother and father. About how he had helped her with the supper dishes. About the fun they'd had together after supper playing ball in the backyard. Even her mama and Clara had played. And the good laugh they had all had when Clara chased a fly ball and almost ended up in the pen with Danny's guinea pigs. But Virginia said nothing about that. She was sure that Jenny would not understand, would simply make fun of her.

Ruthie seemed to be hanging around Jenny all day. In the lineup for the afternoon spelling bee, she even pushed herself between Jenny and Virginia. Normally Jenny would have protested loudly. But she did not. Just cast Virginia a look that warned her that her cherished position was tenuous at best.

Virginia tried to ignore the barbs, the looks, the little titters. But it all hurt. Deep down inside it bothered her a good deal. But she didn't know how to go about regaining her former place at Jenny's side. What could she do to get back in Jenny's good graces again?

"Some of the kids have been visiting the creek."

The comment from her father brought heads up around the supper table. It was her mother who spoke. "Is that a problem?"

"Sheriff Brown thinks it could be."

"The town kids always play at the creek," observed Rodney without slowing his enjoyment of the shepherd's pie.

"But there is still some ice left. Rotten ice. It wouldn't hold anyone's weight and can't be trusted. Yet it's a temptation. Especially to the daring. The creek is already quite high, and there is a lot of snow up in the hills to melt yet. If we get a good rain, it will likely flood again this year. We've had an extra fall of snow this winter."

Virginia listened to the conversation but made no comment of her own. Her school friends had visited the creek a few more times in recent days. Each time they had returned to school triumphant, bragging about the fun they'd had and the daring exploits of their bravest members. So far nothing more than wet pant legs had resulted, although there was much joking laughter about Samuel Boycie nearly sliding in and losing his hat in the process.

"There was this hat floating on down the creek, bobbing up and down in the current," Jenny had said gleefully. "I said, 'What you gonna tell your ma?' and he said,

'I'll tell her ole loony Marshall's pet crow took it.' " More shouts of laughter.

Virginia had passed on out of earshot. She didn't want to hear more. Jenny was intent upon rubbing in the fact that she was missing out on all the fun. Besides, she hated it when folks made fun of Rett Marshall. She knew that in a way the comments were true. He was loony. At least he was not like other folks, if that's what loony meant. Her grandmother had told her Rett's story.

His folks had wanted a child so very much. His mama had lost several babies, and finally God had sent her Rett. She had been so happy, and Rett's pa had been so proud. And then it was discovered that the baby boy was not normal. Oh, he developed physically, though progress was slow, but mentally he stayed a child. Still, they loved him. His mama, Wanda, thought of him as her *forever baby*, and his papa, Cam, took the small boy with him wherever he went.

He wasn't very old when people began to notice that he had an unusual rapport with animals. He gathered the sick and cared for the helpless and communed with the wild things. He soon became known in the community as the boy who could tame the beasts. Folks might not understand him, but they did have a strange respect for him.

He was left to roam the hills and wander the woods to his heart's content. To the community folk he never seemed to age. Rett just stayed as a boy, forever on the move. Forever finding new animal friends. Forever free.

But things around him changed over the years. His folks did not have the same protection against aging. His mama was the first to go. Not an old woman, she took a bad cold that wouldn't leave her chest. All through a long winter she coughed and choked. Virginia's grandma and other neighbors had tried to save her. Her uncle Luke had doctored the sick woman for several months, but nothing that they could do seemed to help. She died early spring and was buried in the little cemetery by the country church.

Her husband and son took it very hard, but they struggled on. Cam took over the cooking and cleaning, and he did a fair job of it, too, surprising even the most critical of neighbors. Folks tried to help him as they could, but each neighbor woman had her own household to attend to, and in time they discovered that he was doing just fine on his own.

Then one day Cam showed up at her grandparents' door. He had just paid a call on Doc Luke, he said, and found that he had a bad heart. He'd been suspicious. Funny little things had been warning him. He wasn't concerned about himself. He was feeling rather tired and lonely, anyway, since Wanda had left. But he was concerned about Rett. What would happen to his boy once he was gone?

The Davis family had talked about it. Prayed about it. At last they went to see Mr. Marshall. Rett was always welcome to live with them, they told him. They would care for him as long as they were able to do so. But the father had other ideas. He thought it might be best for the boy, who in actuality by now was a man well in his forties, to be in town. He'd heard of a new boardinghouse. He was going to sell the farm, set up a trust fund for his son, and move into town to get Rett settled and used to the new dwelling before his heart gave out.

When the plans were carried out, Rett had chaffed at first. Restless and anxious, he paced the one small room that was now their home, and finally his father had realized that he needed to be free. Needed to be able to roam the hills and the woods. He asked the woman who ran the boardinghouse to fix up a lunch for his son, and with that in hand, no matter what the weather, Rett set off each day. "Go ahead," the father told the boy-man. "Just be sure to come back home at night." And he always did, returning at the end of the day satisfied and well. Uncle Luke had said that Rett Marshall had the constitution of an ox. Virginia had no idea what that meant, but Uncle Luke always made the comment as though it was a good thing and something to be admired.

The father and son had lived together at the boardinghouse for almost a year before Mr. Marshall's heart finally failed him. He was gone even before Uncle Luke got there. The loss of his father only increased Rett's wanderings. But he still came home each night. Hungry and often cold and damp—but content.

His only problem was what to do with his pet crow. It was the only bird or beast that Rett attempted to bring in from the wild. All other creatures he insisted on leaving, healing them and returning them to their natural habitat. But the crow went with Rett wherever he went. It perched on his shoulder or flew on ahead of him. His landlady would not allow the bird to be kept in his room. Rett had to build a cage in the backyard, but he fretted some about the bird being left out there alone each night. Folks said that often when a bad storm came their way, Rett stayed right out there with the bird.

Folks said that the crow was better at communicating than Rett himself. Mostly folks' remarks were made without meaning to disparage the strange man. But the schoolboys were an entirely different matter. They teased and tested the man sorely. He had become the butt of many of their cruel jokes. Virginia hated it. When she had been younger, she had quickly come to Rett's defense. At one point she was even known as the *loony lover*. But as she had grown older and understood just how important the approval of her peers was to her, she had stopped publicly defending Rett. She felt cowardly. But she was not brave enough to defy the crowd in order to take a stand against their constant ridicule.

Danny, however, had no such reservations. If anyone

said anything cruel concerning Rett when he was within earshot, he was quick to defend the strange man. Virginia felt both pride and chagrin. She hoped that the school crowd would not link her with her younger brother. Yet she did admire his courage. However, she reminded herself that one day Danny would realize that standing up for society's outcasts came at a big price. She was sure that when that time arrived, Danny, too, would be silent.

CHAPTER 5

"Have you heard what that long-nose Mrs. Parker is saying now?"

Her green eyes flashing, red hair tossed back with an angry flip, Jenny almost flung the words at Virginia. Virginia had no idea. She didn't believe that the folks in their small town paid much attention to anything that came from the lips of Mrs. Parker. Leastwise, her own folks chose to ignore it. "Facts are facts," her papa always said, "and until one has proof, it is merely hearsay."

But then her papa was an attorney. He didn't care much about any information that couldn't be proven solidly enough to hold up in a court of law.

And her mama didn't pay much mind to Mrs. Parker's stories either, but for a totally different reason. She quoted from the Bible about gossiping tongues. Gossip and Christian charity didn't fit together in her mama's mind. Family members in the Simpson household were discouraged from dragging home with them bits of neighborhood gossip.

Virginia looked back at Jenny's flushed face and gave her shoulders a bit of a shrug. She seemed to have been accepted back into Jenny's good graces, but she had no idea what Mrs. Parker had said and wasn't particularly interested. Jenny was sure riled up, though, about something.

"She says my pa's a drunk."

Virginia did not even blink. It was well known in the town that Jenny's father was a drinker. Virginia supposed the bit of information would be seen as undisputed fact even in the eyes of her attorney father. But she did not say so to Jenny.

"She says that he comes home and pushes me around."

Virginia's eyes did widen some at that, remembering days when Jenny appeared at school with bruises here or there and funny little excuses of how she had bumped into this or banged against that.

"She says that's why my ma ran off."

"How did she find out all that?" Virginia asked innocently. An angry glare was her reply.

Too late, she realized the implication of her words. She fumbled mentally for some words to cover her mistake but could think of nothing that would wipe the conversation slate clean again.

It was also commonly known in the town that when Jenny's pa had too much to drink, he babbled on and on to anyone who would listen to him about the hard luck that life had handed him and the fickle wife he'd had the misfortune of being "chained to" for seven long years. The story varied with the telling. Sometimes he'd kicked her out. Other times he sobbed uncontrollably as he told how she'd up and left him—him and his little girl—to run off with a fella she scarcely knew. Virginia's folks never allowed such stories to be passed on at home, but Virginia had heard plenty from talk in the school yard. Would have been no problem at all for Mrs. Parker to get enough information to keep her gossipy tongue in business for weeks.

"I hate it!" Jenny was exclaiming. "I'd love to give that

old biddy something to *really* make her tongue wag."

Virginia frowned and shifted uncomfortably. She didn't like the feel of what was in the air.

The conversation was interrupted by the ringing of the school bell. Virginia could not help but let out her breath in relief, but Jenny was not finished. As they hurried toward the red brick building, she still raged on. "I'll do it, too. I'll think of something. Just you wait. That ole . . ." And Jenny used a word that Virginia had never heard before. Something told her that the term would not be accepted in the hearing of her mother and father. She could tell just by the ring of it, even if she had no idea what its meaning was.

" . . . I'll put her in her place—just you wait." And Jenny angrily flipped her red hair back with that familiar toss of her head.

Virginia was glad to feel the hard seat of her desk beneath her as she slid onto the wooden surface. It felt solid and cool. Almost a comfort after the red-hot anger of Jenny and the out-of-control feel that the girl's flushed face and furious eyes had brought to the early morning. Surely Jenny would not go and do something stupid. Surely not.

But even as Virginia reached for her speller, her stomach knotted. She had the unsettling feeling that Jenny just might, and for reasons she could not explain she also feared that, as Jenny's friend, she was going to be dragged into it. To try to keep herself apart would mean Jenny's anger. And Virginia hated more than anything to see those flashing green eyes turned on her with disdain. It was even worse than facing the punishment meted out by her parents.

Virginia cringed.

The days went by and Jenny did not speak about Mrs.

Parker again. Virginia began to relax. Perhaps she was safe after all. At least safe where plots of revenge on the neighborhood gossip were concerned.

But Jenny was busy with other plans. Constantly Virginia found herself being pushed in awkward corners and uncomfortable situations. The little crowd of malcontents was going across to the pasture of Mr. Moss to tease his big red bull. They set a trap for Crow Man Marshall's pet, just to hear him squawk a bit, laughing over who would squawk the loudest—the bird or the man. Virginia had managed to bow out of these escapades with valid excuses. But it was not so easy to say no when Jenny decided they were going to the town's hardware store to pester old Mr. Lougin. Virginia was told that the man firmly believed all school kids were thieves and that he nearly put his neck out trying to watch them all at the same time whenever they entered his store without the supervision of a parent.

"He thinks anyone under twenty should be kept on a leash," Freddie Crell sputtered, and everyone in the group laughed as though it was a great joke.

"Maybe in a cage," hooted one of the other boys.

"It drives him half mad," Jenny said with great glee, "just for us to mill about a little and pretend to look at this or that. He breaks out in a sweat and his face gets red. It's great sport."

The shouts of laughter seemed out of proportion with the statement, to Virginia's way of thinking.

She had known Mr. Lougin all of her life and had never seen him agitated in such a fashion. But then Virginia had never been in his store except with a parent or on a legitimate errand for a parent.

"What do we do?" she asked, her voice giving away a bit of her concern.

Jenny laughed her giggling, near-hysteria laugh. "That's just it," she finally choked out. "We don't have to do *anything*." She managed to get control of her tongue so she could talk properly and went on, her green eyes dancing with the fun of it all. "We just walk in and scatter. Just *scatter*." She indicated this with a flutter of two small freckled hands. "We scatter and just walk around and look—and he turns into a loony. It's hilarious. He rushes about, here and there, counting items on the counters where we've just been, watching this way, then that—his big ole eyes nearly poppin' from his head. It's *hilarious*."

It sounded mean to Virginia.

"My folks would whup me if they ever caught me at it," muttered Jedd Marlow, who had somehow been tricked into joining the group. Virginia supposed it had something to do with the fact that Ruthie, who was included on some of the escapades, thought Jedd was cute. "I'm not to go in a store unless I got proper business there," explained the boy.

Virginia was just about to open her mouth to agree with Jedd. Her folks would not take kindly to the idea, either, even though they might think of something other than a whipping to express their displeasure. But before she could even get out a word of agreement she saw Jenny whirl around and give Jedd one of her looks.

"We aren't doing any harm to nobody. If this wasn't such a dead town—if the grown-ups were concerned enough to give us something interesting to do with our time—we wouldn't need to look for our own way of making fun, now would we?"

It was funny with Jenny. She could make her arguments for almost anything sound so reasonable. And convincing. Virginia found herself agreeing with the words. It *was* a dull town. The grown-ups didn't do much, or supply much, to entertain the young. Maybe it was their fault that young folks had to hatch up ways to fill their free hours.

But Jedd held his ground. He did not even flinch under Jenny's wrathful glare. He shrugged shoulders that were quickly broadening out in their reach for manhood. "Do what you like," he said matter-of-factly. "Me—I don't need to be looking for something to do. Got plenty of chores waiting for me at home. And when I finish them, I'm gonna meet up with some of the fellas for a game of ball."

Jenny's glare became more intense. But she was now looking at Jedd's full back. He had turned and was walking away, totally unperturbed by Jenny's fury.

"Game of ball," Jenny sputtered to those who remained. "Game of ball—on a dirty ole sandlot. Don't even have a decent backstop. And he thinks that's living." Virginia almost expected her to spit in the dust. But Jenny quickly cast aside her anger with Jedd and let the glint return to her eyes. "Now, who's in? Just a little fun with the good man Mr. Lougin." She emphasized the name of the man, drawing out each syllable and making a face as she did so.

Virginia looked after Jedd. She could hear his whistle as it drifted back on the warmth and stillness of the afternoon spring day. If only she had the nerve to follow suit.

The trip to the hardware store was rather a letdown. Five neighborhood men sat around a large nail keg, checkerboard set out before them as Mr. Telsworth took on Mr. Teigs in what appeared to be a tight match. The others watched, eyes glued to the board, or clucked appreciatively as a brilliant move was made. When the ragtag band of school friends self-consciously entered the store, eyes lifted from the board to focus fully on all the young faces. Even Mr. Lougin himself seemed ready to welcome them if it meant a sale.

"Help you young folks?" he asked good-naturedly as

he moved toward them from his spot on an upturned barrel.

Virginia could hear the shuffling of feet. No one spoke. There seemed to be nothing to say. Then Jenny managed to find her tongue.

"We were wondering if you got in any of those six-inch-tall ink wells—like they carry in the city."

The man shook his head. "No tall ink wells. Have the standard—"

"No, that's not what we wanted. Tall ones hold more. We just thought . . ."

"I'll sure look into it. See what I can do." Mr. Lougin pulled a stubby pencil from behind his ear and tugged the little note pad from the front of his bib coverall. He gave the pencil a bit of a lick before he put it to the paper to make himself a note concerning tall ink wells.

"How many you thinking you might need?" he asked without even looking up.

Jenny was backing slowly toward the door, her little cluster of followers slowly backing with her. For once she seemed to be losing control of the situation. "Uh . . . maybe . . . maybe six or eight."

Mr. Lougin's left eyebrow shot up. "Half a dozen."

Jenny nodded. "They are rather pricey," she said, her chin lifting as she seemed to recover her haughty spirit. "Pro'bly not many folks in this town can afford them."

The right eyebrow joined the left, but Mr. Lougin said nothing as his pencil scratched on. "Maybe a dozen," he muttered to himself as he finished his writing.

The little group backed themselves right out onto the sidewalk. Virginia could feel a collective sigh pass through the entire company.

"Six-inch-tall inkwells," whispered Freddie. "Never heard of six-inch-tall inkwells."

Jenny gave him a scathing look. "Neither will Mr.

Lougin," she said with a toss of her head. "Not any such thing."

"You mean—?" Sammie Boycie began the question that he never did finish. Instead, as the light began to dawn he howled at the fun of it. It seemed to lighten the spirits of the entire little group. Jenny tossed her red hair and emitted a delighted giggle. The situation was redeemed. She was back in charge again. The trip had not been a total disaster after all.

"Maybe *you* could talk to him."

Virginia was already shaking her head even as Jenny broached the suggestion.

"He goes to your church, doesn't he?"

Virginia nodded. That was true. But what did that have to do with it? Besides, she simply could not understand Jenny's determination to get Jamison Curtis to be one of her little set. Jamison had been approached a number of times. It was true that he could be as much fun as anyone, but it was also true that he had vetoed Jenny's plans on more than one occasion. Yet Jenny kept persisting. Virginia could not understand it. She knew that if she had crossed Jenny as many times as Jamison already had, she'd be out. No parole. No forgiveness. No pardon.

"He wouldn't . . . he wouldn't listen to me," she was mumbling to Jenny.

" 'Course he would. I think he likes you," cut in Ruthie and received a look from Jenny that stopped her rush of words. "Sort of," she finished lamely.

Virginia again shook her head. Jamison Curtis was a good two years her senior. He sat with the bigger boys in church. He took his faith seriously. Very seriously. The pastor himself had his eye on Jamison for great things. Oh, he'd never really come right out and said so, but Virginia could tell. He always smiled at Jamison in a special way, and he gave him unique little jobs to do with the young people. Every kid in church knew it—and accepted it. Jamison was geared for leadership—not for following. And especially not for following someone like Jenny.

"He'll never do it—no matter who asks him," Virginia maintained stoutly, chancing Jenny's wrath.

"We aren't going to do anything bad," insisted Jenny. "Just have a bit of fun. Maybe just . . . just go for a malt . . . or soda or something."

Virginia thought back to that other time they had gone for a soda. It had been fun. She loved sodas. But she sure wondered if yielding to the temptation had been worth it. She still remembered all those nights of dish-washing. She didn't like doing dishes. And she didn't like being on the outs with her family.

Her mind hurried on, wondering almost against her will if Freddie might have another nickel that he would be willing to spend so they could share another soda together. That had been fun, too. At the time. But things were changing somehow. She didn't know how or why, but she didn't feel the same way about Freddie that she once had. It bothered her when he pushed close up against her side and seemed to think he had a right to be there. Sort of like she was his girl or something. In one way, it made her feel a bit special. In another way, it made her feel cornered. And what if her parents ever saw that? She wanted to back away—or push Freddie back a step.

But Jenny was speaking again.

"Just a quick soda."

That seemed a rather tame plan after some of the other proposals that Jenny had made. For one moment Virginia considered being Jenny's messenger. Then she hesitated.

"He has chores," she said flatly.

"Every night?"

Virginia nodded.

"Well, he can still do his chores. It only takes a few minutes to have a soda."

"He goes right home."

"Well surely he doesn't need—"

"You ask him," cut in Virginia and was rewarded with a withering glare. She stammered, trying to think of some way to express her thoughts without challenging Jenny.

"I . . . I just . . . well . . ." She shrugged. "What do we need him for anyway? Why bother?"

It was a total mystery to her. What was Jenny's reason for continuing to pursue Jamison? He had made it quite clear that he had no intention of doing her bidding. Or was that what this was all about? Was it a challenge of wills? Did Jenny feel threatened when she wasn't in control—of everyone? Yet there were several of the other fellows and girls that Jenny never bothered with at all. So why Jamison? Virginia couldn't sort it out.

"She thinks he's cute," Ruthie offered, giving a titter as she disclosed the information.

Virginia's eyes opened wide. Never once had she thought of Jenny nursing a crush on Jamison. They were so . . . so different. So totally unlike each other. Surely Ruthie was teasing.

A quick elbow aimed at Ruthie's ribs made the girl gasp. "Shut your mouth, Ruth," Jenny said sharply, but her face was flushed, and there was no denial on her lips.

It was true. It was really true. Jenny had a crush on Jamison. If Virginia had dared, she would have laughed at the very thought. But she did not dare. She only stared, open-mouthed, unable to say a word.

Then she shook her head again.

"He wouldn't come," she insisted, her words carefully chosen and hardly above a whisper. "Not for me, he wouldn't. Not for you, either. He . . . he never crosses his parents. Never."

Jenny gave the angry flip of her red mane. "Is he totally boring?"

"No. He's fun." Virginia was too quick with her answer. She softened her voice and continued because Jenny was staring at her, waiting for her to go on. "He's . . . he's fun at Youth Group. He . . . laughs and . . . everything. Makes us laugh. He—"

But Jenny seemed to have heard enough. She reached out a hand that pushed Virginia aside. "Maybe I'll just have to go to Youth Group," she said with another toss of her head. And as she turned to give Virginia a smug look, her green eyes were flashing again.

CHAPTER 6

"I've got it!" was Jenny's greeting to Virginia the next morning when they met at the corner for the last few blocks to school. Her face was flushed with her excitement, and Virginia felt her own pulse quicken.

"Got what?"

She was sure that the answer would have something to do with Jamison Curtis, so she was surprised when Jenny answered, "A way to get ole nosy Parker."

Virginia blinked. She thought that Jenny had given up on her little plan of revenge. She wanted to ask about the plan, and at the same time she feared to do so. She had a foreboding that she might enter into Jenny's scheme in some way.

"We'll give her something to talk about," Jenny hurried on.

Virginia swallowed. She was right. Jenny was using the word "we."

"What are you. . . ?"

"We," Jenny confirmed. "I'll tell you all about it at recess. I can hardly wait. I sorted it all out last night in bed. Just wait. The whole town will know she's just a meddlin' ole fool."

Virginia's frown deepened. The whole town already

knew about all there was to know concerning Mrs. Parker. Folks just, well, accepted her for the way she was, ignoring most of what she prattled on about. Who paid any mind to Mrs. Parker?

They couldn't talk as they hurried on to reach the school yard before the bell rang. It was too hard to walk fast and talk at the same time.

Virginia did not know if she wanted recess to arrive or not. In some ways, the very thought of Jenny's excitement made her heart quicken in similar fashion. Yet it frightened her a little bit, too. It was sure to be something that would get her in more trouble at home—unless they could lay their plan carefully and not get caught at whatever it was Jenny intended for them to do.

When the bell was given a little tinkle to announce the recess break, Virginia looked up to see Jenny's eyes already upon her. With a nod of her head toward the door, Jenny indicated that Virginia was to leave the room and meet her around the east corner, their usual rendezvous spot.

Wordlessly she slipped her books back in her desk, rose from her seat, and followed Jenny from the room.

Her mouth felt uncomfortably dry. She tried to swallow, but there was nothing there.

Jenny continued walking until she had rounded the corner and turned to lean against the warmth of the brick from the brightness of the early rising sun. A grin spread over her face.

"You know that grove of poplars just down from Parker's house?" she began.

Virginia nodded.

"Well, we're gonna give Mrs. Parker something to *really* set her tongue a waggin'."

"But—"

"We're gonna meet down there—sort of a secret meeting."

"She won't even see us."

"Oh, yes she will. She's always watching whatever's going on."

"She won't even know it's us."

"That's just the point. We don't want her to know. It's the not-knowing part that will drive her near crazy."

Virginia frowned. She was not following Jenny's logic at all.

"She'll get out her spyglass and try and try to figure out who's doing the meeting."

"She has a spyglass?"

"'Course she does. How else do you think she sees everything?"

Virginia shrugged. She had no idea how Mrs. Parker kept track of the goings-on of a whole town.

"If she has a spyglass she *will* know it's us," Virginia argued. "We won't be able to hide that from her. She knows both of us. Has known me since I was born. And you with that red hair. Nobody else in town has hair that color."

"We're gonna be in disguise," Jenny said smugly.

"Disguise?"

It was sounding more and more dangerous to Virginia. What would they be doing that they would need to disguise themselves?

"I have to go right home from school," she argued defensively. "I don't want to get in trouble again."

"We aren't going to do it after school. We'll go on Saturday. Your folks let you out on Saturday, don't they?"

Virginia was angry. Jenny made it sound as though her folks kept her caged up or something. "Of course they let me out Saturday," she exploded. "I can do whatever I want after I finish my chores."

"There," said Jenny with satisfaction, making Virginia wish she hadn't made the bold statement. "When are you finished with your chores?"

Virginia hedged. She still had not heard the plan. After a bit of hesitation she asked, "What are you planning? I don't want anyone to get hurt, and I sure don't want to get in trouble, either."

"No one will get hurt. It's just a harmless little gag, that's all."

Then Jenny turned defensive and angry. "Boy, are you a soggy day. You can't see the fun in anything. I'd hate to live in a family of woe-betiders. Is that what your olc church teaches—that no one never ever has any fun in life? First Jamison—now you. Are you all a bunch of ole cloud-hangers over there?"

Virginia's chin came up. " 'Course not," she responded hotly. "And how would you know a thing about our church? You've never been there. You likely wouldn't know the way if one led you by the hand."

It was as close as they had ever come to open confrontation. Virginia had never challenged Jenny's power so directly before. She didn't really understand why she was bold enough to do so now, but bringing her family and her church into the argument made her upset and ready to stand up to Jenny.

"Maybe I should get Ruthie," Jenny said hotly.

"Maybe you should," responded Virginia with a toss of her own head. "Or maybe you should carry out your silly little scheme all by yourself instead of getting someone else in trouble."

"Nobody's gonna get in trouble. I already told you. It's just a little fun, that's all."

"That's what you always say. Just harmless fun. But you always end up getting someone in trouble. Freddie and George had to clean out Mr. Moss' barns for three weeks after the bull teasing. Sam said he couldn't sit comfortably for a week after you had him passing those notes in school about Mr. Henkel's false hairpiece. And Ruthie got in awful trouble for painting those words on Mercer's fence."

"This is different," insisted Jenny. "This is just harmless fun. To teach Mrs. Parker a lesson. Your folks don't got nothing against teaching people proper lessons, do they?"

"Well . . . their idea of a lesson and your idea might be a fair bit different," said Virginia. She couldn't believe her own boldness now that her back was up.

"Okay, if you don't want to be friends . . ." Jenny began, slowly starting to turn away.

The very words brought a chill to Virginia and took the last bit of rigidity from her spine.

"Of course I—I want to be friends," she stammered. "It's just . . ."

"Be there. One thirty, Saturday. Come in from the back way so that no one will see you. I'll have the disguises."

And with those words, Jenny walked away before Virginia could even respond.

Virginia was not in a good mood when she arrived home. Clara was stirring about the kitchen. Obviously she was making something. But Clara was always making something. Virginia didn't bother to try to figure out what. She cast one glance toward the kitchen table. Likely she would have extra baking dishes to wash at supper. Clara had all of the fun of making her fancy foods, and she, Virginia, got the dirty task of washing up after her. It wasn't fair.

With one doleful look Clara's way, Virginia started for her bedroom.

"Don't you want your milk and . . ."

"No," answered Virginia shortly. "I don't need any more dirty dishes to wash than you are already making."

Clara shrugged and said nothing more. But whatever it was that she was baking did smell awfully good. Virginia's stomach growled in response.

Jenny did not talk again of the coming Saturday. All week long she seemed to tantalize Virginia with her silence about the plans. In fact, they talked very little through the days that led up to Saturday.

Ruthie hung around like a hornet round a water puddle. Her very presence irritated Virginia. She knew that she couldn't ask any questions with Ruthie hanging around. Jenny had made it clear enough that the little outing, whatever it was to be, should be kept totally secret.

The three of them walked the first few blocks from school on Friday. Just as they separated at their usual corner, Jenny turned and looked directly at Virginia. "Be there" was all she said, but Virginia could hear more than a suggestion in the two words.

Ruthie looked from one to the other and opened her mouth as though to speak but changed her mind after staring at the two faces.

And so the next day, feet dragging and heart thumping wildly, Virginia found herself working around the back way to the little patch of poplar trees at the foot of the Parker horse pasture.

"Over here." Virginia heard Jenny's whispery call and swung around to see where the sound was coming from.

Jenny knelt behind a tangled willow bush, her hand resting on a large gunnysack lying on the ground at her side. Virginia cast a nervous look about her, then quickly covered the distance between them.

"What's that?" she whispered, the words coming out in a raspy, breathless fashion.

"Our disguises."

From the depths of the gunnysack Jenny began to

withdraw bits and pieces of odd-looking clothing.

"I don't see how putting on funny clothes is going to keep Mrs. Parker from knowing us," Virginia stated firmly.

"We'll keep our backs to her," replied Jenny.

"Then why do we need these silly clothes at all? She doesn't know . . ."

But Jenny was holding up to herself a red plaid shirt and a pair of boy's overalls. "Here's the plan." She indicated a crumpled, full-skirted dress that lay in a heap on the ground. "You dress in that. And put that hat on to hide your face. I'm a little taller than you. I'll be the man."

"What man?" asked a puzzled Virginia.

"The man you are coming to meet, silly. Your lover."

Virginia could only stare.

"I'm not coming to meet any lover."

"Don't be so dense," chided Jenny. "We're just playing a part. Ole lady Parker will *think* you are. That's part of the joke. She'll be beside herself trying to figure out who it is that is meeting in her woods."

"Why should she care?" asked Virginia. The whole scheme was a total puzzle to her. She could not follow Jenny's reasoning at all.

"Because she's a snoop, that's why. She thinks that she needs to know everything. Don't you see? She'll nearly go crazy trying to figure it out."

Virginia, shaking her head, still could not understand.

"Put it on," Jenny said impatiently. "We don't have all day."

Obediently, Virginia picked up the dress and tried to determine which end was which. It was all ruffles and bows. A disgusting piece of workmanship. Her mama would never ask her to wear such a frilly, overdone thing.

She struggled to get it over her head and settled into place. When she raised her head, she noted that Jenny was already in her plaid shirt and overalls and was busy trying to get her mop of red hair carefully tucked under the ample brim of a beat-up brown hat. In spite of her confusion, Virginia could not suppress the giggles. Jenny lifted her head, took one look at Virginia, then fell into peals of laughter of her own. They were a sight. At least that much of it was rather fun.

"Here's the plan," Jenny said when they were under control again. "You go first. Stand just toward the house by the poplars. Keep your back to the house. Pace back and forth like you're waiting for someone. Keep looking toward the trees. After a little bit I will come out, and you will run to meet me. Got it?"

Virginia nodded. It didn't sound at all complicated.

"Here . . . here's your hat," Jenny called quickly as Virginia turned to go. "You forgot to put it on. You want your face to be hidden—all the time. Don't forget. Don't let her see who you are. That's the point of it."

Virginia nodded. Maybe it was turning out to be a little bit fun.

Virginia started off again, her yards of billowy skirts flouncing out about her ankles. The dress was too long, and more than once she tripped over it. She had to use both hands to hold it up out of the way of her feet.

When she reached the edge of the poplar grove, she made sure that she avoided looking toward the Parker house. Carefully, her head turned slightly away, she made her way out into the open and dropped the handfuls of skirts. She stood there, the full sun beating down upon her head. For a spring day, it felt dreadfully hot with her layers upon layers of clothing. Then she remembered that she was supposed to be pacing. She began to walk back and forth, pretending to peer into the secret depths of the poplar trees. Two horses, feeding at the other end of the pasture, lifted their heads and stared in curiosity. She heard one snort and then they returned to their feeding again.

Back and forth, back and forth Virginia paced. She was

getting tired of the game and terrible impatient with Jenny. Why didn't she come? What was she waiting for? Surely by now Mrs. Parker would have gotten out her spyglass—if indeed she had one—and was focused on the spot down in her own pasture.

As Virginia paced, she got warmer and warmer. Her face flushed beneath the broad-brimmed hat. Her shoulders felt weighted down with the yards of heavy material. Her nose began to tickle from the dust her boots were raising. Why didn't Jenny come?

And then there was a rustling from among the branches and out poked Jenny's brown hat. She looked about stealthily, first checking one way, then the other. Slowly, ever so slowly, she advanced, brushing aside small imaginary bushes, looking, reaching, feeling her way across the short distance, continually turning one way, then the other, as though she were wading through some dense jungle. Virginia was so intent upon watching the strange maneuvers that she totally forgot that she was to rush to meet her.

"Run!" Jenny hissed. Virginia hiked up her skirts and, fearing she was about to be attacked by some beast or run over by the Parker horses, with one wild look about her, would have headed directly toward the Parker house.

"No," squealed Jenny. "To me."

Virginia then remembered and changed her course and her actions. With outstretched arms she headed toward Jenny. It was almost her undoing, for she had taken only two steps when she tripped over the hem of the cumbersome skirt. Quickly she reached to jerk the skirt up from the tanglement of her foot, but she heard the sickening sound of tearing cloth as she did so. She did manage to keep herself from going down, but she staggered along for several steps before she totally regained her balance. Jenny did not look amused.

Virginia plunged into Jenny with such force that both

of them nearly went down. After doing an awkward two-step, trying to support each other, they managed to untangle themselves enough to stand upright.

Virginia could feel Jenny's arms encircling her shoulders and pulling her close. "Kiss me," she hissed in Virginia's ear.

Automatically Virginia pulled back and felt Jenny's arms tighten.

"Kiss me," Jenny hissed again.

"But—?"

"Just do it. Haven't you kissed anyone before?"

Of course she had. She made the rounds each night, giving her mother and father their good-night kiss. But this . . . this was so . . . foolish.

"Kiss me," Jenny ordered for the third time.

Virginia leaned forward and gave Jenny a quick peck on the cheek.

"Not like that. That's not the way lovers kiss," Jenny exploded scornfully.

But Virginia pushed away from Jenny. "How do I know how lovers kiss?" she returned, anger making her own words come hissing forth.

Jenny used some nasty words. "I thought your sister had a boyfriend."

"She does."

"And you've never seen them kiss?"

Virginia's face flushed. The fact was, she had seen Troy kiss Clara. Once. Once when she'd had no business being where she was. She had spied on them. Secretly and disobediently spied. If her mama had known about it—or if Clara had found out—she would have been in enormous trouble. But she was not going to kiss Jenny the way Troy had kissed Clara. Never.

"Kiss me," Jenny said again. "Mrs. Parker will never believe we're lovers if we don't kiss."

"But we're not lovers," insisted Virginia and pushed back from Jenny again.

"We are supposed to pretend, that's all."

"But I can't pretend—that."

"You are a dead fish," Jenny exclaimed disgustedly. "If you aren't going to play the part, what did you even come for?"

"You never told me what the part was—remember?" Virginia shot back heatedly.

"I told you we'd be lovers. What did you think they did?"

But Virginia took another step backward. And as she did her feet again tangled in the hem of her skirts, and this time she could not recover her balance. With a wild grasp for something to hang on to she flung out a hand that sent Jenny's brown hat hurtling toward the poplars at her back. Down tumbled her mass of flaming red hair, reflecting the gold of the afternoon sun.

Virginia gave a gasp, then wildly scrambled for her own broad-brimmed hat that had tumbled away from her with the impact of her fall. Both of them—*both of them* had been totally exposed right before the very eyepiece of Mrs. Parker's spyglass. What in the world would the story about town be now? She could only imagine. What would her father and mother say about this escapade? What about the people of the church? The pastor? Virginia could feel her cheeks heating. They would be the laughing stock of the whole town. Why had she let Jenny talk her into such a ridiculous stunt anyway?

Angrily she scrambled to regain her feet and started toward the cover of the trees. With one backward glance, one that shot arrows of malice Jenny's way, she hiked up the remnants of the tattered skirts.

To her surprise Jenny was not hurrying after her. She was not even clamoring to retrieve the wayward hat. Instead she was standing, fully exposed, facing the yard of the Parkers, dancing from one leg to the other, mane flying, hands up beside her ears as she pulled some of the most hideous faces Virginia had ever seen a human being manage. She even heard her little chant, "Ya, ya, ya, ya, ya."

Virginia sucked in her breath. Harmless fun? They were *sure* to be in great trouble. Without stopping to think she straightened to her full height and yelled in her loudest voice, "Jenny Woods—you stop that this instant and get over here."

Jenny stopped her prancing and spun to look at her, an expression of unbelief on her freckled face.

But Virginia was not finished. "Get over here," she said with an angry jerk of her hand. "You're acting like a moron, and you'll get us both in huge trouble."

Jenny threw her a defiant look, tossed her red hair, and turned back toward the Parker house, starting up her weird sporadic dance and "ya, ya, ya's" again.

"Okay for you, Jenny," Virginia called angrily. "I'll never speak to you again."

She turned to run, trying desperately to draw the cumbersome dress over her head as she did so. It was not an easy task, but at length she was able to wriggle free of it and cast it aside.

"You're right," Jenny's angry voice called after her. "You won't talk to me 'cause I'll never let you that close to me again. Not ever again. Do you hear me, Virginia?"

In spite of her anger, or perhaps because of it, great rasping sobs welled up within Virginia. This was so stupid. So unfair. Why did Jenny think of such dumb things to do anyway? Now they would never be friends again. She had broken off all possibilities of any further relationship, and besides—now she would have to bear the brunt of Mrs. Parker's gossiping tongue. It was all just so totally unfair—and humiliating.

At the end of each day that followed, Virginia breathed an audible sigh as she climbed into bed at night. She still ached for her friendship with Jenny. She so much missed being a part of the little group. But, as yet, there had not been one snippet of gossip about the incident down in the Parker's pasture. Perhaps Mrs. Parker did not spend all of her time with a spyglass in hand after all. Maybe she didn't even have a spyglass.

CHAPTER 7

It rained steadily for four days straight. Virginia humped her shoulders and leaned into the wind and slashing rain. She hated foul weather, and it put her in a very foul mood. She wished she didn't have to go to school. She arrived dripping and out of sorts, face shiny from cold spring rain, hair whipped and plastered against her head. It didn't help one bit that everyone else arrived in the same condition. She hated it.

Many of her peers seemed to share her feeling. The halls of the small school echoed with disgruntled comments. People groused at one another about soggy coats dripping on text books, rubber boots left in the walkway, musty smells from wet coats, and umbrellas left *up* when they should have been *down*. Even the teachers seemed to be affected by the weather. Especially when they attempted to dry out their drenched charges so they wouldn't sit shivering in their desks, too cold and miserable to concentrate on the morning lessons. Mr. Noraway complained that they were burning more firewood now than they had during the cold of the winter months.

Some good did come of the storm, Virginia decided. While cooped up in the classrooms at recess and over the lunch hours, Jenny started talking to her again.

At first it was just little snippets. Small comments that were not quite as acid as they had been of late. Then they became actual bits of conversation. They led to subtle little invitations for Virginia to join the small group again.

Virginia's heart lightened. It seemed so important to be part of the group. Accepted. Her world, even with the continual dump of rain, became a brighter place. And when the clouds finally rolled off to the east and the sun actually came out again, Virginia was in totally different spirits. The world wasn't such a gloomy place after all.

She almost skipped her way home from school that Thursday afternoon. Mr. Adamson, as usual, was out working in his garden. Now his dirty pant knees were not just covered with soil but practically dripping water. Virginia knew it was much too wet for the elderly man to be gardening, but apparently he could stay indoors no longer.

"A little wet, isn't it?" she asked as she looked at his soggy clothing.

"Trees are a bit drippy," he replied.

"But your knees. Your knees are all wet."

"They'll dry."

"But how about your lumbago?"

He shrugged. His little gesture told her that he considered the matter of no importance. "Rain sure been hard on the flowers. Had to spend the day staking 'em up. Awful hard on 'em. Martha would be heartbroken seein' 'em in such a state."

Virginia looked again at his wet pant legs. She figured that his Martha might be a little upset about his own condition as well, but she did not say so.

"They'll come back," she said instead. "Plants are hardy."

She had heard her grandmother make the statement, and though she had no proof, she trusted her grandmother's word for it.

The old man nodded, but his eyes looked doubtful. He

turned from the flower beds and approached the fence. His muddy hands made dirty marks on the pickets.

"You seem chipper today," he commented. "Been goin' by here lately with yer tail between yer legs, chin nearly draggin' on the ground."

Virginia smiled.

"Change of weather make ya feel thet much better?"

Virginia nodded. But she knew that wasn't the whole story. She had her friend back again. Ruthie had been pushed to the side. She, Virginia, had been reinstated. It was good to be back as Jenny's chosen cohort.

"Jenny and me—we're best friends again," she admitted to the old man.

"Jenny? Thet sassy little gal with the carrot hair?"

Oh, thought Virginia, *Jenny would not like that comment*. But she nodded. Mr. Adamson had the right girl.

He stood, looking at her quizzically. She was afraid he was going to take off his hat and scratch his head with his dirt-caked fingers.

"Never could figure out thet one," he went on. "'Bout as different as day and night, the two of you. What makes ya friends?"

It was a startling question. One Virginia was not prepared to answer. She had never even thought about it before. Jenny was just . . . just Jenny. Full of life. Of ideas. A leader. Anyone would have been happy to be Jenny's best friend. The fact that Jenny had chosen her was . . . was some kind of little miracle. She was sure that every girl in her class must envy her.

But an old man like Mr. Adamson could not be expected to understand any of that.

"We like each other," she said with a quick shrug.

He nodded, but he still seemed to be looking deep inside of her. Searching for an answer to the puzzling question.

"So yer friends agin?" he said at last. Virginia sensed

that he did not seem too pleased. "Well, ya best git on home, an' I'd best git on to my gardenin'. Tell yer mama thanks fer thet last batch of ginger cookies."

"Clara likely baked them," said Virginia. Some of the sun had been robbed from her day. Clara. *Clara the good*. The dull. The dependable. Mama's *special helper*.

"Good little cook, Clara," said the man. "Make a good wife."

Yes, thought Virginia, *and the sooner the better, I'm thinking*.

"Well, be off with ya. I've still got some plants to stake."

Virginia nodded. "Good-bye, Mr. Adamson," she said politely as she moved on down the sidewalk.

She glanced back over her shoulder. The old man still stood there, shaking his head. She wasn't sure if the pensive look was because of his chat with her or because of the damage done to his flower beds.

Friday morning brought a return of full sunshine. It felt so good to pull on a light sweater and head off for school without worrying about wind and rain. Virginia even allowed Francine to walk along with her. She was sure nothing could daunt her new spirit of joy. But as she neared the school and Francine scampered on ahead to join some of her little classmates, Ruth seemed to appear from nowhere. She fell into step with Virginia, not waiting for any kind of invitation, spoken or otherwise.

"Ya comin'?" she asked without preamble.

Virginia's head came up, eyes showing her confusion. Ruth seemed to take great pleasure in the fact.

"Hasn't Jenny asked you?" she continued, tipping her head to one side and looking very smug.

Virginia could only shrug.

"She already asked me."

The words were said with such cockiness that Virginia felt the anger rise within her and her cheeks begin to flame.

"She'll ask me," she retorted sharply. "She just hasn't seen me yet."

Ruth gave her a smirky smile that told Virginia she wasn't going to keep her secret. "Maybe not. You've already said no so many times. We're going to the creek after school. Sam says thet the rain has made it a river. It will be perfect for rafting—and other stuff."

Virginia wasn't sure what the other stuff would be, but she suddenly had a sick feeling in the pit of her stomach again. They were all going to the creek. She had just found her way back into the little group, and she would have to say no again.

The temptation to turn around and head for home, pleading illness when her mother confronted her, was almost too much to overcome. But what if her mother knew she was faking? Her mother was a nurse. She knew the signs of real illness. And what if . . . what if her mother decided that she really might be ill? She'd insist on Uncle Luke seeing her. He'd know the difference for sure. No, she couldn't risk that. She'd just have to go on to class.

Ruthie was speaking again. "—an' Georgie knows where we can sneak a raft—ready-made. Mr. Taggart keeps one down by the bridge. What he uses it for—"

"You can't do that," Virginia said, shocked that it would even be considered. She stopped short and stared at the girl before her.

"Wha'dya mean?"

"Can't take something that doesn't belong—"

"Boy, are you stuffy!" Ruth's words were more indignant than Virginia's. "We're only gonna borrow it. Not steal it."

"But you still—"

"We'll put it back. Okay?"

"I still—"

Ruth gave her a withering look. "No wonder Jenny hasn't asked you. She likely doesn't even want you along. Boy! What a dead head."

Virginia swallowed. Was that what Jenny thought? Was there really the danger that she wouldn't even be asked?

Anger filled her again. Anger at Ruth, who had somehow gained the inside edge again. Anger that Jenny might not include her. And though she did not formulate the thought, anger with her parents for bringing her up with such a strict set of do's and don'ts.

She brushed past Ruth and proceeded up the school steps. She had no desire for further discussion.

She was already in her desk when Jenny slipped into her seat. Virginia did not look up. Did not wish to meet the eyes of the girl across the aisle. Would there still be friendship there, or had Ruth eroded it once again?

But as soon as the opening exercises had been completed, the class assignment had been given, and Miss Crook had settled herself with her head bent over correcting lesson books, Virginia felt a little tug on her sleeve. The eraser was being "loaned" again. Self-consciously she accepted it. The small scrap of paper under it nearly scorched her fingers, her anxiety was so heightened.

She laid the eraser on her desk and slipped the paper scrap under the cover of her text. Nervously she cast the smallest glance in Jenny's direction and saw the girl give her a brief nod and a knowing smile.

Virginia turned her eyes back to the front of the classroom. Miss Crook was still busily engaged in correcting. Virginia eased the bit of paper from under her literature book and uncrumpled it.

"After school. At the creek. You coming?"

Virginia bowed her head. Her eyes wanted to shut and block out the words. To allow some kind of concentration.

To think. Think. But she willed them to stay open, staring straight at the small scrap.

Her mind went back to the conversation at their supper table a few weeks back. The creek had been dangerous then. Now with the heavy spring rains, it was swollen and even more so. It was risky to go there. Not just an act of disobedience—but a risk of getting hurt—or worse. But if she didn't, if she failed the test now, she knew she would never be invited to be a part of Jenny's crowd again.

Her head whirled with the enormity of her decision. What should she do? What could she do? At last she picked up her pencil, flipped over the small scrap, and with her chin set firmly in stubborn resolve, she wrote just one word and slipped the note back under the eraser. Without even looking up she passed the small rectangle of rubber back across the aisle to Jenny. She would not meet her eyes. Could not meet her eyes, but she heard the faint rustle of the paper as Jenny unfolded her message, then a contented sigh and Jenny's little exclamation of "Good."

She did not hurry home first for permission. She knew that such permission would never have been granted. Instead, like a fugitive on the run, she sneaked her way out of town, staying to back alleys, ducking from fence to clump of trees.

In a way it was exciting, but her pounding heart also raced with conflict. She would be in trouble. Real trouble when the act was discovered. And it would be discovered—she had no doubt of that.

They had agreed to meet at the small stand of trees down creek from the bridge. As soon as Virginia was past the houses of the town, she struck out directly for the spot. Two of the boys were already there.

"Boy, ya oughta see it," exclaimed Sam. "It's wild!"

Excitement made his voice crack. It also made Virginia shiver. In the distance she could hear the sound of rushing water, and she knew that the boy's words were true.

"Georgie's gone fer the raft," Freddie whispered conspiratorially, edging close to Virginia.

Virginia subconsciously moved away a step. She didn't want Freddie's flannel sleeve brushing against her ginghamed arm.

"Where's Jenny?" she asked. Her voice sounded weak. Squeaky.

"She'll be here. She had to stop fer somethin'."

"What?"

"I dunno. She didn't say."

Virginia cast a nervous glance at the sky, at the sun making its steady decent in the west. Already she would have been missed at home. Each minute that passed put her in further jeopardy. She did hope that Jenny hurried. That they got it all over with quickly.

"Here comes Georgie," shouted Freddie, running to meet the boy who was dragging the raft on a tow rope, panting and puffing with the effort.

"Why didn't ya float it down?" chided Sam. "Stupid to drag it."

"Once you put it in thet creek—you'd never git it stopped, thet's why," Georgie gasped out between breaths.

His words brought more fear to Virginia's heart, but Freddie did not seem to share her concern. He was rubbing his hands together in excited agitation. His eyes shone with anticipation. "Boy," he exclaimed. "This is gonna be heart thumpin'."

Still Jenny did not come. The boys were hard to hold back. They were eager to get the raft in the water. But they knew they had to wait for their leader. Jenny would never forgive them if they went ahead without her.

Virginia paced back and forth, glancing often at the

sky and the lengthening shadows. She was about to tell the fellows that she was going home, that Jenny had taken too long, that she had been there but had to leave, when Jenny and Ruth appeared. They were out of breath, flushed with hurrying and excitement. Jenny held up a full sleeve and shook out the contents. Five licorice sticks and several peppermints tumbled out.

"I wanted six but I could only get five," she said, passing out the licorice. "We'll have to share."

Virginia's eyes grew large. "Where did you get all the money?"

Jenny cast a glance toward Georgie and the two began to whoop with laughter. The others joined in. Virginia frowned. She didn't know what was so funny. She turned her back on the lot of them. "C'mon, let's get this thing in the water. I've gotta get home."

Jenny reached out and roughly grabbed her sleeve.

"Just a minute, Miss Prissy," she hissed. "Who's in charge here?"

They stood facing each other, Jenny's green eyes flashing, Virginia looking confused but angry.

"You are," she finally admitted reluctantly.

"Then I'll give the orders. Understood?"

Virginia could only nod mutely, but she was still upset. Angry enough to dare a further challenge. "I only wanted to hurry."

"I'll decide whether we're in a hurry or not," responded Jenny with a flip of her head. "And it just happens—I'm not."

That was too much. Virginia gave her a cold stare. "That's easy for you to say," she spat out. "But I have to get home."

"She has to get home," Jenny taunted in a singsong tone, turning to her peers. "Little Miss Skirt-hanger has to get home to her mama."

They laughed in unison. That was what they were supposed to do.

Virginia's anger flared. Tears sprang to her eyes. "You don't know what it's like," she flung at the other girl. "You don't have a mama to tell you what to do. You don't know how lucky—" But she stopped. The foolishness of her own words hit her solidly.

She turned on her heel and fled the grove of trees. She didn't belong. She knew that. This wasn't her crowd. The pilfered raft. The defiance of orders. The challenging of the dangerously swollen creek. She didn't belong. She was going home.

Suddenly aware that she was still holding the licorice stick, she glanced down at it and with a sickening feeling finally understood the laughter. The licorice stick was stolen merchandise. The thought brought terror to her heart. She had never stolen. Never. Her folks—her grandparents would be shocked. Mortified.

She wheeled and threw the licorice stick in the direction of the little crowded tangle who stood looking after her. It fell in the grasses, short of its intended destination, but she did not wait to see if it was retrieved. She hiked her skirts and spun around to continue her dash for home.

"Just you wait, Virginia. . . ." She heard Jenny's angry cry after her, but she kept right on running.

CHAPTER 8

All the way home Virginia tried to figure some way that would allow her to slip in quietly—undetected—into the solitude and comfort of her own room. She felt sick inside. Sick and scared. She had disobeyed again. There would be punishment. But it was not the thought of the punishment that bothered her the most.

She was confused. On the one hand, she hated to be an outcast again. On the other, she was relieved to be rid of the bondage of trying to please Jenny. They didn't belong together. She knew that now. They were too different in their upbringing. In their way of looking at things. Why, Jenny did not even believe in God. And though there were times when Virginia wished she could dismiss His presence from her own life, she knew, deep down, that she could not. Whether she wanted Him to exist or not, He did. And because He did, she was—in some way she had not quite figured out yet—responsible to Him. It was a scary thought and one that often troubled her at night when the house was quiet.

But Virginia's mind turned to other things as she hurried toward home. Things tangible. Things visible. Like her mother's upset eyes. Her father's stern voice. Clara's shocked look and Francine's teary face. And her brothers would add their voices to the admonitions, the lectures she was sure to get. She would have it all to face once again. The worst of it was that she had gained nothing in the process. Jenny was even more upset than before. Virginia would never be part of the *in* group again.

The door to the kitchen was ajar. Only the screen door was securely in place. Virginia hesitated for one moment, hand on the latch. She could hear someone stirring about inside. She hated to enter. Hated to face what lay before her.

"Would you like me to check?" she heard Clara ask.

Her mother answered, her voice tight. Worried. "Where would you check?"

"I don't know. I could try The Sweet Shop."

"I don't think you'd find her there. Even a teenager could not drag a soda out to last so long. She's never been this late before."

Virginia shifted nervously. They were right there—fretting about *her*. She was going to have to walk right into the lion's den. She couldn't even pretend. If only they were back in the parlor or out in the garden.

"Do you think I should go get Papa?"

There was a moment of silence. Virginia could envision her mother's eyes lifting to the kitchen clock with its border of blue forget-me-nots. "He will be home anytime. It's late."

"She'll be here, Mama," Clara said with assurance. "It's hard for a young girl to leave her friends. It always seems that the others are having so much fun. Fun you hate to miss."

"Oh, Clara. I worry so about her. I'm not sure that her friendships are—that she has chosen wisely. I hope and pray—I just don't want her to get hurt."

"She's just a kid, Mama. She'll be all right."

"But you never—"

Clara laughed. "Of course I did. I struggled with acceptance just like Virginia. I just wasn't quite brave enough to let it show so openly."

"You—?"

"Of course. I think all kids do. Some just . . . just take it more seriously than others."

"Well, I never remember you being in direct defiance of our rules. I really worry about Virginia. I don't know what to try next. We've prayed. We've reasoned. We've punished. We've—I'm going to have a talk with Grandma. Maybe she has some idea. . . ."

Virginia could not stand any more. With one quick movement she stepped forward and flung open the screen door. She stepped inside, her eyes flashing, her chin up. If they wished to chastise her, she was ready.

At the sound behind her, her mother swung around. Her first reaction was one of intense relief. She moved slightly, and Virginia wondered if her mother was going to rush forward and crush her wayward girl to her breast. But her mother quickly checked herself. The look in her eyes turned to one of frustration.

"Change your clothes, Virginia, and wash up. Supper will be on the table in a few minutes. We will discuss your tardiness after supper."

Virginia turned to go. They were not going to deal with it and get it over. She had to wait. Wait in misery. Suddenly she did not want any supper.

"I'm not hungry," she called back over her shoulder as she left the room.

"You will join the family at table," her mother answered firmly. "Even if you just sit there."

So that little ploy had not worked, either. Anger began to take hold of her again. She might as well have stayed at the creek with her friends and had some fun. She was going to pay for it anyway.

She changed her clothes and washed as she had been bidden, but she did not leave her room for the kitchen until her father called. At the sound of his voice, she dragged herself obediently toward the big kitchen table. It would not do to make her father call a second time.

She slid into her seat and lowered her head. She did not wish to meet the eyes of any family member. She did not need to raise her head to know that her mother had prepared her favorite meal. She could smell the savory fried chicken. It made her stomach growl in spite of her determination. How could she just sit there and listen and smell as the rest of them enjoyed the crispy, succulent chicken? And she was hungry. She had not even had milk and cookies after school.

Her father said the evening grace. Virginia scarcely listened to the words. She heard the Amen and roused herself. The passing of heaping serving bowls was about to begin. She would be tested beyond endurance.

"I want the wishbone," declared Francine, as she always did.

"Please, may I have the wishbone?" her mother reminded, as she always did.

Francine corrected her error.

Virginia could have gone round the table and named the piece of chicken that settled on every plate. Clara would take breast meat, Rodney a thigh, Danny a drumstick, and Francine her wishbone. Her papa would take two wings and a drumstick. Some white, some dark meat. And her mother would take the neck, or the back, insisting that they were her favorite pieces, when all the while the family knew that she was simply cleaning up the ones no one else was interested in.

The other piece of breast meat should have been Virginia's. It made her mouth water just thinking about it. And the steaming mashed potatoes and rich gravy did not help, either. Nor did the thought of the whipped turnips, seasoned with parsley and smoothed with cream.

Without comment her mother slipped the piece of

chicken breast on Virginia's plate as the serving dish went around. Virginia thought about ignoring it, but she could not. Her mother also served her a helping of potatoes, gravy, and turnips, all the while chatting easily with the family. As usual her parents were discovering the highlights from each one's day. Virginia hoped they would not get to her. She had little to say.

There was high-meringued lemon pie for dessert. Virginia was just cleaning up the last bite when there was a sound of running and a loud thumping on the back door.

Before her father could even reach it to admit their caller, they heard a shout. "There's trouble at the crik."

Her father flung the door open and faced an excited Jedd Marlow. The young lad looked ready to plunge on again before even delivering his full message. Virginia's father reached out and grasped his shoulder.

"What it is, son?"

"Doc Luke wants Mrs. Simpson. Some kids went down in the crik. They're hurt."

Virginia felt her world whirling. Her stomach heaved. She wondered if she was going to be able to keep down her fried chicken.

It seemed forever before her mother returned. Clara had taken over the family, sending the younger ones off to bed. But Virginia could not sleep. She paced back and forth in her room, waiting for the sound of the door, her mother's step across the kitchen.

What had happened? Who was hurt? How badly? What if she had stayed with them? The questions hung heavy upon her mind. She could not dismiss them. Her frantic thoughts would not let her rest.

The hall clock had already announced the midnight hour before the door finally opened. Virginia, hearing voices, crept from her bed and ventured toward the kitchen. Her mama was seated at the kitchen table looking weary and sad. Her father was pouring two cups of steaming tea. "You look exhausted," Virginia heard him say to her mother. "Are they going to be okay?"

Her mother shook her head as she drew off her gloves and laid them aside on the corner of the table. "We don't know yet. The one boy is in rather bad condition. If it hadn't been for Rett Marshall, he'd be gone for sure."

"What happened?"

"No one is too sure. Seems they were rafting on the—" Her mother looked up and saw Virginia clinging to the doorframe of the kitchen. She extended her hand without comment. Virginia moved forward. She knew her face must reveal her state of mind.

"It was some of your school friends, Virginia."

Virginia nodded mutely. As much as she needed to know, she could not even ask about them.

Virginia felt her mother's arm slip about her waist. "They had an accident on the creek. Seems they were rafting."

Virginia nodded again.

"One of the boys—the Boycie boy—made it to shore with no problem. He clung to an overhanging tree limb, he said. He also helped one of the girls—the Riant girl—to hang on until help came."

Her mother accepted the cup of tea and turned back to her father. "The Booth boy—George, isn't it?—got a bad gash on his head. Needed a good deal of stitching. That's why Luke wanted me. And the other boy—the Crell's son—he was in the water the longest. We still don't know if he'll make it, and if he does, if he'll be all right mentally."

Her mother seemed to remember Virginia again. She turned back to her, and one hand reached up to smooth the tangled hair. She leaned forward and pressed a kiss against her daughter's forehead. "I'm sorry, sweetheart. I know they are your classmates. This is hard."

But Virginia's mind was whirling. Her heart pounding. "Jenny?" she managed through lips stiff with fear. "What about Jenny?"

Her parents exchanged quick glances. "What do you mean? How did you know—?"

Instantly, Virginia knew that she had given away her secret. For one instant her eyes widened in consternation, and then she leaned against her mother's shoulder and began to sob.

Her mother let her cry, pressing a comforting hand against the small of her back, using the other to smooth the hair back from her face. When the worst of the emotional storm had passed, her father quietly spoke. "I think you need to sit down and tell us about this."

Virginia blew on the hankie her mother offered and sniffed back remaining tears. "We went to the creek after school," she started slowly, twisting the handkerchief around her fingers.

"Why?"

"They knew it was . . . was flooded, so it would . . . would raft good."

"But it *didn't* raft good," protested her father, irritation edging his voice. "It was extremely dangerous and could have—may have—cost someone's life."

Virginia nearly burst into tears again.

"How many?" her mother asked her rather sharply.

"Six," Virginia replied, mentally picturing the group. "Freddie, George, and Sam and Ruthie, Jenny and me."

"Thank God," her mother said with deep emotion. "Then we did find all of them. They were so upset that we weren't sure they were thinking properly. They are all in deep shock."

"They just wanted to raft," defended Virginia.

Her father let the comment pass. "What happened?" he asked instead.

"I don't know. I . . . I . . . Jenny and Ruthie were so late, and I . . . I got mad and came home."

Virginia was well aware of the looks that passed between her parents. With a deep sigh, her mother's arm tightened about her again.

"So you came home before they took the raft?"

"They had it already. They got it from under the bridge. Mr. Taggart's."

"So they filched a raft."

"They were just borrowing it," Virginia quickly tried to explain.

"But they didn't have permission—did they?"

"No-o." The answer came slowly.

"Go ahead," prompted her father.

"Well, they had the raft, and we waited for Jenny and Ruthie to come and when they came—" She hesitated. Did she dare tell her folks that Jenny had also stolen sweets? Did she have to tell? She decided to skip that part. It had little bearing on the accident, and her folks had always told her not to be a tattletale.

"I . . . I got mad, so I came home. The rest of them were going to try the raft."

"So what happened?" Her papa had turned back to her mama.

"We aren't sure. They got into rough water. Something went wrong. Luke thinks they might have hit a submerged rock or caught a tree. The raft must have flipped. They were all thrown into the water. The one boy struck his head sharply—likely on a rock. Like I said, a couple of them managed to hang on to an overhanging limb, but they are still in shock and suffering from exposure to the icy water. The one boy went under. Was swept along. It was Rett who pulled him out. Guess he heard the screams. He had to make three tries before he found the boy, Ruthie said. By then the Crell boy had been under for a long time—maybe too long."

Her mother stopped and shook her head. "Luke doesn't know if he'll make it."

Virginia felt a sickness sweep through her body.

"What awful news to take to parents."

Virginia watched the fingers of her father's hand pass through his hair. She noticed that he looked as drawn and pale as her mother.

"The Crells are with him now—hoping and praying that he will wake up."

"And all for some stupid lark on the creek. They could have drowned. All of them." The tension in her father's voice twisted Virginia's stomach in knots.

"It could have been Virginia." Her mother's voice was also choked with emotion. Her arm tightened around Virginia again, and her eyes filled with tears.

"We never know," said her father, "when we pray for God's protection on our children to what great lengths He will need to go to fulfil our prayers."

Her mother seemed too moved to respond.

Virginia noticed that the poured tea had been forgotten. It sat, getting cold, while her folks exchanged both verbal and silent messages.

"Luke is concerned about Rett as well. He refused any kind of treatment, but he was in that cold water for some time. If it hadn't been for him . . ." The rest of the thought was left unspoken.

Virginia fleetingly wondered what the boys would think of the Crow Man now. He had rescued some of his worst tormenters.

And then she remembered that she still had not heard about Jenny.

"Mama, what . . . what happened to Jenny? Is she—?" She couldn't finish. The thought was too scary.

"Jenny is in pretty bad shape. She took a nasty knock into the rocks. She has some cuts and bruises, a broken arm and collarbone, and two or three broken ribs."

Virginia felt all the air leave her lungs. "Will she—?"

"Uncle Luke hopes that she will make it. But it will be slow. It will take a long time for her to heal from her injuries." Her mother sighed. She hesitated for a moment before going on, her eyes meeting those of her husband, as though seeking his advice on what she was about to say. "She will need your friendship more than ever."

"But—" How could she tell her folks that she and Jenny were no longer friends? That Jenny had pushed too far with the stealing from The Sweet Shop? That Jenny would not even wish to see her again? Parents didn't understand things like that. Virginia closed her mouth tightly. There was nothing she could say.

"It's late," said her father. "You'd best get back to bed. We all need to get some sleep."

Virginia wondered if there would be any sleep for her that night. For any of them.

Her mother pulled her close and kissed her again. More tears had filled her eyes. "You can't know how I thank God that you are safe. That He watched over you. But even while I rejoice, other parents are in pain. Deep pain. Their children are suffering tonight. Are . . . hanging between life and death. Do you understand all this, Virginia? Do you have any idea what those parents are going through? Can you even begin to understand how much we love you? Why we try to protect you?"

Virginia could only nod her head mutely. She was beginning to understand.

But Jenny did not have a mother to care for her. To hover over her, praying for her safety. Her healing. Thoughts of her own cruel, stupid words returned to haunt her. "You don't have a mama. You don't know how lucky—"

Tears filled Virginia's eyes and rolled down her cheeks. "I'm sorry," she whispered against her mother's hair. "Really sorry. I won't do it again. I promise."

She felt her father's arm go about her shoulders. He knelt beside her and gathered her close. Her mother, too, was included in the embrace. She could feel the tears on his cheek as he pressed it against her forehead. "I think that we need to pray before you run off to bed," he said. "We have much to be thankful for. Others have not been so blessed. We need to pray for those families."

Virginia nodded and wiped at her cheeks with her flannel sleeve. Prayer sounded like a good idea.

CHAPTER 9

Virginia was never sure if her mother ever discussed her disobedience with her grandmother or not. But when the family came together for Sunday dinner, she was not surprised to have Grandma Marty pat the seat on the swing beside her and invite the girl for a little chat.

It was not unusual for Grandma to have little visits with her grandchildren, but Virginia had a feeling as she accepted the seat and felt her grandmother's arm tuck around her that this little talk might be different.

They swung back and forth in silence for several moments. The rest of the family seemed to have gone off on little missions of their own. The womenfolk were washing up the dinner dishes and putting babies down for afternoon naps, and the men had headed for the back porch to sit in the shade and talk and laugh about things that only men think are funny.

Even with so many of them scattered across the land, there still was a formidable gathering when the local ones got together for family dinner at the home farm. So Virginia found it peculiar that she and her grandmother were actually all alone on the front porch swing.

"Heard about yer little friends," her grandmother said.

Virginia wished to argue that they were not *little* friends, but she let it pass. She would never argue with her grandmother.

"It be a shame the hurts thet they suffered."

Virginia nodded her head in agreement.

"Youth can sometimes be too daring."

Virginia admitted with a nod that perhaps that was true.

"Yet it seems so important to belong—to be a part of all this—the goings-on. Doesn't it?"

Virginia only nodded again.

"Why, do ya think?"

Virginia frowned. Was her grandmother really expecting an answer?

"Why do you feel it's so important like to be a part of this . . . group that feels it is so . . . so necessary to flirt with excitement—danger even?" Grandma Marty continued.

"I dunno," replied Virginia.

"Study on it a minute. See iffen you can come up with an answer."

Virginia put her mind to "studying" on it.

"I guess just 'cause I want them to like me," she said at length.

"An' you think thet works? To give in? Go along with any plan they come up with? Even when it means that someone might get hurt?"

"Well, when I didn't do what they wanted, I know *that* didn't work."

"Were they roiled about it?"

"You mean mad?"

"Yes, mad. Were they upset? Nasty?"

Virginia nodded. Jenny had been nasty all right. "Jenny didn't even want me for her friend. She picked Ruthie."

"And that made you feel bad?"

Virginia nodded.

"Left out—like?"

Virginia nodded again.

"Not a nice feelin', bein' left out," agreed her grandmother. "I remember once whenst I was a girl. My best friend—well, I thought she was my best friend at the time. Turned out she wasn't my friend much a'tall. But anyway, she was a right smart little thing. Popular, too. All the girls thought they could be somebody by havin' her as a friend, an' all the boys thought she was . . . perky. But she was a little foxy, too. Rather mean-like—snippy, when she put her mind to it.

"My ma thought that she meant trouble, an' it turned out Ma was right. Sometimes grown-ups seem to have a nose fer sech things. I hated to admit it at the time—in fact, I didn't. Jest got right stubborn about the whole thing. Figured my ma didn't understand about sech things."

She stopped for a few minutes, and Virginia waited.

"Well, one day this here 'best friend,' she tells me thet the melons were ripe in the neighbor's garden. One big one looked especially good. She figured as how we could slip on in and sneak it off and have our own private melon party. I was scared. But I knew I had to do it. That is, iffen I was gonna keep her fer a friend. But iffen I did do it—and got caught—I'd sure git me one awful tanning from my pa. I knew thet, too."

"What did you do?" asked Virginia.

"Well, now. I couldn't lose my best friend, could I? So I says 'yes.' She made all the plans . . . how we'd sneak in as soon as it got dark. I had to crawl out of my bedroom winder after I'd been sent to bed. Got a great big sliver in the palm of my hand sliding on over the windersill. I can feel it burn yet—whenever I think about it."

She shivered, and Virginia could almost feel the sliver, too.

"Well, there was one thing we didn't know. Old man Wilchuck kept his huntin' dogs in the garden at nighttime. We no sooner lowered ourselves on the other side of the fence than those two ole dogs came a flyin' at us, bayin' an' a barkin' up a storm. Thought they'd waken the whole neighborhood—those thet claimed the cemetery as home included."

Virginia looked up into her grandmother's face to see if she was serious about her story or just funning. Her grandmother seemed to understand the question in her eyes.

"This is the truth now," she added. "Jest as it happened. Well, I turned to my friend—my best friend—and says 'Run,' and she ran and I was right on her heels runnin' as fast as my legs could fly. But I hadn't taken but a few steps when I tripped, and there was those big ole dogs right on my heels. I yelled for my friend, but she jest kept right on a runnin'. Lucky fer me those two ole dogs were more bark than bite. But I thought they were gonna lick the freckles right offen my face. Never have I had sech a complete slobberin'.

"But thet weren't the worst of it. When ole man Wilchuck came out to see what was frettin' his dogs—shotgun in hand, mind ya—he found me there sprawled on the ground, those two ole dogs slopping me up with their drippin' red tongues. He asked what I was doin' there. 'Course I didn't have a good answer, so I said nothin'. But later this here 'friend,' she spread the story all around thet I was in the garden to steal melons. Thet I had been boastin' to her of how I was gonna do it. Thet I said ole Mr. Wilchuck was too dumb to catch anybody. Well, I got the lickin' of my life, an' I'm not just talking 'bout the one those ole coon dogs gave me, either. My pa had his own kind, you can be sure of thet."

Virginia squirmed.

"Well, I decided right then and there thet any friend

who wants to git ya into trouble isn't really a friend at all. An' yer a heap better off without 'em. But I learned somethin' else, too. Though I haven't ever admitted it to a soul—until now. My ma was right all along. Thet girl was trouble."

She stopped talking and seemed to be listening to the creak of the swing.

"Peaceful out here. I love it." She looked down at Virginia and smiled. Her arm tightened about the young girl's shoulder. "Especially when I have sech good company."

Virginia managed a grin. She loved the time spent with her grandmother. But there was a funny little tightness in her stomach that did not want to go away.

Virginia had thought her thirteenth birthday had been the most important birthday she would ever have, so it was surprising to her when her excitement grew as her fourteenth birthday neared. Fourteen seemed so much more grown-up than thirteen.

But even as the excitement grew, so did the sadness within her. Her friends, her very best friends, were suffering the effects of the rafting incident the Friday before.

Virginia had not admitted it to anyone—it was a hard thing to talk about—but she had not been sleeping well at all. She kept thinking back to the day at the creek. It hadn't been her idea, but she had gone along with it. What if she had said no? Would they have gone anyway? Was there any way that she could have talked them out of it? Should she have informed an adult? But she wasn't to be a tattletale. Still—that was no excuse. Her folks had always told her that if someone's life was endangered, it was all right to tell. No, more than all right. It was one's duty.

But she hadn't told. Had not tried to talk them out of it. Yet she knew that the creek was dangerous. Had heard her father say so with concern in his voice. She should have tried to warn them. It would have cost her Jenny's friendship, of that she was sure, but she should have tried to warn them, or stop them in some way.

And she had nearly pushed Freddie away. Why? He had been nothing but nice to her, and yet she had suddenly felt miffed with him. Not even wanting him to stand close to her. Was she really that fickle in her friendship? It bothered her. Bothered far more than she would have ever imagined. Now he lay, still and unaware, between life and death. It kept her awake at night trying to sort it through. She felt drained and anxious.

And now her fourteenth birthday was approaching—such a special birthday, and she wouldn't even be able to enjoy it. Life was so totally unfair.

"How would you like to celebrate your birthday?" her mother asked at the evening supper table.

Virginia could tell by the tone of her voice that she was making an effort to be especially cheerful.

Virginia swallowed hard. Their mother usually did not let them choose how they would celebrate. The celebrating was always done just as it had been done for the many birthdays before. With family. And perhaps a few friends.

Virginia did not have time to reply before Francine squealed. "I know. Have a great big party."

Virginia felt like giving Francine a nasty look. Party? At such a time? But before she could even raise her head, Danny proposed another idea. "Let's go to Grandpa and Grandma's."

Danny never could get enough of the farm. Had Virginia not been feeling so down, she might have heartily agreed. As it was, she only sighed and bit at her lip to keep it from trembling.

"We'll talk about it later," her mother said quickly, her eyes watching her young daughter fight for control.

In the end, they did very little. A family supper with

Virginia's favorite meal of fried chicken was served around the family table. Grandma and Grandpa came. That made it special. They did have cake—with fourteen candles—and Virginia did get a pleasing round of presents from family members. But still—in spite of everyone's effort—the event seemed hollow. Almost a mockery.

Virginia wondered if things would ever be the same again. The whole town was in turmoil over the accident. Confusion and conflicting reports seemed to surface on every hand. Each story had a new twist—new rumors about the incident. Virginia heard things that were absolutely outlandish. There had been six on the raft, and one body had never been found. Old Mr. Taggart had taken four shots at the youngsters as they tried to steal his raft, but had luckily missed each time. Rett Marshall had swum after the raft for miles, overtaking it in the deepest and most turbulent water. Rett Marshall had hid in the bushes at the side of the creek and waylaid the rafters, deliberately overturning the raft and letting the passengers flounder in the churning water without even so much as offering any assistance.

The stories went on and on. It both frightened and sickened Virginia.

Ruthie and Sam were well enough to return to school near the end of the week. Ruthie seemed nervous and self-conscious about her bruised cheek and stitches, but Sam swaggered just a bit, enjoying the attention and assuming a role of great bravado.

Georgie returned the next week, a bandage covering a good deal of his forehead. Virginia could not help but wonder just what kind of damage the white patch hid from view, but George seemed to prefer to not talk about it.

The reports on Jenny sounded better than the initial

concerns about her condition. In spite of her lacerations and broken bones, she seemed to be healing nicely. Virginia wondered if she should pay a call, but she was hesitant. She did not know if the girl would welcome her at all into her sickroom.

On the other hand, the news on Freddie was still cause for deep concern. Virginia could not keep his face from appearing in her troubled dreams, haunting her night after night. The young lad's face was always serious, almost begging. Never once did she see in her dreams the crooked smile or the teasing eyes. When folks in town asked for reports on Freddie Crell, no one seemed to have any real answers. Even her uncle Luke, in his hushed doctor's voice, did not know if the boy would recover. Freddie was still unconscious, needing around-the-clock nursing care. Virginia's mother took shifts along with two other area women.

School finally finished, and the warmer days of summer settled in. Virginia hoped that the world would now return to some kind of normalcy. But that was not to be. Just as she began to relax, word came that Freddie Crell had passed away. He had never regained consciousness.

It was a sad funeral. Virginia sat and bit her trembling lip as she watched Freddie's family mourn their dead. His two sisters wept uncontrollably, and his younger brother, looking straightforward, sat with his face fixed in a grim set. He seemed determined not to cry, but it likely was anger that simmered in his eyes in place of the sorrow that should have been there. His mother wiped tears until she had sopped several hankies, and his father, a big barrel-chested man, looked about to explode in grief and rage at any moment.

Folks worried about the Crell family. What long-range effects would the deep grief of the parents have on the rest of the family? Virginia heard her parents discussing it in hushed tones.

And now her nightly dreams turned into agonizing nightmares. On more than one occasion Virginia awoke in a cold sweat, sobs shaking her body. She had seen Freddie's face again, and now it was not just somber, it was filled with panic. And always, always, he was slipping away from her, over a precipice, into a deep hole, inside a whirling eddy . . . and always, he was just out of reach of her hand.

It wasn't until summer was half over that Virginia saw Jenny. They both seemed frozen in place on the boardwalk outside the local grocers. Virginia wasn't sure just how to act. What to say. Would Jenny still be her enemy?

Jenny did not exactly smile, but she didn't turn away, either. She looked older. Sadder. There was no more bubbling mirth ready to spill out at the least provocation.

"Hello," Virginia at last dared to say, almost shyly. "Are you—is your arm better?"

Jenny shrugged. She still carried her arm in a sling. Uncle Luke said that she would need some therapy to get the hand working well again.

"Does it still hurt?"

"Not much," responded Jenny.

That seemed to be the end of the conversation. Jenny turned away, and Virginia swallowed her disappointment and entered the store.

The next week Virginia saw Jenny again at a community picnic. She looked so alone and forlorn that Virginia could not help but feel pity. Still, she could not get up the courage to make any kind of friendly overture. She was surprised when Jenny approached her.

"Are you still mad?"

Virginia looked at her evenly. "No."

"Me neither."

It was all that was said. Perhaps it was all that needed to be said—for the time. They just stood there, silently, beside each other, not talking, not even touching, but no longer alone.

But Virginia was still not sure just what the relationship should be. Were they really friends? Were they just not enemies? She knew she didn't want to get into trouble with Jenny again. Would that be a temptation? So she held herself aloof, wishing to assure Jenny that there were no hard feelings, but not daring to take the new friendship any further.

"How is that little Woods girl?" her mother asked one afternoon as she busied herself in the kitchen and Virginia poured a glass of milk to go with some of Clara's fresh gingerbread.

Virginia shrugged. "She's okay."

"Is her arm healed?"

"Not completely, I guess. Her hand still doesn't work quite right."

"That's a shame."

There was silence for a few moments while her mother chopped some onions for the stew.

"You should invite her over."

The words surprised Virginia.

"I don't think she'd come."

"Why not?"

"I dunno. She doesn't visit much."

"Maybe she's not had invitations."

Virginia thought about that. Maybe that was the reason.

"She doesn't have a ma."

"I know. That must be very hard for her."

Virginia thought about that, too. While she was thinking her mother spoke again. "I understand that her father is almost always away from home."

Virginia had not known that, but she wasn't surprised.

"He works," she answered after another sip of milk.

"Most fathers work. But some of them have more time for family than others."

Virginia thought of her own father. She knew that he was a very busy man, yet he always seemed to find time to spend with the family.

"I think her father is still mad," she offered.

"Mad?" Her mother turned to face her.

"About her ma. She left them and ran off."

"Oh." Her mama must have known the local gossip. The one word was spoken softly, yet somehow it carried with it a great deal of feeling. Her mother turned back to her stew again. She lifted a spoonful and tasted it for seasoning.

"Then Jenny *really* needs a friend. She must be dreadfully lonely."

Virginia's impatience flared. "Mama," she said more candidly than she had ever spoken to her mother before. "She's the one that got me in all the trouble. She coaxed me to go to The Sweet Shop, and . . . and . . ." She decided to let all of the minor things that Jenny had talked her crowd into doing go unsaid and went straight to the big event. "She thought of the idea to go to the creek. She stole the—"

"I see."

Silence again.

"You feel it was Jenny's fault that you got into trouble?" When Virginia didn't answer, her mother went on, "Jenny *forced* you to go along with her plans?"

"Well, no." Virginia finally acknowledged.

"But now you don't want to be her friend?"

That wasn't it at all. She had thought her mother would not *want* her to have Jenny for her friend.

"You don't think you are strong enough—have grown up enough—to resist her coaxing, is that it?"

Virginia honestly didn't know. She had made out just fine over the summer months without Jenny. She had not been in trouble with her parents once. At least not much. There had been a few little incidents—but nothing major. Nothing even near trips down swollen creeks on stolen rafts.

Her mama turned to her, wiping her hands on her apron as she approached the table where Virginia sat. "I know that this is—this can be confusing . . . in a way. But, Virginia, there is a vast difference between befriending someone who needs our friendship, and being a part of joining in with them in things that we know to be wrong."

She hesitated.

"Do you understand what I'm trying to say?"

Virginia reached up to wipe the milk from her mouth. She wasn't sure. But yes—yes, she thought she could understand the difference. She nodded slowly.

"Do you suppose we might be able to help her—if we work together?"

Virginia frowned. She had no idea what her mother wanted. Jenny was not looking for a grown-up friend.

"You can invite her over here. Then the temptations won't be so great. Invite some of your other friends with her if she won't come alone. I have the feeling that she is a very lonely little girl."

"Mama, she's not *little*. She's already had her fourteenth birthday. She's even older than me."

Her mother smiled. "I know, Virginia. I'm sorry, but someday you'll know why parents talk about their youngsters that way." She paused a moment, then suggested, "We could invite her to join us for church."

"She'd never go to church."

"How do you know? Have you asked her?"

"Well . . . no . . . but . . ."

"There, you see. We'll never know until we ask her."

Virginia remembered Jenny's comment about going to the church Youth Group. But that was so she could be near Jamison and wasn't really meant to be serious. Of course she had never come. Virginia was sure that she *would* never come. Jenny wasn't the type to enjoy anything to do with church. She even used bad words. She wouldn't fit.

Virginia supposed she should be glad that her mother was interested in helping Jenny. But for some reason she felt pushed into a corner again. She already knew Jenny. Jenny would not want to be crowded and pressured toward becoming part of the church. Virginia knew that. Yet she knew what she'd been taught. That Christians were to be healers. Helpers. Sharers of their faith. How could she be that for Jenny? She wasn't even sure if she had a faith. At least not the kind of faith that her mother and father had. Not the kind that Clara's Troy spoke of to the Youth Group.

Virginia crossed to the sink to rinse out her milk glass. Her mother was still waiting for her answer. But it would never work. She had no idea how to be a disciple. Not really. And if she was going to try to be one, she certainly would not start with Jenny. Not Jenny. Never. Jenny didn't need friends pushing their way into her life. Jenny picked her own friends. And at the moment, Virginia did not feel that she would be comfortable being one of them.

CHAPTER 10

More rumors began to circulate round town. Mr. Crell was not at all sure that the facts of the creek accident were as stated. Reports varied as to what Mr. Crell was actually saying, but always Rett Marshall's name came up in some accusatory way. Folks initially were shaking their heads in total denial, but gradually even those who immediately rejected such possibilities were not quite so quick to dismiss the scraps of poor evidence. It was unsettling to say the least.

Normally such bits of neighborhood gossip would never have been discussed in the Simpson household, but one night at their supper table the topic was tentatively brought up by Danny, who could not have missed hearing bits and pieces of the buzzing about town.

"They are saying awful things about Rett. Crazy things."

Virginia saw her father and mother exchange glances.

"We don't need to believe all we hear," her father replied calmly.

"But it isn't right to say it. Rett would never do anything like that."

"Like what?" asked Francine innocently. She was too

young to have been part of the gossip mill in the local school system.

"That he would hurt someone."

Francine's eyes grew larger. Virginia saw first fear, then determined dismissal. "He wouldn't," said Francine with some confidence. "One time I fell and scraped my knee, and he came and helped me up and brushed me off and put some salve from a little tin in his coat pocket on it. It felt better right away."

"See," Danny said with a look of defiance around the table, as though speaking to Rett's accusers.

Virginia had heard the rumors, too. It made her feel uneasy. After all, no one knew for sure just what had happened at the creek.

"They say he tipped the raft," Danny explained.

"No one has any evidence to substantiate that," put in their father quickly.

Francine frowned.

"They say he was just mad at the boys for always teasing him and wanted to get even," Danny continued.

"That is pure speculation." Again from their father.

"They say—"

Their father pushed back his chair and cleared his throat. Danny paused in midsentence.

"I think it's time to put a few facts before us here," said their father as all eyes turned to his face, "as they have been related by those involved."

There was total silence.

"Now, we had an accident at the creek this spring," he began in his best lawyer fashion.

Virginia sighed. Was the terrible incident never going to go away? Would it haunt her forever? Maybe *everyone*—forever. She still was having trouble sleeping, and she had heard that George had lost weight. He wasn't able to eat properly and often screamed out in the night. His folks were worried about him.

But her father was continuing.

"There were five young people on the raft. They were all thrown into the water and rescued—in one way or another—in various conditions. Rett was there—we know that. All four of the remaining members have testified to that.

"Rett did not tip the raft. George clearly remembers the raft hitting something and flipping. Ruth Riant verifies that story. Ruth also says that she saw Rett come running from the bushes *after* she was clinging to the branch. At that point, his clothing was not wet. It was Ruth who yelled to Rett, 'Freddie's in there.' That was when Rett plunged into the water.

"He stayed in the water for some time, feeling his way, totally going under, but could not find the boy. When he came out, Sam Boycie was on the bank by then. Sam was confused, but he does remember Ruthie screaming that Jenny was hurt. Rett turned from looking for Freddie and brought Jenny up on the bank. Then he went back in.

"He still could not find Freddie, so he came out, ran farther downstream, and went in again. That time he kept working his way on downstream, feeling his way, going under every now and then. He was almost to the bend in the creek when he finally came up with Freddie in his arms. He carried him back and laid him beside the others. Then he went and helped Ruthie. Then he left."

"See!" said Danny.

Francine was busy brushing away tears that streamed down her cheeks. Her tender heart still could not bear to hear the story.

Virginia sat trembling. In spite of the time that had passed, it was too real—too personal. It made her feel sick inside.

"Now, we do admit that there are a few discrepancies in the stories that the four young folks tell—but nothing of significance. It all seems to add up to a full and quite acceptable account. There is no doubt in my mind that what Rett did was only in the best interest of the accident victims.''

It seemed so settled—so clear—that Virginia could not help but wonder why all the silly rumors had even gotten started. But her father cleared his throat again.

''Now, the fact also remains that Mr. Crell is not satisfied with that story. He says that Rett has never liked his son—and even admits that Freddie, 'in the mischievousness of youth,' sometimes teased Rett a bit.''

''Teased?'' scoffed Rodney. ''Those boys were downright monsters to Rett.''

Danny looked ready to add his piece, but their father held up his hand.

''Mr. Crell asked for a full investigation. We've done that—as much as possible. Our piecing together of the facts—as we were given them—still does not satisfy Mr. Crell. He wanted to go to court over the matter. I assured him there was no evidence to indicate that the events were contrary to what I have just stated, therefore, there was no reasonable indication that it should go further. For the time it has been dropped, but I don't believe that Mr. Crell is happy with the decision. He may try again.''

''It's not fair,'' Danny stated stoutly. ''Rett is a hero, and they treat him like a crook.''

''Life is not always fair,'' agreed their father. ''On the other hand, the Crells lost a son. One cannot deal with such a loss without some scars. I can understand the anger. The pain. It's natural to want to fight back. To find some reason. Even if it means hurting another individual. We don't always reason correctly when we have been deeply hurt.''

Virginia's eyes fell on her father's empty sleeve. Had he reasoned correctly after his accident? she wondered. Had he looked for someone to blame for what had happened to him?

But her mother's voice interrupted those thoughts. "We all need to pray for the Crell family," she said softly. "It is a terrible thing to lose a child. His parents are hurt and confused and striking out. It is not an uncommon thing. Don't be too harsh in your criticism. Remember—we never know how we will respond to suffering. The Crells seem to have refused the comfort that God could give. And the church. The pastor has tried to call, but he's always been firmly and coolly turned away. We must pray."

Her father cleared his throat again. His eyes circled the table.

"You know that you have always been told to disregard gossip. But this time—this once—we are changing that rule." His eyes sought out their mother's, then he went on, a solemnness to his voice that made Virginia's spine tingle. "If you hear of anything at school—or around town—that you think might be important, that might mean danger to . . . to anyone, then please don't discuss it with others. Bring it to your mother or me."

"I can't see how Mr. Crell can possibly feel ill will toward the man who pulled his son from the water," Clara stated, tossing her napkin beside her plate with an agitated flip. "It doesn't make sense."

Their father took a deep breath.

"Well, the Crells say that Rett shouldn't have left Freddie. That if he had immediately tried to revive him, Freddie would have made it."

"Is that true?" asked Rodney, his eyes wide.

"We will never know."

"But . . . but Rett. How would he know to do that? He's never had training."

"He's always worked with animals. Seems to have natural instincts about how to deal with injury."

"But this is so different," put in Clara.

"How can he be blamed for not doing something he

doesn't even know how to do?" asked Danny.

Again their father hesitated, then seemed to feel they should have all the facts.

"Mr. Crell suggested that perhaps, when Rett found Freddie, rather than bringing him quickly up—he held him under for a time."

Virginia felt the air leave her lungs. *That would be—that would be*—but she couldn't even let the word form in her thoughts.

"You mean—?" asked Rodney. But he, too, was unable to go on.

Their father nodded. "Mr. Crell has accused Rett of murder."

When school started again, Virginia had never been so happy to get back to her studies. She hoped it would give her something else to think about.

But it didn't quite work that way. Jenny was there. Her hand still could not hold the pencil properly. Each time that Virginia let her eyes fall upon the damaged fingers, she felt her insides churn again.

And Jenny looked so sad. Gone was the sparkle in her eyes. The girlish giggle. In its place was a look of total sadness, as though the whole world had turned on Jenny Woods. Worse yet, she looked as if she had accepted the fact and no longer even wanted to fight against it.

For the first few days, Virginia felt herself pulling away from Jenny. She avoided contact as much as possible, taking up with Ida Cross and Myrtle Alwood, two girls from church. They were younger than Virginia, and previously she would not have bothered much with them. But her views about friendships had been changing since her experience with Jenny.

Her mother, however, kept asking about Jenny. How was she doing? Did Virginia want to invite her to the house? To church? For Sunday dinner? Virginia wished her mother would just let it rest. But she didn't.

"Are you and Jenny still on the outs?" she asked one day as Virginia helped peel vegetables for their supper.

Virginia looked up, confusion on her face, even though she fully understood the question.

"No-o," she said slowly.

"I never hear of her anymore."

"There's nothing to say."

"How's her arm?"

"Okay." Even as she said the terse word, she knew that it wasn't. Not really. Nor would it likely ever be okay again. She corrected her statement. "Well, it's still stiff, and she has to go in to have it limbered up every week, but she's gonna stop. Her pa says it's costing too much money and isn't doing any good anyway."

"Oh."

They peeled in silence.

"I have an idea," her mother said, turning toward her, and Virginia paused with her peeling. Was she going to like this?

"I think I'll talk to Jenny's father. I will be happy to help Jenny with her arm and hand—and it won't cost him a cent."

Virginia blinked.

"She can come on home from school with you, and we'll do the exercises here."

Virginia swallowed hard. "I don't know if Jenny will like that," she said slowly.

"Well, we'll see. I'll have a chat with Mr. Woods the first chance I get, and we'll see."

It seemed that it was settled. Virginia found herself secretly hoping that Mr. Woods would forbid it without giving the offer much consideration. To have Jenny here—in her own home—working on that damaged arm would be just too, too upsetting. It was hard enough to avoid her at school.

"How's school?"

Virginia's head snapped around at the question. She had been deep in thought, mulling through her new problem. Mr. Adamson stood at his pickets, hands on the boards, his hat perched askew on his begrimed hair.

She stopped and managed to gather her scattered thoughts to concentrate on the elderly man.

"Fine," she answered almost automatically.

"Heard you have a new teacher."

Virginia nodded. "Miss Crook got married."

"So what's this new one like?"

Virginia thought about it. A teacher was just a teacher. She hadn't given the new one much thought. "She's already married," she replied, feeling that was enough information for Mr. Adamson.

"Haven't seen you and thet little redhead together recently."

Virginia shook her head. *Oh, but you will,* she could have said. *My mama has taken it upon herself to get involved. Jenny's to come home with me every night of the week now*.

But she didn't say that. Instead she said slowly, "Jenny's doing fine."

"Thet's good news," said the elderly man. "She got quite banged up, I hear, in thet there accident."

Virginia nodded.

"You still friends?"

"Of course."

Virginia's answer came too abruptly. The elderly man's eyes darkened slightly.

"How's the family?" he asked, completely catching Virginia off guard. She swallowed and nodded.

"Fine."

"Hear your sister's plannin' a weddin'."

Yes, it was true. Clara was finally going to marry her Troy.

"Next April," Virginia said without emotion.

"She'll make a fine wife. Good cook."

Virginia nodded. Mr. Adamson should know about the cooking part. Clara was always running over with little plates of this or trays of that.

"Suppose you'll miss her."

Virginia had not stopped to think about that. A few short months before, she could not wait for Clara to leave the house. But so much had changed. So much. Clara and her bossiness didn't seem quite so important now. In fact, maybe she *would* miss her—just a bit. Who would come to her room in the middle of the night if she had another bad dream? Her mother's room was too far away for her to hear Virginia's restless stirring. Clara's room that she shared with Francine was just next door.

She looked up at Mr. Adamson and nodded slowly.

"The dahlias are doin' good this year. I know you gotta run on home, but if you come back in 'bout twenty minutes I'll have a bouquet ready for your mama."

For the first time, Virginia smiled. "She'd like that. She loves dahlias."

"You run then. Scat."

Virginia gave him another hesitant smile and then ran. Her mama would be pleased—and the afternoon snack would be waiting to buoy her up for chore time.

The very next Monday Jenny walked home with Virginia. At first they were awkward and strained with each other. They did not talk much. There seemed to be so little to say. When they reached Virginia's home, an extra snack had been placed on the table.

Virginia's mother and sister Clara were both busy

about the kitchen. Danny and Francine were already eating, and Danny was making short work of his lemonade and spice cake. Virginia assumed he was in a rush to get out to his little menagerie.

Francine, as usual, was slowly sipping and nibbling, talking in between sporadic bites as she told about every little detail of her rather uneventful day.

"And Mrs. Howard said that we should bring a fresh hankie every day—and take it home again at the end. Clarisa had seven hankies in her desk—seven—and all of them were already used up and—"

"Francine," scolded Virginia as she and Jenny entered the large, welcoming kitchen. "Don't talk about such things when you're eating."

Francine seemed to consider the comment—and the manner in which it was spoken. "Oh," she said meekly, her eyes beginning to brim. Virginia wished she had not spoken so sharply. The last thing Jenny needed to see was her little sister in tears. It made Virginia feel even angrier with the young girl.

Her mother intervened. "Hello, Jenny. Come right in. I hope you like spice cake."

Jenny nodded, looking around at the scene.

"Excuse me, please," said Danny to no one in particular and pushed himself up from the table, reaching for his hat in the same motion.

"Put your dishes on the cupboard, please," reminded Clara.

Danny did as told and bolted from the kitchen.

"He has animals to feed," Francine informed Jenny, already recovered from her recent chastising.

Jenny's eyes widened in interest.

"A young fox kit," explained Francine. "It was hurt. A hawk almost got it—or something. An' a rabbit that looks old. An' a sparrow. An' a—"

"I don't think Jenny is interested," cut in Virginia, but

this time she tried to keep her voice from being harsh. She did not want to risk more of Francine's tears.

Looking repentant, Francine stopped, though Virginia knew that the little girl would never understand how someone would not be interested in small animals.

But Jenny turned to Virginia. "I'd like to see them—after," she said. "Would your brother mind?"

CHAPTER 11

Things settled into a rather humdrum routine. There was school to rule their day, chores that needed to be attended to after returning home, and Jenny's daily exercises and massaging with Belinda. Then Jenny helped out on things she could do with limited arm movement, like setting the table for supper. Occasionally she even joined the family for the meal when her father was gone.

Virginia began to adjust to the new schedule. She even began to feel more comfortable with it, and Jenny acted as though she could hardly wait to get to the Simpson home. Virginia had the feeling that Jenny enjoyed having Belinda fuss over her, and at times she felt a twinge of jealousy. After all, Belinda was *her* mother. It wasn't Virginia's fault that Jenny's mother had run off when she'd been just a little thing.

It wasn't long until Jenny was appearing around on Saturdays, too. She seemed to find any excuse to come to the Simpson home. She listened to Francine's chatter, watched Danny take care of his little critters, and helped Clara bake.

Virginia's feelings shifted back and forth. On the one hand, she felt that Jenny was making too deep an inroad into the family. It was *her* family, not Jenny's. But her attitude brought guilt. She knew she was wrong to feel that way. It made her a little hesitant when she said her prayers each night. Would God even listen to someone who harbored selfish thoughts? Might He decide that she needed punishment of some kind? It was rather scary.

Francine came skipping to meet Virginia as she returned home from the grocery on an errand for her mother. "We're going to Grandpa's farm," she called before reaching her sister.

Virginia, feeling hot and sticky on the warm Indian summer day, managed a smile. A trip to the farm was always welcome. And on a Saturday—that meant that not so many cousins would be present and she could have her grandparents almost to herself.

"Mama wants to talk to Grandma 'bout Clara's wedding, and she says we can go along."

Virginia felt her pace quicken. Francine whirled around and skipped along beside her.

"Are the boys going?" asked Virginia.

"Nope. Just the ladies."

Virginia smiled indulgently at Francine's including of herself with "the ladies." But she nearly started skipping, too, in the excitement of a females-only outing.

"When?" she asked the little girl

"Mama is just waiting for you to get home. Clara already has her hat on."

Oh, it was just too wonderful.

Jenny. Her steps slowed momentarily as she remembered that they would already be gone when Jenny found some excuse to slip over to the house. Virginia felt a bit smug. She ignored her conscience and decided it would serve Jenny right. She had practically been living with them lately. She did have a home of her own.

"Mama is gonna pick Jenny up, too," Francine enthused. Virginia stopped short.

"Jenny?"

"Yep. She thinks a visit to Grandma's would be good for her."

Virginia felt her anger rise. Why? Why let Jenny intrude even further? She had already taken over the Simpson household. It seemed that there was hardly ever a time they were just a family anymore. And now her mama was taking her to Grandma and Grandpa's as well. It wasn't fair. They were *her* grandparents. Not Jenny's. Jenny had no right to be included. Grandma might end up fussing over Jenny just like her mother did. *It wasn't fair.*

Virginia felt such a knot in her stomach that she feared she might be sick. Francine, normally so sensitive to others' feelings, seemed not to notice as she took up her skipping again.

"Do you think Jenny will like the porch swing?" she asked innocently. "I like the porch swing. 'Specially when Grandma swings, too."

The knot in Virginia's stomach tightened. She did not want to share her grandmother with Jenny. And she certainly didn't want to share her grandmother's swing.

"I'm not going," she announced firmly, stopping on the boardwalk.

Francine, too shocked to even speak, swung around and looked at her big sister as if she had taken leave of her senses.

Virginia glowered at her. "Go tell Mama I'm not going."

It was an order, but Francine did not move.

"Go," said Virginia, almost shrieking. "She's in a hurry—go tell her."

"She's not in *that* big a hurry," Francine finally managed to say. "She's waiting for you."

"I'm not going."

Francine began to blink, and Virginia knew tears were on the way. She felt like slapping Francine. The young girl's face just brought further guilty feelings.

"Mama is taking Jenny—just for you," Francine tried to explain.

"No," declared Virginia hotly. "Mama is taking Jenny just for Jenny. That's all she ever thinks about anymore." Her voice turned to mocking. "Jenny needs friends. Jenny needs family. Jenny needs church. Jenny needs a nurse." It sounded like a chant. "I am so sick of it I could . . . could just throw up."

Francine's chin began to tremble. But now it was not only Francine who cried. Virginia could feel the hot tears running down her own cheeks.

"I'm not going," she flung at Francine. "And you can just tell Mama that."

"She needs . . . needs the packages," Francine wept. "She's been waiting . . . for the packages."

"Here!" said Virginia, thrusting the two bundles into Francine's arms. "Now go."

With one more anguished look at her older sister, Francine turned and started for the house. Virginia could hear the childish sobs even as she spun around and began to run toward the outskirts of the town and the creek beyond.

Virginia did not stop running until she reached the trees along the creek bank. By then her chest was heaving as she fought for breath, and her legs felt like jelly. Streaming tears had wet her hair that was tangled about her face. She flung herself down on a grassy knoll and gave into the sobs constricting her throat. Jenny. She hated Jenny. Everything bad that had ever happened to her was because of Jenny.

First she got her into all kinds of trouble—then she turned her whole family against her. Her mama spent more time taking care of Jenny's bad hand than she ever did with her. She fussed over her and fixed her special things to eat and sent little packages of goodies home with her and talked to her about how God loved her and how the church and—the woeful list went on and on.

And now this. Jenny was about to steal away her grandmother. That was more than Virginia could bear. Much more. To see Grandma Marty fussing over Jenny would be the final straw. For a dreadful moment she wished it had been Jenny who had been under the water—not Freddie Crell. The thought was so terrible that she rushed inwardly on to another one. *What did Freddie do to deserve to die? It was all Jenny's idea anyway*. . . . But her terrible guilt at such a wish made her nearly choke on the sobs pouring from her shaking chest.

Her whole secure world was slowly unraveling, and there was nothing—*nothing*—that she could do about it.

Suddenly she felt something touching her shoulder—gently, yet firmly. Fear pushed through her veins like fire. Was some wild animal—?

She lay absolutely still holding her breath, fearful to move a muscle. A soft murmur reached her ears. It was hardly audible. Not distinguishable sounds. Certainly not understandable. But then the feather-light brushing of hair and patting of shoulder reminded her of Danny stroking one of his little animals. She moved just enough to peek through her fingers and see a booted foot near her head.

For one moment she didn't know whether to be relieved or more frightened. The little sound came again. A gentle, soothing, wordless sound.

Virginia could hold herself in check no longer. She pushed up slightly and lifted her head.

Rett Marshall knelt beside her, one hand stroking her head and shoulder. The look of intense sympathy on his face and a gentleness in his eyes melted her heart that had felt like a stone in her chest. She lay her head back down on the dried grass and newly fallen leaves and let the sobs once again shake her body.

He stayed with her as long as she continued to cry. When her shoulders quit their convulsive shaking and the tears no longer ran down her cheeks, she gradually became aware that she was now alone. When he had left her and how he had gone was totally a mystery. But for some strange reason she could not have explained, she felt comforted.

At last she sat up and wiped her face on her sleeve. She must look a mess. And she felt awfully warm. She struggled to her feet and made her way to the creek.

No longer the raging torrent that had claimed her friend, it was now subdued—almost silent. It murmured and whispered as it flowed at a gentle pace. Virginia stood and studied it for a moment before falling to her knees on the grassy bank and scooping its cool water to rinse her flushed face. The grass along the banks was still soft and green, even though the neighboring countryside was burnished with the colors of fall.

Virginia let her hands nestle into the grasses, stretching her fingers deep into the coolness. She wished she could just sit there forever. Cool and comforted. Away from all the hurts of the world. The confusion. The pain.

"Virginia?"

The voice was soft. Gentle. Loving. Virginia did not turn her head. She didn't have to. She knew it was Clara. Her big sister. Virginia felt the tears threaten again. She willed them back.

Clara said nothing more. Virginia felt, more than saw, the figure of her sister lower herself down beside her on the creek bank. She felt an arm slip companionably about her waist as Clara drew her close. She felt Clara's cheek pressed against her hair.

They sat together for what seemed like a long time, quietly watching the water trickle around a fallen log, listening to the gentle murmur of the stream. A frog came up and almost hopped over Virginia's foot. She would have laughed in other circumstances. She did not laugh now. Just sat and watched. A hornet dipped over the water, reenergizing his body, then buzzed on. A soft stirring in the tree branches sent a scattering of colored leaves twisting and turning in a sprightly dance to the ground.

At last Clara spoke. "Do you want to talk?"

Virginia shook her head. No, she did not want to talk. Her own conscience condemned her evil thinking. Clara would never understand. Clara would have to condemn her also.

Clara waited.

"It's just—" began Virginia, but she had no idea how to go on.

Clara brushed at the hair against her cheek.

"Jenny?"

Clara's voice was so soft, Virginia could have wondered if she had really spoken. Without wanting to, she nodded her head.

"She's been at our home a lot lately, hasn't she?"

Virginia nodded again.

"Too much?"

Oh, that was an impossible question. If she said no, she'd be lying, but if she said yes, she'd lay bear her evil heart. Clara was bound to lecture.

But Clara went right on. "You know why Mama is trying to help her. The poor girl has had a hard life. Her own mama having left her and her papa . . . well, he hasn't taken very good care of her."

Clara sighed, then bent her head to look into Virginia's face.

"But that's not the most important reason. Mama feels that by loving her—accepting her—there will be a better chance to help her see that God loves her. That He wants to forgive her—accept her as one of His family. You know that, don't you?"

Virginia managed to nod.

"Forgiveness is a precious thing," Clara went on. "One can never have . . . peace, until one has been forgiven. Really forgiven. All the help we give Jenny will really be . . . only temporary in meeting her real need—the forgiveness, the peace of God."

Virginia squirmed and stared at the creek.

"Without that forgiveness, that peace, no heart is ever happy. There is always an inner struggle. Pain. Only when God has been invited in—to manage one's life, to direct one's thinking, to be in control—can one ever get away from all the conflicts inside. We have to stop struggling against His will before we can find real joy. That's what Mama wants for Jenny. So then, whatever life brings to her, wherever she might go in the future, she can take that deep, inward happiness, that peace with her. That's what we are all praying for."

Virginia sat silently as the words sank slowly in.

"That's what Mama and Papa want for each one of their own, too," Clara said with a soft squeeze for emphasis.

Virginia began to sob anew. She turned in her sister's arms and let all the conflicts pour forth in large, cascading tears. She didn't have that peace. She hadn't been willing to let God control her life. She had been fighting against Him. Wishing that He didn't even exist so she could be in control of her own life—her own universe. But it hadn't worked. It hadn't. She just got more and more miserable with each passing day. Her heart was evil. Her thoughts were wrong. She was selfish. Cruel. Mean.

Clara held her. Virginia could feel Clara's tears mingling with her own.

"I love you, little sister. I love you so much," she heard Clara whisper.

Virginia could hold herself apart from God no longer.

There was no way she could continue to carry her deep burdens alone. She did not want to. Fighting the truth only made it harder to bear.

"Would you pray with me?" she heard her own voice saying, and she felt Clara's arms tighten about her.

It turned out they all went to the farm. In honesty, Virginia would not have claimed that it was easy to include Jenny, but she no longer had the deep anger and jealousy burning within.

She was glad to be pulled close by her grandmother and greeted warmly. Jenny was simply welcomed as Virginia's friend. Clara, her mother, and her grandmother gathered around the kitchen table, teacups in hand, and quickly began animated plans for the coming wedding. At Francine's plea the three girls headed for the barn in search of mother cats with new kittens. The farm dog loped along beside them, glad to have someone to romp with.

Later, they made lemonade and cut pumpkin loaf, which they took to the porch swing. They settled in the swing together, each with a barn kitten curled up in her lap. Grandmother was still busy with the womenfolk, and Virginia could not help but feel relieved in spite of her newfound peace.

But she would work on her feelings. She had promised Clara. Had promised God.

When it was time to go home, her grandmother held her again. Virginia felt sure that Grandma Marty had been told the little secret of her prayer at the creek for she held her extra long, extra close, then leaned over and looked into Virginia's eyes and whispered, "I love you. I'll keep praying." Virginia found it hard to hold back tears.

Her grandfather joined the little group, a broad smile bringing crinkles to his face while Virginia blinked and swallowed to get her emotions under control.

"I hear there's to be a baptism on a Sunday soon," he said, and it was his turn to give Virginia a warm hug. "Best news I've heard me for a long time," he whispered into her hair. "We'll be there, you can just count on thet. Grandma and me'll be there."

Virginia managed a thankful smile. It felt good—so good to make her grandparents happy. And even better to have the heavy load of fears and doubts finally off her shoulders. If it was true as her mother said—and Virginia finally believed that it was—that God loved her even more than her family, she was blessed indeed. With His peace in her heart she felt wrapped in love. Loved and protected and totally filled with joy. It was wonderful. She hugged her grandpa back.

"Well," said her mother as they settled into the buggy for the return to town. "I feel good about what we accomplished. I knew that Mama would be a big help."

Clara laughed. "I guess if experience makes a good teacher, we've got us some awful good counsel," she said. She sounded light. Excited. Virginia supposed that the coming wedding would keep her that way over the winter months.

"I can hardly wait to discuss it all with Troy," Clara went on, her voice dreamy.

Virginia lifted her head and looked at her older sister. Her cheeks were flushed, her voice bubbly, and there was a lively sparkle in her violet eyes. She was getting married. It was finally sinking in. Just as Clara was getting to be—to be nice, she was getting married.

She would not be living at home anymore. She would be moving out to the little house on Elm Street with the green shutters and the cobblestone walk.

Virginia felt a lump rising in her throat. She was really going to miss her.

CHAPTER 12

"Would you like to come with me to Youth Group?"

Virginia asked the question as she and Jenny walked home together. Jenny seemed to hear and understand the honest invitation in her voice. She looked at Virginia long and carefully before she chose her reply.

"I . . . I think I'd like to. I mean . . . I . . . Are you sure they . . . they'd want me?"

" 'Course!" Virginia's answer was so quick and emphatic that it surprised even herself. Would they want her? All of them? Jenny was an outsider. Different. Jenny had a bad-talking pa who drank too much. Jenny herself used some of his words. Was a thief. A rebel. Would the other young people be comfortable with Jenny among them?

Virginia thought through her next words more carefully. "I am sure you will be welcome. We have been praying for you and . . . and the others ever since . . . the accident."

It was now mid-winter. Christmas had already come and gone, and folks had settled in to getting themselves through the chill and snow until spring came. At the Simpsons', the thoughts and dreams of spring also included the coming marriage of Clara and Troy. Her excited preparations helped to keep the household filled with anticipation, relieving some of the dreariness of the short, cold days.

"I'd kind of like to," Jenny said again, "but it's a little scary, too."

"Will your father let you?"

Jenny paused. "I don't suppose he'd even know," she answered slowly. "He never seems to pay much mind to where I am or what I'm doing."

"Then there's no problem." Virginia tried to put some spirit into her voice to make Jenny feel more comfortable. "You already know all the young people—from school. We're having a skating party on Friday night down at Conner's pond."

"I . . . I don't have any skates."

Virginia, surprised, had thought that every kid in town owned skates. There seemed to be no way to surmount this obstacle.

"Maybe you could just . . . just come . . . and watch," she offered.

Jenny shook her head and wrinkled her nose. "That wouldn't be much fun." She hesitated, then said, "Someone would think they had to watch with me, and that would spoil their fun, too."

Virginia supposed that Jenny might be referring to her, and she likely was right. It wouldn't feel fair for her to spend her time skating if Jenny was sitting alone by the campfire.

"Maybe next time," Jenny said quietly. Virginia was sure she detected disappointment in the girl's voice.

"Next time we are having a Valentine party at the church."

Jenny nodded, then turned toward Virginia. "Will you need to have a valentine?"

Virginia frowned, then shrugged. "Some exchange valentines, but you don't need to."

"I mean, do you need a—you know—boyfriend?"

"Boyfriend? No. 'Course not. Pastor Doyle doesn't even want us to . . . to pair off or anything. Not at our age."

"Oh," said Jenny. Her voice sounded a little flat.

They walked on in silence. It was Jenny who broke it. "Would your ma and pa let you?"

"Let me what?"

"You know—see a boy? Go out with him or let him call or something?"

Virginia had not even thought about courting.

"I'm only fourteen," she answered.

"Fourteen and a half," corrected Jenny. "Some girls have beaus by then."

"I don't think my folks would let me."

"When did Clara?"

Virginia had to think back. When was it that Troy had started to call?

"Sixteen. Almost seventeen."

"Seventeen? That's old."

"She'll be nineteen when they marry. Going on twenty even."

"That's old."

"Mama was older than that."

"Yeah? My mama was just past sixteen."

Virginia stopped and looked at Jenny. Why, that wasn't much older than Jenny herself. But things had not worked well for Jenny's mama. Virginia did not mention the fact. She did not wish to hurt her friend.

"Would you like to?" Jenny pressed the question. "I mean, would you have a beau if they'd let you?"

Virginia shifted her load of books to her other arm. She had never bothered to think much about going out. Would she like to? Go to Youth Group with a fellow? Hold hands? Let him put his arm around her? Maybe even kiss? She found the thoughts a bit embarrassing—but rather exciting, too. She began to laugh, a nervous, tittering sound.

"I went with Freddie to—"

But she stopped. The memory of the soda shared at the local Sweet Shop with the now missing Freddie was still a painful one.

"I don't think that really counts," put in Jenny. "We were with other people."

"Oh."

"Did you know that Mr. Crell is still mad? He says that he's gonna get that Marshall man back for what he did to his son."

Virginia swung around to face Jenny. "He didn't *do* anything."

"How do you know? No one remembers for sure. I sure don't. I was knocked nearly silly on the rocks."

"And he saved your life," Virginia said, her voice trembling with emotion. "Wouldn't have been for him, you'd been in the same fix as Freddie. And . . . he did too try to save Freddie."

"How do you know that?"

"'Cause. 'Cause he wouldn't do anything to hurt anybody. He couldn't. He's not like that."

"How do you know?"

It was as near to a fight as they had come since renewing their friendship. Virginia felt anger rising within her. She thought back to the day in the woods. To her devastating sobs and Rett Marshall's hand gently trying to soothe her. He *couldn't* do something mean. Something wicked. She just knew it. But how could she ever explain that to Jenny?

"You weren't there, were you?" Jenny pressed further.

"No, but—"

"See—no one really knows."

"Ruth remembers."

"Ruth has moved away. Her folks are way off in the city now. And maybe she didn't even remember it right before. Folks say you can think strange things when you've been in an accident."

"Well, Rett wouldn't hurt anybody. I'm sure of it."

Jenny gave her a knowing look. "Thinking you're sure don't count, Virginia. You should know that with your pa in law. You gotta have proof."

"And that . . . that works both ways," fumed Virginia. "You gotta have proof that he did it, too."

"Well, maybe they'll find it. Mr. Crell is still workin' on it. He says he won't stop until that dangerous loony is locked away."

The words brought a pang of fear to Virginia's heart.

"That's a pretty mean thing for you to be saying," she threw at Jenny. "He did save your life. I would think that you'd be grateful."

Jenny shrugged carelessly. "Maybe they are right. Maybe he dumped us in to begin with."

Virginia gave her a withering look and turned toward home. She hoped Jenny would not be foolish enough to follow. And maybe it wasn't a very good idea for Jenny to come to Youth Group.

"Where's Jenny?" Clara asked as Virginia tossed her books on the stand by the door and settled at the table.

Virginia's thoughts still tumbled one over the other and her face still felt hot with the anger that filled her.

"I don't think she's coming today," she answered, keeping her voice as even as she could.

She felt Clara's gaze upon her, but she refused to turn to meet it.

"Why?" asked Francine, her mouth full of cookies. "Did she have chores?"

Jenny never had chores. At least not a regular schedule of them. Virginia often wondered who took care of all the little tasks around the house. Perhaps they simply did not get done.

"Did you have a fight?" asked Danny candidly, staring at her face.

Virginia wanted to tell him to mind his own business, but she bit back the remark. She had promised Clara that she would work on trying to be more considerate of others.

"Danny, Mr. Adamson says that there is a blue jay in his yard with an injured wing," Clara said. "He thought you might like to come over and have a look."

Danny pushed the last of his cookie into his mouth and reached for his milk glass, nodding as he did so.

Danny was barely out the door when there was a light rap. Jenny entered. She cast one glance toward Virginia, giving a tentative smile of reconciliation, then nodded to Clara.

"Mama had to go uptown, but she said she would be back in plenty of time to work on your hand," Clara said as she put another glass of milk on the table.

Jenny slipped into the seat.

"There's going to be a skating party on Friday," Clara said. Virginia guessed that her sister was fishing for some topic to lower the tension in the room.

"She doesn't have skates," Virginia said flatly.

"Oh!"

Even Clara seemed to be at loss for something more to say.

"I might go to the Valentine party later," said Jenny in what Virginia judged to be an attempt at politeness.

"Well, that will be nice." Clara smiled and reached out a hand to smooth Francine's hair. It didn't seem to want to go back into place, so Clara stepped closer and removed the clip, stroking the hair in place, then repinning it.

"That's rather a while to wait. Too bad you couldn't go skating. Skating parties are always so much fun."

Francine giggled. "It was at a skating party that Troy first kissed Clara," she informed those around the table.

Clara flushed. "How do you know that?" Her hands fluffed the hair she had just smoothed.

"I heard you tell Josie Biers."

"You little sneak," said Clara, lifting Francine's chin to look into her face. But there was warmth in her voice.

"It's true," sang Francine. "It's true."

Clara did not try to deny it.

Virginia could feel Jenny's eyes upon her. She knew it had something to do with their little discussion about boys and courting, but she wasn't sure just what she was trying to communicate.

"Valentine parties are fun, too," Virginia said to fill the silence.

"Wait a minute." Clara swung around to face them, new excitement in her voice. "What size is your shoe, Jenny?"

Jenny looked puzzled but extended a foot for Clara to see for herself.

"I think my skates might fit you. Wait here."

Virginia fleetingly wondered why Clara would need to instruct Jenny to wait. She was always at their home of late. She did well to sleep under her own roof.

Soon Clara was back, a pair of ice skates in her hands. She knelt before Jenny's chair, and Jenny turned to her and slipped off the boot on her left foot.

"Umm. A little big perhaps, but you can wear another pair of stockings. Actually, they'll do quite well. There! You can go to that skating party after all."

Clara looked very pleased as she stood to her feet and handed the pair of ice skates to Jenny.

"Aren't you and Troy going?" asked Virginia. She could not hide her disappointment.

"Well . . . yes . . . we are. But we'll be busy taking care of the fire and fixing the hot chocolate."

Virginia knew how much Clara was giving up. She loved to skate, and folks said she was the smoothest skater on the pond.

"She can kiss by the fire 'stead of on the pond," announced Francine with an impish look toward her older sister and was given a playful punch in response.

The night was cold, with a melon-sized moon hanging low in the sky. Its soft shadows across the frozen expanse outlined the trees at the rim of the snowbank around the patch of cleared ice.

Excited voices echoed across the crisp night air as the bundled young people began to gather at the pond. Already a brisk fire threw its flaming fingers toward the sky, its shards of golden sparks dancing momentarily, then dying out in one quick moment.

It was a perfect night for skating. Virginia could feel the anticipation in her chest as she laced on her bladed boots. She was not the skater that her older sister was, but she loved the feel of gliding over the smooth surface.

"Where are your skates?" she heard more than one person call to Clara. Clara always had a cheerful response. She and Troy would keep the fire. Fix the hot chocolate. Folks seemed to accept it. Clara was older now. She would be married come spring. Maybe she didn't care to skate anymore.

But Virginia knew better. She cast a glance toward Jenny, who sat on a log, lacing on Clara's carefully maintained skates. Did Jenny have any idea of the care and concern that had prompted the loan of the skates? She supposed not. But then Jenny could be a little . . . little insensitive at times. Why, Jenny actually thought that Rett Marshall could bring harm to someone. The unfair accusation still rankled in Virginia's heart.

But even as she remembered her annoyance with

Jenny, she remembered one of her talks with Clara.

"We must never be too harsh in our judgment of folks," Clara had said. "They may not have had all the blessings of proper training—of concerned parents—or truth from Scripture that we have enjoyed. We should not judge them for things they do not know. For making mistakes that they do not recognize."

Maybe it was that way with Jenny. Maybe she had never been taught to look for the good in people, to be kind and appreciative. . . .

Virginia finished lacing her skates and stood up.

"You need some help?" she called to her friend. She was determined to make Jenny's introduction into the Youth Group as enjoyable as possible.

"Did Jenny have a good time?" Virginia's mother asked the question as she helped her off with her lengthy scarf and knit hat.

"I think she did," Clara answered before Virginia could. "I was proud of our group. Proud of Virginia. Everyone went out of their way to make Jenny feel at home."

Their mother smiled. "Do you think she'll continue to go with you now that the ice has been broken at the skating party?"

Belinda stopped and laughed at her own little pun.

"Ice didn't break tonight," offered Rodney, rubbing his hands briskly over the big stove. "It was too cold."

"Was it really chilly?" This from their father.

"It was cold all right—but perfect for skating," Clara assured them. "The ice looked good and fast tonight."

Virginia thought again of Clara's gift to Jenny. She wondered if she would ever be that unselfish.

"Well, I am so pleased," her mother commented. "I feel that you have finally made a breakthrough, Virginia.

Now that Jenny has been to one youth outing, I hope that she will feel more confident to join us for church. I think that sometimes people outside the church can have some very strange ideas about us—and about what happens there."

"They think we're . . . we're monsters or something," put in Danny, who had been allowed to stay up for his siblings' return. He could hardly wait for his turn to join the Youth Group.

"Well . . . I don't know about monsters," their father said, "but anything new and unknown can be rather frightening at first. I'm glad Jenny had a good time, her first time out. You've made us very proud, Virginia."

"It wasn't me," Virginia admitted as she drew off her heavy leggings. "She wouldn't have been able to go if it hadn't been for Clara. I never even thought to offer her my skates."

She was still selfish and thoughtless. She still had a long, long way to go.

CHAPTER 13

Virginia was surprised that Jenny seemed more excited about the upcoming Valentine party than she herself. Jenny didn't seem to be able to talk of anything else. But when Jamison's name came up so often in those one-sided conversations, Virginia began to understand just what the attraction for Jenny might be.

She wanted to say something. To warn Jenny that Jamison was one of the "older boys." That he wasn't one bit interested in a girl two years his junior. That Nelly Bent already had her eye on Jamison, though Jamison seemed to be totally ignorant of the fact. That Jamison would not think of pursuing a girl who did not share his faith. But she said nothing. She did not wish to make Jenny angry with her. That might cause her to refuse to continue in the Youth Group.

"I told Pa I need a new dress," Jenny said excitedly as they walked home from school together on the rather chilly February afternoon.

Virginia had not even thought of asking for a new dress.

"What did he say?"

"He said, 'See to it then.' "

"He did?"

Virginia wished it was that easy for her to add to her wardrobe.

"So are you getting one?"

"Of course," Jenny answered.

Virginia felt a twinge of envy.

"You can come with me to choose it," offered Jenny generously.

"I'll have to ask Mama."

The following Saturday they set out for the mercantile so Jenny could pick out her yard goods. The local seamstress was already engaged for the sewing. Not having a mama at home to teach her, Jenny had not learned the art of sewing.

In spite of herself, Virginia felt some excitement, too. Perhaps it was contagious.

"This is the first dress I've picked out for a—you know—for a boy," Jenny's words enthusiastically tumbled over each other.

Virginia frowned. She had thought the dress was for Jenny. "What do you mean?"

"You know," said Jenny with that flip of her red hair. "This is the first time I need to . . . to think about what he'll like best."

"Who?"

Jenny cast her a disdainful look. "Are you a dullhead!"

Virginia finally understood that Jenny was speaking of Jamison. "Oh."

The one word came out sounding flat and reproachful. Jenny gave her another hard look. Then said a bad word. Virginia had hoped that Jenny had put aside all that language borrowed from her father. She felt the frown pucker her forehead.

"I'm sorry," cut in Jenny. But she didn't look sorry. She looked angry. "But sometimes you can be so . . . so very childish. Someday you're going to have to grow up."

Virginia felt her chin lift. "If growing up means using bad words and—" She was going to say, *swooning over boys*, but she caught herself in time. The latter might indeed be part of the growing-up process and didn't belong in the same category with the first accusation. She changed to, "Well, I just don't use those words. Mama and Papa—"

Jenny gave her another cold stare. "I know, I know. They don't let their little girl use grown-up talk."

"That's not grown-up talk," Virginia insisted. "That's . . . that's gutter talk. My folks—my grandpa—none of them need those words. And they are grown-up and—"

"All right," Jenny interrupted. "I said I'm sorry. Let's not fight."

They walked in silence, tempers cooling along with their faces in the biting wind that blew from the north.

Virginia was glad to reach the store and step inside. It felt warm and sheltered, and she found herself drawn to the big potbellied stove in the middle of the room. Sharing its warmth with the few customers who gathered around it, she chaffed chilly hands and listened to stories about harsh winters of the past.

Mr. Eddy raised his head and gave a nod and a smile. "What can I do for you girls? Bit cold to be out strolling this morning."

"I need yard goods," Jenny said quickly, the excitement back in her voice.

"Yard goods? Mrs. Eddy helps with that."

He turned and bellowed, "Cora! Customer needs some help."

Virginia moved as close to the stove as the others would allow and tapped her feet lightly to get some circulation back in her toes. It was too cold to be out buying material for a new dress just to impress a boy at a Valentine party. She felt an elbow in her side.

"C'mon," Jenny said. "She's here."

Virginia obediently followed toward the shelf of ginghams and calicos, flannels and wools.

Mrs. Eddy had not spoken nor smiled. She began to lift down bolts of sturdy material, placing them on the counter in front of Jenny. Jenny looked at them, fingered one, then frowned.

"Haven't you got anything . . . nicer? This is for a party dress," she told the woman.

"Party dress?"

Virginia heard the words and the agitation that accompanied them. Had the woman been called away from her baking or mending? She seemed annoyed, and they hadn't even done anything. And then Virginia remembered that, according to Mrs. Parker, Mrs. Eddy spent the greatest share of her time reading penny novels. Perhaps she had been called from the pages of one of those. No wonder she was out-of-sorts.

"What about that . . . that blue?" Jenny was pointing up on the shelf.

"It's too fussy for a schoolgirl," Mrs. Eddy snapped.

Jenny seemed to ignore her. "Or the green there—or that . . . that creamy color."

"It's too light for winter wear. There's a nice cinnamon here."

Jenny scowled. Though the face was meant for Virginia, Mrs. Eddy saw it and bristled. Virginia was afraid there was going to be trouble. It was rumored—again by Mrs. Parker—that Mrs. Eddy could be rather overbearing if she put her mind to it.

Virginia stepped forward and, in her most conciliatory voice, said softly, "I think she is afraid the nice cinnamon would not suit her hair color."

Mrs. Eddy humphed as she turned to stare at Jenny's hair, but she didn't say a word.

"The blue, the green, and the cream," Jenny repeated.

Without a word the woman reached for them and plopped the bolts firmly on the measuring counter.

"Ah," said Jenny, her face brightening as one hand touched the fabric of the cream-colored material.

Mrs. Eddy quickly pushed aside her hand. "Don't fondle it. You'll soil the fabric." The words were sharp.

For one awful moment, Virginia thought that Jenny was going to explode. She might use some of those bad words again. Or worse. But instead, Jenny reached into her pocket and withdrew a little roll of money. She laid it firmly on the counter, all the time her eyes full on Mrs. Eddy. The woman seemed to get the message. Jenny was a paying customer. Then with another look that firmly announced she was well within her rights, Jenny reached out and gently fingered the cream material.

She turned back to Virginia. *What do you think?* her eyes asked.

"It *is* light—for winter," Virginia finally said.

"But it is pretty."

"The blue is nice, too. And I think the green would suit your . . . your eyes."

Jenny lifted the bolt of blue and held it against her chest. Then she laid it aside and picked up the green. "Watch closely," she told Virginia. "Which one is best? The blue, the green?" She switched them again. "Or the cream." She reached for the cream and held it up against her, close to her face.

There was no doubt in Virginia's mind. The cream did wonderful things for Jenny.

But Mrs. Eddy was right. It was much too light for winter. It would not be a proper choice. Her mama would never have selected it. It was like material for a bridal gown.

"Maybe the green," Virginia mused.

But Jenny swung around to the storekeeper. "Do you have a mirror?"

The woman looked surprised but nodded stiffly. She produced one from beneath the counter.

Jenny began her own investigation. Virginia turned away. She knew what the choice would be. Jenny could not help but see that the creamy material brightened her green eyes and brought out the rosy flush of her cheeks. It would be the cream material, and everyone would think that she was a simpleton for wearing such flimsy material in the dead of winter—and to a church youth party. It was silliness. Pure silliness.

If she had a mama . . . Virginia's thoughts began. But Jenny did not have a mama.

"Why don't you let my mama come down and help you choose." Virginia heard herself saying as she tugged on Jenny's sleeve. "She's really good at picking material, and I bet she'd even sew up the dress."

But Jenny turned to her, a look of pure delight on her face. "She don't have to. I've already made up my mind."

Jenny modeled the dress for Virginia the day before the Valentine party. It was beautiful. Beautiful and totally inappropriate. But Virginia did not say so.

"It's lovely," she said instead, which was a perfectly truthful statement.

"Do you think that . . . that he'll like it?"

By now Virginia fully understood who *he* was. But she couldn't say. Not really. She had no idea what Jamison might think of the dress. "It's lovely," she said again.

"But will he like it?" Jenny persisted.

Virginia swallowed. She wished she could tell Jenny that she was far too concerned about the impression of a boy who couldn't care less. But she could not say the words. "I . . . don't know why not," she said lamely. "It really is lovely."

That seemed to be enough for Jenny.

The night of the Valentine party was even colder than the skating outing had been. Virginia bundled up under the supervision of her mother. "Be sure to wear your heavy stockings and your warm sweater under your coat," her mother advised. "It's cold out there. Even inside the church it will be chilly. The stove will never be able to keep up to the cold from the windows."

Virginia thought of Jenny. How would she survive in the frilly, lightweight dress?

The two were to meet at the corner and walk the short distance together. Rodney would already be at the church, having volunteered to make sure the fire was built in the big cast-iron stove. Clara had also left early. She was on the refreshment committee.

As Virginia moved along the frosty walk, she hoped Jenny would not keep her waiting. It was much too cold to be standing on a street corner.

But Jenny was already there. Hopping back and forth from one foot to another, clapping her hands, and blowing out streams of silvery breath each time she exhaled.

"I thought you'd never come," she said impatiently.

"I'm on time," Virginia countered. "You're early."

Jenny spun away and started off down the boardwalk before Virginia even reached her side. Virginia noticed that the girl was wearing her light coat.

"Where's your winter coat? You'll freeze," she exclaimed.

"It would rumple the dress," said Jenny simply.

"But—"

"Hurry."

That did seem like a good idea.

They removed their coats and scarfs and hung them on the pegs in the church's entry. Virginia thought Jenny looked almost blue with cold. She kept rubbing her hands, blowing on her fingers, and shifting back and forth from one foot to the other. And then Virginia noticed that

Jenny was wearing light stockings and shoes as well.

"Jenny, you'll freeze. You'll be sick," she said in concern but was rewarded with one of Jenny's famous *looks*. They moved in to join the other young people who had already gathered.

The room had been completely changed. The hard-backed benches had all been moved to the sides, leaving the room open and empty. Cheerful red hearts and white lacy bows had been skillfully hung by the decorating committee. Cheerful red candles burned on each window ledge, fluttering a fragile flame with each small draught of air. In spite of Rodney's careful attention to the fire, the large room still held a chill. Virginia was glad for her warm stockings and wool sweater. She cast another glance Jenny's way and saw her friend noticeably shiver.

But Jenny did look lovely in the creamy gown.

If getting attention had been Jenny's purpose, she was completely successful. In a room filled with young girls in sensible, dark winter wools and flannels, Jenny stood out like a butterfly in a garden full of moths. Virginia noticed the various reactions. Girls looked at Jenny with sly glances, pretending not to be impressed but just a bit uncertain as to how they should respond to her appearance. Boys, too, stole quick looks, flushed, then turned quickly away to pretend that they really hadn't noticed anything out of the ordinary.

The party began with a round of games. Virginia was glad to be moving about and guessed that Jenny would be even more so. In spite of chattering teeth, Jenny did appear to be having fun, even though her announced goal of capturing Jamison's attention did not appear to be meeting with success.

When refreshment time arrived, Clara handed out "broken hearts" that had to be "mended" by finding the partner with the other half. The two would then share the evening's hot apple cider and heart-shaped ginger cookies.

Virginia felt her pulse race. Did the parents know that Clara was about to match up the young people?

But yes, she supposed they did. It was all in good, clean fun, in a totally supervised and lighthearted atmosphere. Still, it was rather unnerving to think that one would have to sit with a boy while enjoying the food of the evening.

She looked about for Jenny. Would this be the girl's chance? If Jenny's half of the broken heart were to match up with Jamison's, she would be ecstatic.

There was a good deal of milling about the room as young people, nervously and excitedly, found the other half of the heart they held and paired off for their steaming cups of hot cider. Virginia noticed several blushing faces and a few upset looks as one or another girl watched the fellow she had her eyes on teamed up with another. A few of the boys looked equally disturbed. Virginia saw Rodney, red-faced and obviously nervous, lead a young Ida Cross to one of the side benches, a steaming cup in each hand.

Several other couples began to find their places. Much too interested in what was going on about her, Virginia had not moved from where she had stood when the hearts had been passed out.

She caught Jenny's eye. As yet Jenny had not found her partner, either, but she was making her way toward Jamison, broken heart extended. Just as she neared her hoped-for escort, a tall, thin, somewhat awkward-looking fellow, good-naturedly known as String Bean, stepped forward, grinning. He shoved the half of his heart against Jenny's, and to his seeming delight and Jenny's dismay, the two halves fit neatly together. Virginia turned away. She could not bear to see Jenny's face.

She looked down at her own heart. She still had made no effort to find her own partner. Most everyone else had already been matched up. She hated looking for a partner.

Hated it. It was most embarrassing. Why did Clara have to go and set everyone up in pairs anyway?

She was about to move away when a voice right before her said, "Hey, it looks like we have a fit."

Virginia, startled, looked up directly into the eyes of Jamison Curtis.

CHAPTER 14

She did not dare to look at Jenny. She had chosen her pretty party dress especially to impress Jamison, had tried furtively to catch his eyes all evening, had been led off by the less-than-desired String Bean, and now . . . now she, Virginia, was matched up with the very fellow that Jenny had set her cap for. The girl would be furious.

Virginia swallowed. She felt her face flush, her palms go suddenly sticky. There was no denying it. The two pieces of the Valentine heart matched neatly together.

"Shall we get some cider?" Jamison was asking.

Virginia nodded dumbly and shuffled behind him to the table where Clara dished out the steaming cups. Clara gave her a sisterly smile, but Virginia did not even respond.

"Cookies?"

Virginia nodded mutely.

"Two—or three?"

"One. One will do." Virginia was sure she would do well to get one choked down. Jamison took three.

"Where would you like to sit?" he inquired.

Virginia did look around then. The thought came to her that if they were to join Jenny and her partner, perhaps Jenny would be able to get Jamison's attention after all.

But that hardly seemed fair. Not to poor String Bean. And, besides, it might mean that she herself would be stuck with him. She had nothing against the young man, in fact thought him a fun member of the Youth Group, but she did not wish to be paired with anyone. She was almost relieved to see that there was no room beside Jenny. Other couples had joined the pair on the bench, and Jenny was totally surrounded. They all were determined to make the new girl feel welcome, even in her unusual outfit.

Virginia let her eyes drift up to Jamison's face. She had never noticed how tall he was. He was a good eight inches taller than she was. But then she had never stood that close to him before.

"I—" she began but never did finish.

"There's room over there by Clara and Troy," he said, pointing the way with the cup he held in his hand.

Virginia had no desire to join her big sister and her beau, but there didn't seem to be a place anywhere else. She followed meekly.

Clara moved over and tucked in her flowing skirt, patting the spot beside her. Immediately the three were engaged in easy conversation, and Virginia found herself relaxing in spite of herself. Maybe it wasn't such bad luck to end up here with Clara after all.

By the time Virginia was included in the little chat, she felt quite free to answer the question directed her way by Troy. Yes, school was going fine. She liked the new teacher. Jamison responded that some kids said Mrs. Murray was strict, but he didn't mind strict teachers. Not as long as they were also fair. Then you knew exactly what was expected, he explained.

Virginia nodded. She didn't suppose Jamison did mind strict teachers. He had never been in trouble at school as far as she knew. She'd had a few little run-ins with the new teacher, but nothing that had needed to be reported to her parents. Virginia was relieved about that. Perhaps Mrs. Murray *was* fair. She had never thought of it before.

Very quickly the refreshment time was over, and Troy stood to lead the youth in the evening devotion. Again Virginia wished she could be seated by Jenny. She hoped her friend would not be uncomfortable as Troy talked about what the Bible had to say concerning the human heart.

He had several hearts to display to the group. A black one represented the sinner's condition, a white-washed one showed human attempt to make things right with a holy God. It was rather messy, with the white paint still letting the black show through in blots and spots and ugly splotches. A broken one needed obvious mending. A red one showed the pain and suffering of a Christ who was willing to die in order to obtain forgiveness for the sinful human race. Then Troy held up a pure white one.

" 'Create in me a clean heart,' King David prayed. And that is the only way that we will ever have a clean one," said Troy. "Only God can take care of the sins of man. Only He can forgive and give to us a clean, pure heart. But we must ask Him to. Just like King David. God will only come into our life and clean up our sinful hearts upon our invitation. We must pray for His forgiveness."

It was not a new lesson for Virginia. She had heard it many times over the years. Both at home and at her little church. But this was the first that she had listened to the familiar words and not squirmed a bit. She was glad that she was no longer plagued by guilt. She had done what Troy was talking about. Had finally done that. She had prayed, and God had forgiven.

She gave Clara just a hint of a smile.

But what about Jenny? Was Jenny squirming? Or was Jenny just shivering, ready to freeze to death in the ridiculously inappropriate summer-weather dress?

"Did you get lucky?" Jenny wanted to know, her voice an angry hiss. "Or did big sister rig the valentines?"

Virginia frowned.

They were hurrying into their wraps, preparing for the walk home in the cold. Already most of the crowd had left.

Virginia had offered to help Clara with the cleanup. Jenny also had pitched in. Virginia thought that it might have had something to do with the fact that Jamison was helping, too.

"Well?" Jenny demanded.

"I don't know what you're talking about."

Jenny retorted. "Don't be so innocent, Virginia. You got Jamison. I got String Bean."

"Clara did not rig anything," Virginia declared hotly. "She'd never do that. In case you didn't notice, she had two other girls pass out the hearts."

Jenny's expression acknowledged that she had to concede the point.

"Well, you didn't seem to mind one bit," she accused instead.

"I thought you looked like you were having a good time, too," Virginia responded.

It was true. Each time she had glanced toward Jenny, the girl was laughing. Sometimes a bit too hilariously. Maybe it was keeping her teeth from chattering.

Jenny just tossed her head. "Sort of," she admitted. "He is kinda fun."

They were just heading out the door when Jamison appeared. "See you at church Sunday, Virginia," he called with a wave. Virginia pulled the door tightly behind her. Oh, dear. What was Jenny going to say about that?

It was a quiet walk home. Each step they took crunched the snow beneath their feet. Virginia hunched into her wraps, her body shivering anyway. *How does Jenny stand it?* she wondered to herself, but she dared not ask. She hoped with all her heart that Jenny would not be sick. She wondered if she should speak with her mother about it when she got home.

As they neared the corner and the parting of their ways, Virginia felt that she must speak. Jenny still seemed upset with her. That was no way to end the evening.

"I hope you enjoyed the party." She tried to put lightness in her voice.

"I did." Jenny could hardly get the simple answer out, she was shaking so badly.

"I hope you'll come next time."

"I will."

They were at their corner.

Virginia turned and spoke once more. "Your dress was really pretty, Jenny. Everyone noticed it."

Jenny said nothing, but the corner streetlight picked up the hopeful glint in her eyes.

Virginia watched Jenny hurry away and then turned her own steps homeward.

She had only taken a few steps when she heard Jenny call her name. She wheeled. "Virginia," Jenny called again. "I think I'll go to church with you on Sunday."

For a moment Virginia struggled to fully comprehend the brief message, then grinned, hardly able to contain an expression of triumph. This was what she had been praying for. What they had all been praying for. Her mother would be so excited.

Jenny was hurrying off before Virginia could even respond. She turned toward home, her thoughts chasing each other. Jenny was going to go to church. Was it because of the warm welcome given by the young people of the church? Maybe it was because of Troy's message about hearts.

But perhaps . . . perhaps it was Jamison's comment as they had left the church.

"See you at church on Sunday, Virginia."

The next day, Saturday, cleaning rag in hand, Virginia answered a knock on the door. Jenny was standing there. At least she was wearing her warm winter coat.

"Are you all right?" Virginia's question was out even before Jenny was able to move into the warmth of the kitchen.

Jenny frowned. "'Course I'm all right. What do you mean?"

"I was worried. Worried that you might catch pneumonia—or something."

Jenny still frowned.

"It was so cold last night I was afraid . . ."

At Jenny's scowl Virginia's words faded away. She would not again make reference to Jenny's poor choice of clothing.

"Jenny," said Virginia's mother, entering the kitchen with a duster in her hand. "I didn't expect to see you today. It's so cold out there." She turned to Virginia. "Fix Jenny some hot cider," she instructed. "Take the chill from her bones."

She laid aside her duster and wiped her hands on her apron. "How's that hand doing?" she asked as she approached the young girl.

"Good."

"I think it is. I think it gets just a little bit better each week."

She stopped before Jenny, who obediently thrust out the injured arm. Virginia's mother took the hand in her own two hands and gently began to massage it.

"My . . . you *are* chilly. Your fingers are almost blue. I didn't think you'd brave the cold for your treatment today. It could have waited. Are you continuing with the exercises?"

Jenny nodded, then said, "I didn't really come for the—the treatment. I came to find out about church."

Virginia saw her mother's eyebrows raise. She smiled softly, continuing to massage the still-stiff fingers.

"The Bible lesson starts at ten o'clock. Then we have the morning sermon. I think you'll like Pastor Doyle. He has the most interesting sermons. Even the children listen."

Then there was silence. Virginia wondered if her mother might feel she had to fill the silence with more words. But she did not. Just kept right on gently massaging the arm, the hand, the fingers.

Jenny finally spoke. "What—how do—what do the girls wear?"

"Well, unless the weather changes drastically overnight, I would suggest the warmest thing you own," Virginia's mother said lightly. "It's cold out there. The poor old heater is not able to keep up with weather this cold. I expect folks will wear their coats right through the sermon tomorrow."

"Do—will school clothes do—or do people dress fancy?"

Virginia noted that it was rather strange Jenny was addressing the personal question to her mother and not to her. Over the weeks that Jenny had been coming to the Simpson home for medical treatment, she seemed to have become quite comfortable with her mother. The jealousy that Virginia once felt had now been replaced with honest concern for her friend. She was glad Jenny could talk to her mother. Especially when she did not have a mother of her own.

The cider began to steam, and Virginia went to get a

heavy mug from the cupboard.

"School clothes are just fine," her mother said. "Many of the girls wear simple dresses to church. We do not make a point of 'dressing up,' nor do we study one another to see what is being worn. Nor does God. It's our hearts He views as we enter the doors to His church. Not our clothing."

Virginia set the mug before Jenny. Her mother let go of Jenny's hand with one final pat. She smiled.

"There. You need to have two hands to enjoy your cider."

She turned to Virginia. "Did you fix enough that we can join Jenny?"

Virginia nodded. There was plenty in the steaming pot.

"Good. I could use a break from my cleaning. Why don't you run and call Clara? She is working on the bedrooms."

While Virginia moved to do as bidden, her mother poured three more cups of cider and set a large-mouthed cookie jar on the table.

"Will you join us for dinner following church?" Virginia heard her mother asking as she and Clara entered the kitchen.

Jenny nodded.

"We'd love to have your father as well." Mrs. Simpson had offered that invitation on several occasions.

Jenny shook her head.

"Even if he isn't able to go with us to church, he still would be most welcome for dinner." Virginia's mother had said that before, as well.

"He sleeps most of Sunday. The paper keeps him working through most nights. When Sunday comes he sorta just . . . flops."

"Of course. It must be very hard running a paper."

Jenny nodded. She didn't comment that the bottle at

her father's elbow also had some bearing on his deep sleep.

From the cellar came a sharp squeal. "Danny, you cheated!"

"Never did" was the quick denial.

Soon hasty tramping sounded on the boards of the wooden steps and the door was flung open. Francine emerged, her hair in disarray and her hands smudged with dust. She was so used to Jenny being there, she did not even hesitate when she saw her sitting at the kitchen table.

"Mama. Danny cheated," she insisted. "We were having a race to see who would finish first, and he—"

"I never did, either," shouted a voice from somewhere down below.

"Did too."

Francine seemed unable to decide whom she should address. The cellar and Danny or the table and her mother.

"Now, now," chided their mother.

Francine turned misty eyes to her mother's face.

"Now let's start at the beginning. What's the problem?" the woman asked.

"Well, I had the fruit jars and shelves to dust. . . ."

Their mother nodded. She knew the Saturday task that had been assigned to Francine.

"An' Danny was cleaning the veg'table bins."

Another nod.

"So, Danny said, 'Let's race.' An' I said yes. But Danny skipped the 'tata bin. He just went right from the turnips to the carrots. An' now he will beat me."

"Come," said their mother, taking Francine by the hand and leading her back toward the cellar. Virginia knew that the dispute would be settled. As Mrs. Simpson left, she paused long enough to say, "Why don't we stop by and pick you up tomorrow, Jenny? About twenty to ten?" Jenny nodded.

Clara stood, stretched her back, one hand on a hip, and turned to go. "That was a nice break, but if I'm going to be done before dinner, I'd better get back at it."

Virginia thought of the cupboards she had been wiping out. She'd have to hurry, too, to get done in time for dinner.

"Boy, you are lucky," she said with a sigh, turning her eyes on her friend. "No chores. No one to fight—"

But she stopped short. There was a strange look in Jenny's eyes. A look of longing. Of loneliness. As though she missed being part of a large, busy, boisterous family. Virginia bit her tongue.

Virginia saw her mother's eyes widen the next morning when she appeared for breakfast. But it was Rodney who spoke. "How come you aren't ready for church?"

"I . . . I am ready," Virginia answered. Her voice was gentle but held an underlying hint of don't-challenge-me.

"No, you're not," Rodney insisted in spite of her unspoken warning. "You're wearing a school dress. An everyday dress."

Virginia did not even look down at her dark blue wool. Plain and drab, it had never been a favorite. It had been one of Clara's, handed-down and resewn. Now it was beginning to show wear on the cuffs and elbows.

She would have felt so much more church-ready in her new green and orange print. Those colors didn't really describe it. It was more . . . more a soft minty green with even softer shades of melon. Sort of like sun-warmed peaches and ripe apricots. It had lace cuffs and leg-o'-mutton sleeves. Such a pretty gown, and it made her feel so grown-up. Everyone had complimented her on it. But . . .

Her eyes lifted to her mother's. Did she understand?

The eyes that met hers were shiny with unshed tears. A hand reached out to gently brush her shoulder, pat just a little, then recede. Her mother was nodding. Just nodding. She blinked once and raised a handkerchief to her eye.

She not only understood. She approved. Jenny would not be the only girl at church wearing a simple school dress.

CHAPTER 15

The weather finally warmed. Not all at once. Gradually, each day a little bit, so that one hardly noticed the difference at all. But then a morning came when one suddenly realized that it was no longer bone-chilling to step out of the house. A sure sign of early spring, school children began to argue against wearing heavy woolen stockings and scarfs that covered chins and noses.

Virginia was glad for the change. She was tired of winter. Of hearing her mother's reminders about bundling up every time she stepped toward the door.

She was looking forward to the tobogganing party that the Youth Group had planned. And Jenny was going. She had made that clear enough—pestering Virginia almost daily about the plans. Jenny already knew every detail there was to know, but she still insisted on asking questions that Virginia couldn't answer. How was Virginia to know what Ida intended to wear or if Jamison had his very own toboggan?

"I hope, if he does, it's just a two-seater," Jenny sighed.

Virginia was perplexed—then quickly understood. Jenny did not want company along on her trip down the hill with Jamison.

Virginia had never given Jamison much thought before Jenny arrived. He was just one of the Youth Group. One of the older boys who pestered or ignored the girls as the mood seemed to strike. Now Virginia was forced to take another look at him. She supposed that most of it was due to Jenny's constant prattling about him, but the Valentine party had certainly increased the awareness. And there was the fact that Jamison almost always made some kind of contact each Sunday. Often it was just a nod, or a simple hello. But once he had actually spoken, and one other Sunday, he had helped her find a hook and hung her heavy coat up for her. Virginia had blushed slightly.

But Jenny—Jenny never let up about Jamison. Jamison this and Jamison that. Virginia was weary of it. At the same time she did not want to say or do anything that would offend Jenny. Jenny was coming to church every Sunday now. She even had a nice dress. It was a rich green that had been Clara's. Clara had been rather artful about it. Virginia remembered it well. She and Jenny had been seated at the kitchen table, school books spread out before them in pretense of studying. Actually, Jenny was just using it as an excuse to fantasize concerning Jamison again.

"He looked right at me on Sunday. I expect him to speak any day now."

Virginia had winced.

"Did you see him look at me? Do you think he likes me? C'mon, be honest now."

Virginia swallowed. How was she to answer that?

Clara had entered the kitchen at that precise moment. Virginia sighed in relief. Clara held her green dress over one arm.

"Jenny, I've been wondering," she began and lifted the dress up for Jenny to see. Virginia could see the expression on Jenny's face. She knew her friend well enough to know that Jenny thought the dress was very pretty.

"This is getting a bit tight. Virginia is built so slight, my dresses are never . . . just right for her."

Virginia knew that Clara's carefully chosen words, though true as far as they went, were just a bit slanted. She and Clara had never been "built alike," but that had not stopped her mama from remaking every dress that Clara had ever outgrown. It was always made over to look new, but it was Clara's old material just the same. And this dress—this pretty green material that Clara had saved her very own money to purchase—was not *that* tight on Clara.

"You and I are . . . almost the same build. Through the shoulders," Clara went on. "I wondered—do you mind hand-me-downs? We could change the collar and the cuffs and maybe cut the waist a little different. It's a little fussy for school, but it would do—nicely—for church and such. Mama is a skilled seamstress and—"

Jenny's eyes had spoken for her.

It was Clara who actually did the sewing. Jenny whirled and spun and admired herself with flushed cheeks each time there was a fitting. The color suited Jenny's green eyes and fair skin. It made her red hair look gloriously bright. Like polished bronze, Virginia's mother had said.

Virginia had decided that if ever Jamison was to take notice of Jenny, it would be accomplished by that green dress. Every other boy in the church certainly had already noticed her. Virginia could see the stares and hear the husky whispers that first Sunday when she and Jenny had walked into church together. Jenny looked almost giddy with the power she had suddenly found. But she had expected Jamison to fall at her feet, and she had been disappointed.

Virginia stirred from her reverie. It seemed that her thoughts were too often directed toward Jamison.

But perhaps that wasn't strange—considering the amount of time that Jenny spent with her and the fact that Jenny was always going on about the young man. Virginia smiled. Jenny always referred to Jamison now as a "young man." Virginia decided that it probably made Jenny feel more like a "young woman." And she still had not reached her fifteenth birthday.

"I'll soon be fifteen," she liked to remind Virginia, totally ignoring the fact that Virginia would be fast on her heels in reaching that significant milestone.

"My mama was—"

Virginia found it hard to be patient with Jenny's chattering. Sure, her mama had married early, but where was her mama now?

But it would have been cruel to make such remarks to Jenny. The Simpson family prayed regularly for Jenny. The girl was still much on her mother's heart. Jenny remained a deep concern to Virginia herself. Jenny persisted in pushing away from spiritual truth and life. In spite of her involvement with the youth, in spite of her newly established church attendance, Jenny had not seemed to soften one bit toward God. It made Virginia uneasy. Her mother encouraged her to continue to pray—and trust.

The moon chose to hide its face behind a ribbon of cloud on the night of the tobogganing party. The young people compensated by building little bonfires at intervals along the hillside run. At least there would be enough light to keep flying toboggans and sleds from running into one another. That is, if the occupants kept their heads up and their wits about them.

It was a pleasant evening, stars beginning to twinkle against the darkening northern sky. Just cold enough to make the snow crunchy under the heel of a boot or the runners of a sleigh. A big plus for the sledders was the fact that there was no wind.

Virginia and Jenny were already breathless by the time

they joined the excited group on the hill. Virginia was not sure her pounding heart was from the hurry through the night, burdened with warm clothing so she could hardly move, or the thought of the fun that was ahead.

She saw Jenny begin her usual scan of faces and knew without asking that Jenny was searching for Jamison.

"There he is," Jenny said, giving Virginia's arm a hard squeeze. "Over there—and he does have a toboggan." But to Jenny's disappointment, Jamison's toboggan looked like it would carry four or five passengers. Maybe even six, if they crowded.

Jamison was heading their way.

"Hi," he called with a wave of a mittened hand. "Just get here? Do you want to go down?"

The question was really directed to Virginia, but the sweep of his glance included Jenny. Virginia did not have to guess what Jenny's answer would be.

Jamison was already lining up his toboggan for the run down the hill. Jenny was excitedly bouncing from one foot to the other, hardly able to contain herself as she clapped mittened hands together.

Jamison settled himself at the front of the toboggan, carefully tucking in his feet and adjusting the tension on the rope in his hands.

"Tuck in close behind me, Virginia—"

Virginia did not catch the rest of Jamison's directions to her as to how she should sit, how to best hang on.

Her mind was frozen. Jenny was expecting to *tuck in*. What should she do now?

Without stopping to think, she gave Jenny a little push on the back that indicated that she was to move forward and take a seat directly behind the young man. Jenny did not need a second invitation. She snuggled up against Jamison's back, her arms reaching around his middle to cling firmly for the ride down the hill. Virginia could only stand and stare. She did hope Jamison realized that it was not she who clung so tightly to him.

"Load it up," called Jamison, and Virginia stirred from her daze to climb on behind Jenny. Two boys noisily and clumsily piled on behind them.

"Give us a start," called Jamison to no one in particular, and hands were soon at their backs, giving them a running start down the hill.

It was a thrilling ride. Virginia's thoughts concentrated on the sharp wind in her face and the bumps and jolts of the hillside flying beneath them as they careened down, snow stinging their faces where they were not hidden behind scarves.

Virginia heard Jenny's shrill, excited screams. She could imagine that the girl was using this excuse to give Jamison the tightest bear hug he'd ever been given. She felt her face flush again.

They didn't quite make it all the way to the bottom. In the increasing darkness, the flames of the bonfires did not reveal all the obstacles on the course. Just as they reached maximum speed, they hit a large bump under the snow. The toboggan flew into the air, and when they all landed, sled and people had parted company.

Soft snowbanks cushioned the fall, and the laughing, breathless bodies wriggled out, brushing snow out of faces, getting limbs untangled, and their feet properly under them again.

Jamison reached down a hand to assist his companion to her feet. Virginia, just clambering to her own feet, saw the surprised look on his face. He had thought that it was she, Virginia, who had crowded in behind him, clinging firmly and squealing in his ear all the way down the hill. She saw the quick dart of his glance around the group as he tried to sort through how this switch of girls had happened. When he caught Virginia's eye, she couldn't really be sure what he was thinking. Did he look disappointed? She continued to brush at the snow on her coat, letting her eyes drop away from Jamison's.

Jenny had not noticed. Still giggling, she had not even started to clean off the snow. "What a ride," she squealed. "Jamison, you were terrific! How can you ever steer when we're going so fast? And in the air half the time?" She giggled again.

Virginia turned away. She really didn't want to hear any more.

"Let's go again," Jenny's voice followed her. "It's . . . it's *superb*! It's the most fun I've ever had."

Virginia wasn't sure that her own sentiments were expressed by Jenny's words.

Virginia could never remember just how the quarrel started. One minute they were walking home under the stars together, Jenny bubbling on and on about all the trips down the hill on Jamison's toboggan, how he always gave her a hand to help her up from the snow, how he brought her a cup of hot chocolate, how his eyes looked by the light of the dancing fire—and suddenly Virginia could take no more.

"You made rather a fool of yourself," she said without any preamble, her voice tight.

Jenny whirled to look at her, defense then defiance quickly flashing in her green eyes.

"You practically chased him all night. He . . . he couldn't move without you," Virginia went on, shaking her head in disgust.

"I did no such—"

"You did too, and you know it. Every time he took the toboggan to the top of the hill, you piled on before he even asked you to."

Jenny's eyes were smoldering. "I got on because he wanted me to," she countered.

"I never heard him say so."

"He didn't have to say so."

"What makes you think—"

"Did you hear him ask me to stay off?"

"Of course not. He's too polite for that."

"Did he ask you?"

Virginia could have said yes. Yes, he had asked her. The very first time when she had nudged Jenny forward. It was to her that Jamison's eyes had been turned. To her that he had issued the initial invitation.

She was tempted to say it. To tell Jenny that the place she had usurped for the whole evening had really been meant for her, Virginia. But she bit her tongue just in time. She couldn't say that. She couldn't. It would make Jenny angry. Hurt her deeply. She might never go to church with them again. And if she didn't go to church, they had slim hope of ever winning her to a faith in God.

"I just think you were too bold," Virginia said instead, making a conscious effort to control her voice and her emotions.

Jenny cocked her head saucily. "Jamison didn't think I was too bold."

"How do you know?"

"He would have said."

"He would not have. He's too—"

"Polite. I know."

They were almost yelling at each other.

Then Jenny took another tack. "Grow up, Virginia. You don't always need to *say* something. You can tell—without words—how a boy feels."

Virginia did not have a rebuttal. What did she know about such things? She had never had a beau. Not really. Freddie's invitation to The Sweet Shop certainly didn't provide her with much knowledge.

"Besides," went on Jenny loftily, "I really think that what goes on between Jamison and me is our business."

Virginia did have an answer for that. She had heard it

from her folks often enough. The conduct on youth activities was to be open and above-board. One could be dismissed from the Youth Group if one behaved badly.

"Not when you're with the Youth Group."

"What do you mean?" At least Jenny's attention was now fully on Virginia.

"Proper conduct. The pastor will not allow—" how was she to describe it for Jenny? "—fondling—mauling—in the Youth Group."

"I was not mauling."

"You were. You squeezed Jamison so tight he could hardly catch his breath."

"How do you know?"

"I could tell. I was just behind you—remember?"

Their voices had risen again.

"I'm fifteen—" began Jenny and was cut off sharply.

"Not yet."

"I am as good as fifteen, Virginia Simpson. I am quite old enough to be courting, and I—"

"Not in our Youth Group," Virginia countered quickly. Her voice was now louder than Jenny's.

"Then maybe I won't go to the Youth Group anymore."

Virginia had many conflicting emotions crowding to the fore. That would be a relief. No, that would be a shame. It would be her fault. She needed to apologize. Quickly. But she didn't want to. Jenny was being so difficult.

"Fine," she said before she could stop the words. "If that's what you want."

She was about to remind Jenny that Jamison would be going to the Youth Group, but she decided against mentioning that fact.

Jenny tossed her red hair, almost shaking the wool hat from her head.

"You are just jealous. You wish that Jamison had

picked you. That's all. You wanted to be the one huggin' him."

"That's a big, bold lie. I never would have squeezed him like that. Never. It was totally . . . completely . . . too forward."

Jenny was laughing. Laughing—right in the middle of an out-and-out war.

But Virginia failed to see the humor in the situation.

"Someday you will grow up," Jenny said when she could control her voice again. "You'll—aw, never mind. You wouldn't understand. You're such a child."

Jenny's last words were said soberly, caustically. They cut Virginia to the quick.

"You are—" she faltered for a description, but Jenny saved her from having to think of one.

"And you are jealous," Jenny flung into the air between them.

Virginia was relieved they were at their parting corner.

Virginia wanted to hurry home to the safety of her own bedroom. But she knew that before she reached her place of privacy, she would need to pass through the warmth of the big kitchen. Her father and mother would be waiting up with questions about the night's outing. Her steps slowed in her reluctance to face them.

How could she tell them that Jenny and she had fought? That she had been cruel and self-serving? That Jenny had vowed not to come to Youth Group anymore? It was her fault. What had made her so touchy? So critical? She had just dashed the chances of her own prayers being answered. It was foolish. So foolish. She had lost all hope of being the right influence in Jenny's life. How would she ever win Jenny back again? How could she have risked it? And why? Why?

Her racing thoughts went back to the evening that had

just passed. It had started out with such high hopes. They had not been able to wait to reach the hill together. And then, then everything seemed to go wrong. Jamison's invitation. Jenny's response to her push forward. And then things just seemed to get worse and worse. Jenny had spent the entire night fluttering around Jamison. He had hardly been able to move without bumping into her.

Virginia felt her cheeks flush. Anger pushed through her again. Anger and something more. *Was it jealousy?* Jealousy? She had never even considered it before. Had not realized just how it felt. But yes. Maybe. Maybe that's what it was called. Jealousy.

She only knew that she did not want Jenny fussing over Jamison in such a way. It made her uncomfortable. And not for the sake of the Youth Group. She didn't want Jamison smiling at Jenny. Helping her from the snow. Bringing her hot chocolate. It made her feel angry. A little sick.

Jealousy? She wasn't sure what to call the feeling. But she did know one thing for sure. She kind of liked Jamison Curtis.

CHAPTER 16

Virginia made the first move toward a reconciliation. Jenny seemed tremendously relieved. They had endured one miserable day of trying to stay angry—of passing each other in the school hallways, heads held high, eyes averted. The next day Virginia made a tentative approach. Jenny did not turn her back.

Virginia spoke quietly. "I'm sorry. I shouldn't have said such mean things."

Jenny nodded.

"I would like you to come to church with us on Sunday. Will you?"

Jenny acted as though she was giving it careful thought.

"And the Youth Group," Virginia went on. She knew what she was saying. It meant that she would need to be willing to back away and let Jenny establish the desired relationship with Jamison. Virginia had battled long and hard with her feelings and even now found it difficult to choke out the words.

Jenny nodded again.

"Mama wants to know if you will be over today?"

"Sure," said Jenny.

"Good."

It was all settled so simply. It was hard to remember just how wide the breach had been.

Winter seriously began to give way to spring. Jenny's fifteenth birthday came and went. Activity in the Simpson household increased with Clara's wedding plans now seeming to include them all. Even Francine was "helping" to fold linens and tea towels for the hope chest that had to be totally furnished by the special day in April.

Jenny's exercises and massages were reduced to twice a week. Virginia's mother thought the girl had progressed quite nicely and would continue to do so if she kept up the special exercises at home. Virginia wondered if Jenny really fulfilled the assignment or just said that she did. She knew that Jenny told little fibs about other things. Jenny didn't seem to worry too much about the consequences of lying. Only about being caught.

But she was still coming to Youth Group and also to church. Virginia was quite sure that Jenny had been disappointed regarding Jamison. Since the night of the tobogganing party, Jamison seemed to almost ignore Jenny. In fact, Virginia thought that he rather ignored them both.

But she had little time to think about Jamison. With her mother and Clara both busy with the trousseau and hope chest items, more of the household duties fell on Virginia.

"With Clara gone, you will now be my chief help," her mother had said cheerily and seemed to expect that Virginia would be flattered by the prospect.

Virginia was not. She had never cared that much for housework and certainly didn't enjoy kitchen puttering as Clara had always done.

Sometimes Jenny came over under the guise of being Virginia's helper. In truth Jenny was mostly in the way.

She had never learned to do housework efficiently and properly. Virginia had to give careful directions about everything that was to be done. It was even worse than trying to work with Francine.

So as she peeled the potatoes for supper, Virginia was not surprised to hear Jenny's customary tap on the door.

"Come," she called without even drying her hands on her apron.

"My word," Jenny exclaimed before she even closed the door behind her. "They're at it again."

Virginia's head came up. What was Jenny talking about now?

She didn't have to ask. Jenny went right on. "The Crells are out after Loony Marshall again."

Virginia felt her hand tighten on the potato she held. "What are you talking about?"

"They are. Oh, not the old story. It's a new one now. Guess they gave up on the other one. Now they say he's a thief."

"A thief?"

Jenny nodded, her eyes gleaming with the impact of her news.

"That's ridiculous," exclaimed Virginia.

"Ridiculous or not—that's what they're saying."

"He'd never steal."

Jenny looked cocky. "That's what you *think*, Virginia."

"That's what I know."

Jenny hesitated for a moment as the tension built.

"Crell has already been to see your pa."

"Papa would never even listen to such silly charges," Virginia declared hotly.

"Well, some folks are listening. Mrs. Parker says she has never really trusted the man, and Mrs.—"

"Mrs. Parker. Who listens to Mrs. Parker? You certainly don't."

Jenny seemed to stop to plan her next attack. "Mrs.

Parker isn't the only one to be talking, Virginia. Other folks are beginning to wonder about ole Loony."

"I wish you wouldn't call him that."

"That's what he is."

Jenny tipped her head slightly and gave Virginia a smug stare, then moved to lift an apple from the bowl on the cupboard. After taking a crisp-sounding bite, she went on. Virginia could barely sort out Jenny's words around the apple in her mouth.

"Several folks in town have had things turn up missing lately. Now that isn't hearsay. That's fact. The sheriff has had several reports of stolen property, and he has had an eye out for some time."

"How come we've never heard about it?"

Jenny shrugged. "Sheriffs like to keep those things quiet until they get a lead."

"A lead?"

"Yeah. Someone that looks guilty. Things that just don't fit. That kind of thing."

"So he has a lead?"

Virginia felt a strange queasiness in the pit of her stomach. Surely—surely Rett Marshall had not done anything to be under suspicion.

"Guess so." Jenny gave a shrug again. "He wouldn't let folks talk like that if he didn't, would he?"

"You can't stop folks from talking, you know that," Virginia responded.

She looked down at the hand that still held the unpeeled potato. She would be late with supper if she didn't get busy.

"Well, the sheriff was in to see my pa. Told him to please hold printing anything until things could be sorted out. 'Course my pa agreed, but folks pretty well know that it's gotta come out some time."

Jenny looked so knowing and self-righteous about it all that Virginia had a hard time biting back a sharp retort.

She turned back to her potato peeling, hurrying to get the task done so she could get the kettle on the stove.

But her thoughts were heavy. Mixed and jumbled all together in one huge whirl that made her head spin and her stomach feel sick. Surely it couldn't be true. Rett couldn't steal things. He had never even cared about *things*. Just animals. Why, his pa had said that all the time he was growing up there wasn't even any gift that they could get him. He just looked at it briefly, then laid it down and walked away. Why would he start wanting to gather things now? It didn't make a bit of sense to Virginia.

At last she turned to Jenny, who had been standing watching her, munching steadily on the apple.

"What sort of things have been missing?"

"I dunno. Little things mostly. Crell lost a cowbell. One fella some fishhooks. Another a new wrench."

"Maybe they misplaced them," put in Virginia.

"Oh, Virginia!"

"They do. Folks misplace things all the time. Doesn't mean they've been stolen."

"Mrs. Parker lost that red pin that she treasured so highly and wore on every dress she owns. Don't know who would want it. Have to be someone *loony*. It's an ugly thing." Jenny shivered to show her disgust.

"Why would Rett want a pin? That's pure silliness!" Virginia felt her case had been won.

"How do you ever know why loony people do what they do?" responded Jenny.

It was a point well taken and one that even Virginia, with her staunch loyalty, could not dispute.

She had thought the whole matter of charges against Rett had finally been put behind them. Apparently it had all been dredged up again. Would it never end?

"Afternoon."

Mr. Adamson hung on the pickets of his fence like a limp sheet. But even though his back seemed to bend more with every passing season, his near-toothless smile was still intact. Virginia had no problem bringing her dragging feet to a halt.

"Afternoon," she responded, but there was no brightness in the word.

"You're lookin' a mite down in the mouth," the elderly man observed.

Virginia nodded. She could not deny it. She was feeling discouraged and sad. Every place she went as she fulfilled her mother's errands she heard the whispered innuendos, and at times outright charges, against Rett Marshall. He was a thief—but, said the more lenient and forgiving, one could not really hold it against the man. He could not really be held responsible. He hardly knew what he was doing. He just needed help.

Such statements did nothing to erase Virginia's heaviness. She was sure that Rett Marshall would never steal—from anyone. But the poor man was not even capable of coming to his own defense. She wondered if he was even aware of the serious charges that were being laid at his door.

Now she nodded to Mr. Adamson. "I guess I am—a bit," she acknowledged. "I've—I'm worried."

He seemed to read her thoughts. "That Marshall fella?"

She nodded again. "He didn't do it, Mr. Adamson, I'm sure he didn't."

"I've a notion to agree with you," said the man. Now it was his turn to shake his head. "He's gonna have a hard time clearing himself, I'm afraid."

Virginia brightened some. "Papa says that he won't have to prove he *didn't* do it. They will have to prove—beyond reasonable doubt—that he *did*."

"They don't have no proof?"

" 'Course they don't. And they never will, either, unless . . ."

"Unless?"

"Unless someone mean goes and trumps up some false charges."

"You think someone would do that?"

Virginia stirred restlessly. "I don't know. They've had it in for Rett, and that's for sure. They have wanted him put away for a long time."

"Well—expect the sheriff will get it all cleared up real soon." He sounded so cheery that Virginia wanted to believe him.

"Those hothouse roses are coming along just fine. They should be ready for Clara's wedding, no problem," he went on.

Virginia managed a smile. "I'll tell her," she promised. "She'll be pleased."

Clara's wedding was only a week away. Virginia had been excited about it. She was to be the bridesmaid. She was thrilled when her older sister had asked her to share her wedding in the honored position. Her mama had sewn her the most lovely dress in a soft, almost weightless silk material. It floated about her when she moved, making her feel that she was next to walking on air. Jenny had oohed and aahed over the dress, telling Virginia over and over just how lucky she was. Virginia had come to believe her.

And now . . . now this awful story that rumbled and tumbled over the whole town, seeming to smother all the joy out of Clara's approaching wedding day. It didn't seem fair. Not to Rett. Not to Clara. And not to Virginia.

Clara's April wedding day dawned bright, quickly spilling bright sunshine over the entire area. Virginia's pulse quickened as she arose from her bed and went to her window. It was earlier than she normally awoke, but excitement coursing through her would not allow her further sleep.

Already she could hear voices from the kitchen. Other members of the family were up before her.

Quickly she slipped out of her nightie and dressed in clothes she had laid out the night before. There would be many small tasks to accomplish before she could turn to the lovely pink dress that hung from the cloth-covered hook in her wardrobe.

Her mother turned her head as she entered the kitchen. "Virginia. I was going to let you sleep for another half hour."

"I couldn't sleep. I'm too excited."

Clara gave a little laugh, the closest to a girlish giggle Virginia had ever heard from her practical sister. She gave Clara a quick glance to assure herself that she was still the same person. She was. A flushed, bright-eyed Clara, looking more nervous than Virginia had ever seen her.

"*You're* excited," said Clara. "I could just . . . *fly away*."

Virginia agreed that Clara just might do that.

Her father, passing by Clara's chair, stopped and reached out his hand.

"Relax, Dumplin'," he said good-naturedly with fatherly assurance. "I've never known a bride to actually leave the ground."

Clara laughed again. The same high, excited laugh. "Well, I might well be the first," she cautioned.

Rodney came into the room, still fighting the hair that wanted to flop forward into his face. "What's all the ruckus?" he asked sleepily. "Sounds like a pen of clacking chickens out here."

That brought another titter from Clara.

Rodney stared, then yawned. "So it *was* you," he said

around his gaping mouth. "I thought Jenny had already arrived."

Warm laughter filled the kitchen, signaling the close family bond. Rodney poured himself a cup of coffee and joined the others at the table.

"Speaking of Jenny, I saw her in town yesterday. She said the sheriff has a man watching Rett's every move."

The words ushered in a dark cloud over the day. Virginia looked at her father for some kind of rebuttal. An expression of his outrage over such preposterous monitoring. But her father was smiling. She even heard a slight chuckle.

"I sure hope the man is in good shape," he said, a smile twitching his mouth. "He'll have to be if he's to keep up with Rett."

The words eased the tension of the room as family members began to picture the scene. Rett moved ceaselessly, sometimes covering many miles before returning home at night. Up hill, down hill, through swamps, over bogs, pushing his way through dense undergrowth or fighting his way across rocky outcroppings. It would be rather comical to watch another man try to keep up. The smiles turned to chuckles, the chuckles to outright laughter.

But in spite of their merriment, Virginia still felt uneasy. Rodney's few simple words had managed to shadow her day. She would not be able to fully enjoy the excitement of being Clara's bridesmaid or the swish of the soft material against her ankles. In spite of her aim to concentrate on the joys of the event at hand, her mind would keep going back to Rett. Rett and the man who tailed him, stalking, watching, hounding him as he waited for him to make some kind of self-condemning mistake.

The family and friends who gathered to witness the

wedding filled the little church with their warmth and love. Virginia watched her sister's face during the service, and as the vows were said, she thought she had never seen someone look so beautiful.

It's not just the dress, Virginia thought, though it was lovely, too. She had watched Clara and her mother as they carefully stitched and embroidered the exquisite gown. *It's . . . it's like Clara's face shines from inside*, she decided. *I wonder if I'll ever feel like that about someone*, she mused as she looked from Clara to Troy.

CHAPTER 17

Life had settled back into more normal routines during the week following the wedding. One evening there came a sharp rap on the kitchen door. Before Virginia's father could rise from his chair to answer it, Aaron, Luke's son, had pushed it open and stuck his head in.

"Aaron," invited her mother. "Come in. We were just finishing supper. Could I get you—"

A look at the young man's face stopped the flow of words. "Something's wrong," she finished quietly.

"It's Grandpa. Pa hopes it's not serious, but he wanted you to know."

"What's happened? Where is he?" Virginia's father asked the questions that were on everyone's mind. A somber silence had instantly stilled the family chatter from around the table.

"Uncle Clare brought him in."

"Where's Mama?" asked Virginia's mother, pushing back from the table. Her face was white.

"She's with him."

"Do they know—?"

"Pa thinks it's a stroke."

Aaron had not come into the room or closed the door. He just stood there, one hand on the doorknob, as if he was about to bolt as soon as he had delivered the message.

Virginia's mother had fully risen now. Virginia could tell that it was the daughter rather than the nurse as her mother fought to control her emotions and her fear.

"Virginia, you do the cleaning up," she instructed through trembling lips. "See that Francine reviews her spelling words before she goes to bed. I may not be home tonight. You might have to look after things in the morning, too. Rodney, you help with the school lunches. Danny—" She stopped with visible effort. "You all know your chores, there's no need for me to go on so." Quickly she lifted her eyes to her husband as though in quiet apology. "Your father will be here."

He understood her anxiety and reached out a hand. She seemed about to burst into tears as she went to him. "I'll go with you," he said as he pulled her close. "Just . . . just hold steady." He was patting her shoulder, pressing his lips to her forehead. "We'll go—right away—as quickly as we can. But first . . . first let's have a short word of prayer together."

The prayer *was* short. Just a brief but emotional plea for God to be with their grandfather—to be with him and sustain him. To be with Uncle Luke and give him special wisdom. To be with each family member, especially Grandma—in Jesus' name.

"Danny, run get your mother's light shawl," Virginia's father said as he lifted his head.

No one had noticed when the door closed or when Aaron left them to carry his sad news to other family members.

It was a long, agonizing evening for Virginia. She went through the routine of cleaning up the table and doing the supper dishes by rote. Danny cared for his animals and pulled out his homework, which he spread across the kitchen table. He seemed to be doing more fidgeting than solving arithmetic problems, Virginia noticed. Rodney paced about after having volunteered to dry the supper dishes, seeming to feel that he should be doing something for his younger siblings but unsure of what it was that he could do.

Virginia hung up the dishpan and turned to Francine. Francine had not stopped weeping since the arrival of the news. The tears rolled down her cheeks, soaking handkerchief after handkerchief.

"What will we do if Grandpa dies?" Francine asked in a wobbly voice.

Danny looked up, fear in his own eyes. "Aaron told us that Uncle Luke said it wasn't serious," he reminded the small girl, and his voice was sharp with reprimand at such an awful suggestion.

It just brought fresh tears. Virginia had a hard time choking back her own.

"Come on, Francine," she said in what she hoped was a patient tone. "We need to work on your spelling words."

"How can we do spelling—now?" cried Francine.

It was a question that Virginia had been asking herself. Her mama had set her an almost impossible task.

"We must do it. You will be asked to spell them tomorrow."

She cast a glance at Danny, who sat with eyes unfocused, chewing on the end of his pencil. "And, Danny, you best finish up your arithmetic."

She was beginning to sound like Clara. Clara, who had now been married for a full week. Clara, whom she was missing more than she ever could have imagined. Clara, the one she used to accuse of being bossy. And now *she* was giving the orders. But how else could one take charge? Suddenly Virginia realized that it was not easy being the one responsible for the rest.

"Come," she said again to Francine as she extended

her hand. "We'll work in the parlor and let Danny finish his work here."

Francine followed, dabbing at her cheeks and eyes as she did so.

They got through the spelling words. Virginia had her doubts at first, but gradually Francine was able to settle down and think about the task at hand. She hoped that when the time for testing arrived, Francine would be prepared.

She put Francine to bed—in the big bed that the young girl had formerly shared with Clara but now had all to herself. She looked small and alone. Virginia decided to stay with her until she fell asleep.

"Would you like me to read to you?" she asked.

Francine looked surprised. It had always been Mama or Clara who had read to her—or occasionally Papa if he had the time. Virginia had never offered to read to her before.

But Francine shook her head. "I don't think I could listen good."

"Well," corrected Virginia softly.

"Listen well."

Virginia sat down on the edge of the bed and stroked Francine's hair back from her face. Francine had already sobbed her way through her evening prayers, so she did not have to remind the small girl of that.

"Do you think Grandpa might die?" Francine whispered, her eyes solemnly on Virginia's face.

"I hope not." Virginia's voice quivered.

"But he could—couldn't he?"

Virginia nodded. It would be foolish to try to deny it.

"He's old, isn't he?"

"Pretty old."

"And strokes are bad."

Again Virginia nodded.

"Minnie's grandma died 'cause she caught stroke."

Virginia did not correct her.

"People don't always die," Virginia said, as much to assure her own heart as to comfort her younger sister.

Then her thoughts went further. It was a stroke that had put Mrs. Harmon in her bed, unable to move or talk or even care for her own needs. Her mama, who had done much of the nursing, had quietly confided to their father that it would have been a blessing if death would have taken the elderly woman. Virginia had overheard the murmured words, even though at the time she had found them confusing.

"If Grandpa dies—" Francine began.

But Virginia interrupted gently, "If Grandpa dies, God will take care of him. We don't need to worry about Grandpa, Francine. He—"

"I know," said Francine with a fresh burst of tears. "But I will miss him."

"We will all miss him—terribly—but . . ."

What could she say? Her own heart was aching with the possibility that they might lose their grandfather. Life would be so different without him. She wanted to cling to him. To demand that God leave him with them. Yet what if God were to leave him like old Mrs. Harmon? She didn't want that. No, she wanted him back—just like he had always been.

It was almost one o'clock in the morning before Virginia heard the door. She had not been able to go to sleep. Her father had been back once, about ten o'clock. He had checked on all of them, brought the news that their grandfather seemed to be resting comfortably, advised them all to go to bed and try to get some sleep, then had left again, assuring them that he and their mother would return later.

But as Virginia strained to hear the small movements through the darkness, she could hear only one pair of footsteps. There were no whispered conversations. Only one person was stirring about, carefully muffling sounds. Virginia crawled from her bed. She met her father in the hallway, the kitchen lamp in hand.

"Virginia. Sorry to waken you."

Virginia did not bother to explain that she couldn't sleep. Instead, she asked quietly, "Is he any better?"

"Well, it's a little early to be talking about being better. But your uncle Luke is encouraged. He thinks that things—that he's holding steady."

Virginia was not sure if that was good news.

Her father put the lamp down on a hall table and reached to draw her close.

"It's late," he whispered as he held her. "Are the others sleeping?"

Virginia nodded against his chest.

"You need sleep, too."

He pushed her back slightly and looked into her face. "Look—why don't you slip in and join Francine?"

Virginia was the one who had insisted on her own room. Her own bed. Her privacy. Clara had willingly shared her room with their younger sister. Now Francine had her own room, though the little girl did not really seem to fully appreciate the fact.

Virginia found herself nodding. Sharing it sounded like a good idea.

The next several days were a blur. Grandma moved into Francine's room for those hours that she was coaxed to get some much-needed rest, and Francine shared Virginia's. Virginia somehow managed to keep things going at home. Oh, not as efficiently as her mother did. But a routine, of sorts, was established. They all were fed and clothed and went off to school. Her father came and went often, and her mother occasionally. The chores were supervised, and the school lessons done. Clara came over frequently to help make a meal or deliver a casserole and a loaf of fresh bread. Neighbors sent in baking.

When Grandma Marty was there for a meal, her eyes had a faraway look in them, though Virginia could tell she tried to engage her grandchildren in conversation as usual.

The day finally arrived when Virginia's mother, pale and exhausted from many nights of nursing, came home, sank into a kitchen chair, pushed a tired hand through neglected hair, and announced to an anxious family, "He's on the mend now."

It was the news they had all been waiting for.

But if they had expected life to return to normal, they were to be disappointed. There was still the disruption of the family as their mother's services were needed. Day after day their grandfather had to be given nursing care and helped through endless hours of exercises and treatments to get his damaged limbs to once again cooperate, his muffled words to once again become clearly enunciated.

And with all the emotional upset, Virginia almost forgot about Rett Marshall and the unfair accusations. She seldom had time to spend with her friend Jenny, whose visits to the household had dropped back considerably, as though being in a home that was in upheaval was too unsettling for her. Virginia almost forgot about her secret discovery of having a crush on Jamison Curtis. Life seemed to consist of making it through another day. Even her fifteenth birthday passed almost without notice. Almost.

Virginia thought of it, but it really didn't seem worth bringing up. Her mother came home looking tired but trying to be cheerful. She held Francine close for a long time as she watched Virginia prepare a pot of steaming tea.

"You have become so . . . so grown-up, Virginia. So efficient. I don't know what we would have done without you over the last while."

Virginia looked at her mother sitting there, clinging to Francine as though she was afraid to let her go.

"I have not forgotten that today is your birthday. Fifteen. I can scarcely believe it."

She hesitated as Virginia set the pot and a rose-patterned teacup in front of her. Virginia turned to slice some cinnamon bread that the pastor's wife had sent over.

"I'm sorry things are—that it has worked this way," her mother continued. "Last year your birthday was spoiled with the accident and all, and this year . . . this year . . ."

"It's all right," Virginia said quickly. Her mother certainly didn't need the extra burden of feeling guilty.

"Oh, Virginia. You've had to grow up much too quickly. I'm sorry. I pray that . . . that things will soon return to normal. That I can let you be a . . . a girl again. This has been hard for you."

Her mother allowed Francine to move from her and stirred to pour the rich, golden tea.

Virginia moved self-consciously as she took the few steps from the cupboard counter to the table with the plate of cinnamon bread.

"Who do we thank for this?" asked her mother, who was trying to keep a running list.

"Mrs. Doyle."

"Bless her heart. She has more than enough to take her time."

Virginia nodded

"We'll plan a party," said her mother, returning to her former thoughts. "Just as soon as your grandfather gets back on his feet."

"Foot," corrected Francine without a smile.

Virginia and her mother looked at each other and burst into laughter. It may not have been funny, to think of Clark Davis and his missing leg, but the family had long ago adjusted to the thumping of his cane or the sight of his slight limp when he wore his artificial leg. The grandchildren were even used to running to "fetch my leg" or "put this thing out of the way in the corner." So Francine's gentle, sober reminder lightened the tension and served as an excuse for a good laugh.

It was much better than crying.

"How's your grandfather?" Jamison asked as Virginia entered the church the next Sunday.

She managed a smile. It had been a number of weeks since she had spoken to Jamison.

"He's . . . getting better," she answered. In truth the progress seemed so slow that it was hard to judge from day to day.

"Good."

The door opened again, and Virginia was surprised to see Jenny. She had been missing church services over the last Sundays, not having open invitations to join the Simpsons for Sunday dinner. Virginia saw Jamison's eyes turn to the door as well.

"Hello," he said easily with a smile. "Good to see you back."

Jenny flushed and shrugged out of her light sweater. She hung it on a peg and turned to them. Virginia noticed that she was wearing the creamy dress, much more suited to the warmth of the summer day then it had been for the mid-winter Valentine party.

Jenny's cheeks glowed. She looked at Jamison, blinked the long lashes that rimmed her green eyes, and flipped back her red hair.

Virginia, whose own locks were pinned neatly in place at the nape of her neck, felt a twinge of envy. Jenny did look so . . . so feminine. So pert and appealing.

Jamison turned away. "See you later," he said, and Virginia was not sure which one of them he was speaking to.

Jenny could not hide her disappointment, but she quickly covered her feelings.

"How is it going with your grandpa?" Jenny asked, watching Jamison's retreating back. But the question was not really a question. Simply a way to fill up the silence and get past the awkward moment.

Jenny did not wait for an answer. She turned to look at Virginia, then used a word that should never have been used, particularly in the church foyer. ". . . Virginia! You look pale as a ghost. Haven't you even been out of the house?"

Virginia wanted to retort with something cutting. Sarcastic. But she bit her tongue. It would not help anything to lash out at Jenny. After all, she was still praying for her friend. Still hoping to win her to the faith.

"Not much," she said quietly. "There hasn't been time for anything but school and . . ."

She let the words trail off. Jenny wasn't really listening. She was much too busy watching the line of boys who were filing in, in rather rowdy fashion, to the last row on the right side.

"Let's sit over there," she said, giving Virginia an elbow and a nod in that direction.

"My family expects me to sit with them," answered Virginia.

Jenny used the unacceptable word again, softly and under her breath, but Virginia heard it. It brought a frown to her forehead and a hope to her heart that no one else in the building had overheard.

Virginia's grandfather continued to improve slowly. He was moved home and was working hard to get back on his *one foot*. Virginia's mother still spent much of her time out at the farm, supervising his daily exercise treatments, but in some ways things began to gradually return to some kind of normalcy.

Virginia was really not too surprised when her mother came home one evening, a smile touching her lips, a new lightness to her step.

"I think it's about time for me to take over my duties as mother of the home again," she said as she hung her shawl on the wall peg and unpinned her everyday hat.

"Grandpa's better?"

The apprehensive words came from Francine, but Virginia felt them echoed in her own heart.

"He's getting a bit better every day. He told me today that it's about time that I went home and minded my own household and left him in peace." She smiled again. "I think he's getting better."

The mood around the supper table that night was one of relief. It seemed that they had weathered the storm. Had, with God's help, somehow come through the trying, anxious days. Now it was time to get on with normal living.

They teased and joked and caught up on one another's lives. It was like old times. Almost like old times. Clara's chair was no longer at the table. Virginia felt a sad little ache accompanying the thought. She had really missed Clara with the busy days that had just passed.

"Now. . ." her mother was saying. "I think it is about time for us to do some serious planning for an important birthday party."

CHAPTER 18

The party was scheduled for the last Saturday before school started in the fall. Virginia could have as many of her church and school friends as she wished to invite. Rather than try to pick and choose from the list, she decided to invite the entire Youth Group. She was glad that Jenny would be counted in the number.

Clara promised to help her mother with the food. There would be corn to roast, crispy cold chicken, garden salads, and plenty of home-baked bread. Her grandmother was sending in some of Virginia's favorite spiced fruit cider, and there would be fresh-turned ice cream to go with the birthday cake. She knew there would be plenty for everyone.

The guests were invited to be at the Simpson home at six o'clock for the picnic meal together, then spend the evening playing party games in the backyard.

Virginia became more and more excited with each passing day. Though it was weeks since her actual birthday, that did not matter. What did matter was that she was going to be able to enjoy some time with friends at a rather "grown-up" party. Looking back over the recent weeks and months, she felt as if she had been stuck at home with kitchen chores for *years*.

Jenny was almost as excited as Virginia.

"I'll wear my cream," she enthused.

Virginia shook her head. "It's much too nice for outside games."

"You are wearing your pink, aren't you?"

"No. I'm wearing my blue calico." Virginia never would have dreamed of wearing the filmy pink bridesmaid dress to an outside lawn party. Things often could get a little rambunctious, dashing for a seat in musical chairs or hopping on one foot in the one-legged race.

Jenny looked disappointed. "Why don't you have an inside party?"

"We've already given the invitations."

"But I don't have another fancy dress."

"You don't need a fancy dress for a picnic. It's just the church youth, and none of them are dressing fancy."

"How do you know?"

"I've been to parties before. So have you. We come for fun, not for . . . fashion."

Jenny glowered at her. It was Jamison again. Jenny thought that the only reason to make an appearance anywhere was to make an impression on the young man.

"Oh, Jenny, stop it," Virginia said in exasperation. "Mama and Clara have gone to a lot of trouble to make this a nice party for me. Don't you go and spoil it."

Jenny, still put out, pouted for the rest of the morning. Virginia began to wish she'd go home.

When Jenny did finally decide to go, she threw one last barb at Virginia. "I still think it's unfair that you've made your party an outside one. You know I have only one party dress."

"No one will be wearing a party dress," Virginia shot back. "And besides—" She almost said that the party was not really designed to accommodate Jenny. It was, after all, her birthday party. But she managed to stop herself in time.

"I'm sorry," she said instead. "I didn't think about dresses."

Jenny gave her a miffed look and flounced out the door with a toss of her head.

Virginia felt anger flush her cheeks. Right then her mother came into the room.

"Something wrong?" she asked.

"Oh, Jenny. She left mad. She's angry that I didn't plan an inside ladies tea instead of a youthful party. She wants to wear her cream dress—the one that is flouncy and frilly so she can impress Jamison Curtis."

Her mother stood looking at her with a puzzled face.

"She is so petty," complained Virginia. Now that she had an outlet for her anger she was ready to express deeply buried feelings. "No matter what I do she wants it her way, and I have to give in and give in just because I'm afraid she will leave the Youth Group and the church and not come back, and then she will never accept the Christian faith." Virginia's words tumbled over each other in their rush to be heard.

Her mother moved to stand beside her and slip an arm around her shoulders. "I know it's . . . it's easy to become impatient. Discouraged. But you have been *sowing seeds*. Little by little Jenny is hearing the *truth*. But sometimes . . . sometimes we must work . . . and pray for many years for someone we care about. You must not give up, Virginia. Just keep on loving Jenny and trying your best to—"

"I've done everything I know to do, and she just . . . she just goes to church, goes to Youth Group, but keeps right on living the same old way, not changing one bit. She even swears yet. Ugly words. Papa would wash our mouths out with soap if we dared to say them."

"She won't change on the outside until she lets God change her on the inside. A heart change is what Jenny needs."

"I know, but she just—she ignores that. She even

makes fun of what Pastor Doyle says in his sermons. I think she really knows that she is a sinner. She knows she does wrong things. And she doesn't care. Not a whit. All she thinks about is Jamison. The only reason she goes to church is so she can see him. She stands there and makes eyes at him and tries to get him to smile at her and—she's shameless about it. It's just—"

"She likes Jamison?"

"She's crazy about him. He's all she ever talks about anymore."

"Does he like her?"

Virginia stopped her tirade and thought about her mother's question. She shook her head and shrugged her shoulders.

"I don't know," she answered truthfully. "Maybe. He does smile at her and talk to her—and he did spend a lot of time with her at the toboggan party."

"The toboggan party was a long time ago."

Virginia admitted that with a nod.

"It seems if Jamison really liked Jenny he would have let her know by now."

"How?"

Her mother smiled. "Oh—boys have ways. Offer their help. Bring a little gift from The Sweet Shop. Maybe walk a girl home from church. Just hang around and talk. Jamison been doing things like that?"

"I don't know. Jenny has hardly been around this summer. I've been too busy."

"Would . . . would it . . . bother you if Jamison did?"

Virginia's eyes came up. She felt her cheeks warm. Her mother had guessed her little secret. She didn't have to answer the question.

"I thought so," her mother continued softly. "Does Jamison know that you both like him?"

Virginia felt the tears sting her eyes. "No," she said,

quite certain of the fact. "I . . . I can't let him know. Jenny would be so angry. So hurt."

"You do have a difficult problem."

Virginia said nothing. She fought to control the tears that wanted to come. She was much too old to be crying over trivial things.

"And you would—give up Jamison—rather than hurt Jenny?"

Virginia nodded glumly. "I—she'd never come to church again. I just know it."

Her mother put both of her arms around Virginia and held her quietly for some time, then brushed the wispy curls from her face. "You have grown up far more than even I guessed, Virginia," she whispered. "I'm proud of you, but a little worried, too. As your mother, I feel you are still much too young to be . . . plagued by this boy-girl thing. Clara was older before she began to think about courtships, and I guess your father and I expected . . . I wish you could put off all thoughts of . . . of boys, too, and just be one of the group for a long time yet." She paused and searched her daughter's face.

"But I fear you have already been thinking—well—it appears a little late for my motherly lecture. I still don't want you . . . courting. Not yet. Your father would never allow it at your age.

"And you know that Jamison will be in his last year of school. He's older—more mature. He might even think that he's ready to . . . to start seeing a . . . a . . . someone. I don't know. But whether he is, and whether it will be Jenny or . . . or perhaps . . . You really can't decide such things. You see, it's not just your life involved here. There is Jenny, and I'm glad you are so concerned about her—and there is Jamison. Virginia, you cannot make choices for him. If he doesn't care for Jenny—in that way—your backing away is not going to fix things. And if Jamison should happen to care for you, you are still too young to think about—anything other than friendship. Friendship is a wonderful thing, Virginia, and I see no reason why Jamison couldn't be friends with more than one girl at this time. It doesn't have to be Jenny *or* you. It can be—well, it can be both of you, and others as well."

The carefully chosen words were being heard. It would be so much easier if that was the way it could really be. Virginia knew she would like to have Jamison as a friend.

The partygoers began to gather a little before six, coming in singles or little groups of two or three. The church youth group was less than twenty members, so it would not be a large crowd that gathered. On this night no members were missing. Everyone looked forward to a last summer party and a chance to help Virginia celebrate the missed birthday.

Jenny was already there when the others arrived. She had spent most of Saturday afternoon at the Simpsons, pretending to offer her services with the preparations. She wore the green dress that Clara had given her, and to Virginia she seemed overdressed, but she did look stunning. Virginia was sure that Jenny would get noticed.

Virginia offered to help her pin up her hair. It really wasn't proper for a girl at her age to be swinging her hair freely with each toss of her head. At first Jenny looked offended, but as she eyed Virginia's swept-up curls, the results of Clara's careful pinning, she changed her mind.

"Just leave little strands loose over my ears," she whispered when they were alone. "I do not have pretty ears. They are just like my pa's."

Virginia had never noticed, but as she pinned Jenny's hair, she had to admit that Jenny's ears were just a little too prominent to be attractive.

She let Jenny have her side curls, and as Jenny looked in the mirror, she seemed pleased with the result.

By the time the others arrived, Jenny acted as if she were the one who had come up with the idea of the upsweep. She tossed her red head until Virginia feared that the pins would fall out of place.

By the time Virginia's father called that supper was ready, all were in attendance. Francine, though not old enough to join the Youth Group, was allowed to be a part of her sister's celebration and took full advantage of the situation.

There was much laughter and good-natured teasing. Virginia caught Rodney giving a plate of food to pretty little Margie Warden. She remembered the words of her mother. Was Rodney announcing to the young girl that he was interested in beginning a relationship? But Rodney was a bit older even than Jamison, and Margie was—well—she was close to seventeen. Maybe her folks would allow her to be courted at sixteen years. Or maybe she and Rodney would just sort of make eyes at each other until they were old enough to really be serious.

Virginia was unwrapping a cob of hot corn when she felt someone brush against her elbow. "Let me give you a hand," came a warm male voice that Virginia recognized at once as belonging to Jamison. Her first reaction was to cast a nervous glance toward Jenny. The girl was flirting outlandishly with Ken Troyer, every now and then casting a sideways glance toward Jamison in case he was watching.

Virginia's next thought was to move slowly away, declining the kind offer. Then she remembered the words of her mother. They could be friends. It would be silly to refuse a friendship with Jamison just because Jenny had decided to set her cap for him. She smiled.

"Thank you," she said, blowing on the fingers of one hand. "It's hot."

Jamison took the cob and finished the unwrapping. "Did you get butter?" he asked as he placed it on her plate.

"Not yet, but I will."

"I'll get it for you. Salt and pepper?"

"Just salt. I don't much like pepper."

He was soon back with the salt shaker.

To Virginia's surprise he motioned to the log bench that had been set up for the occasion.

"There's room there. Shall we sit?"

Virginia nodded.

"Nice that things have finally settled down so you can enjoy your birthday," he commented as they sat and began work on the cold chicken and hot corn.

Virginia nodded again. She felt a little tongue-tied.

"Your grandfather is much better, I hear."

Another nod.

"Bet you're relieved."

Virginia finally found her tongue. "We are. We feared that we might lose him, or that he'd be—you know—sort of . . . crippled." Virginia wondered if Jamison considered a man with only one leg already crippled.

"And it's so good to have Mama back home again, too," Virginia went on.

"I don't know how you managed it—with schooling and the cooking and all."

Virginia grimaced. "Well, I'm glad it's over, I can truthfully state."

They talked of other things. Virginia found herself forgetting her nervousness. It was easy to talk to Jamison. Her mother had been right. They *could* be friends.

"Want another cob?"

"No, thank you. I'd never have room for cake, and I probably should eat a piece of my own birthday cake." They both laughed. "But you go ahead," she said. "I know how much Rodney and Danny can put away. Papa says it's like trying to fill up a sinkhole. No end to it."

Jamison laughed as though her comment was terribly witty. Virginia smiled.

It was a wonderful party. All around her was laughter and teasing as the people of her Youth Group enjoyed the evening together and the delicious food that her mama and Clara had provided.

Birthday cake and ice cream followed. They were all so full they could hardly start the planned games.

Two members of the group had been asked to plan the evening's fun time. They were wise enough to start with slower activities, allowing their supper to settle a bit before becoming a little more boisterous. Virginia was not the only one who was thankful to ease into the activities.

As the evening wore on, Virginia realized that more and more often she turned to find Jamison close beside her, offering to assist her, holding a chair, asking if she wanted more of her grandmother's fruit cider. It began to feel natural to have him by. And then through the maze of bodies, Virginia's brown eyes met the green eyes of Jenny. They cast a clear message across the distance that separated them. Jenny looked furious. She reached up and tore the pins from her long red hair, shaking it out with deliberate rebellion. It was her little message to Virginia that she no longer wanted to have anything to do with her. Neither have friendship nor her assistance.

Virginia felt her stomach tighten. If Jenny was throwing aside their friendship—just like she threw the unwanted hair pins in the thick grass of the Simpson backyard—would she also discard the church? The Youth Group? Virginia felt deep apprehension sweep all through her body.

CHAPTER 19

"You are *some friend*."

Jenny's words were hot and accusatory. The others had all left for home. Only Jenny stood, facing Virginia, eyes flaming, hair in disarray around her shoulders. Virginia bit her lip.

"You know how I feel about Jamison."

That was true. Jenny had not kept her feelings a well-guarded secret.

"But I—"

"You openly chased him all evening."

This did send words tumbling out. "I did no such thing. You've no call to make such a totally untruthful statement. You were the one doing all of the flirting. You practically threw yourself at—"

But Virginia's words were halted as Jenny's hand slapped sharply across her cheek. Jenny looked as surprised at the action as Virginia, who raised a trembling hand to her stinging face.

Jenny quickly recovered. "I'll never speak to you again, Virginia. You pretend to be a friend . . . a . . . a perfect little saint, and then you go and double-cross like that."

Virginia was still rubbing the smarting cheek. Her eyes

were tear-filled and her throat tight. She had never been struck across the cheek before. She felt confused. Along with the pain was anger and humiliation and an underlying desire for retaliation. Virginia took a deep breath and prayed for control.

"I did nothing," she managed to say firmly, blinking back tears. "Nothing but be a friend to a boy whom I have known for many years. If that offends you, Jenny, I'm sorry. I have tried—" She stopped to draw a breath so she could go on. "I have tried to . . . to be *your* friend, too, Jenny. Honestly I have. If it hasn't been enough for you—again, I'm sorry."

Virginia stopped and took a deep breath. What could she say to Jenny? What would wipe away the intense anger? "I . . . I will be happy to continue our friendship—if you wish. That's entirely up to you. But I . . . I cannot let you dictate my life. I have to be free to make my own choices. I will still pray for you. Will hope that you will want to find peace with God. But I . . . I cannot throw away all other friendships just—just to please you."

Jenny stood listening, one emotion after another sweeping across her face. When Virginia ended the speech, Jenny's anger pressed forward once again.

"You'll see him again?"

"I see him every Sunday."

"You know I'm not talking about church."

"As a friend—yes. If he wishes."

Jenny's eyes blazed.

"As a friend? Hah."

"As a friend."

Jenny looked as if she wished she could reach out and slap the other cheek. Her eyes were smoldering. "You stupid—" She added a couple words that Virginia did not understand. Did not wish to understand. They were spit out like venom. "That's not how *he* sees it. He likes you."

Virginia could only stare.

Jenny wheeled to go. But as she was leaving she turned for one last shot. "And I hope they string up your dear ole Loony Marshall. They've taken him in, you know. They found the stolen goods in his room."

"Is it true, Papa?"

Virginia, trembling, stood in front of her father. The deep agitation in her voice caused him to lower *The Weekly Chronicle*, and he raised his eyes to hers.

"Is it true? Has the sheriff really arrested Rett?"

He nodded slowly, laid aside the paper, and reached for her hand.

"Did they really find the things in his room?"

He was slow in replying. When he did speak it was not to answer her question. "Virginia, I'm sorry that you've heard about this tonight. Your mother and I had hoped you could enjoy your birthday party without—well, without being troubled by all the—"

"Then it's true."

He nodded.

"Where is he?"

"In the local jail."

"That will kill him—being locked up like that."

"He's having a hard time, yes."

"Where's his crow?"

"Danny has him."

"That's Rett's crow out there?"

Her father nodded.

All the guests had shown interest in Danny's little collection of pens and recuperating animals and birds. Many of the pens were now empty, but Danny was happy to tell them of the former occupants that had now gone back to the wilds. Someone had questioned Danny about the crow, which looked perfectly healthy.

"When you gonna let him go?" they had questioned,

but Danny had seemed evasive.

"Don't know," he had answered and passed on to another pen. Now Virginia understood the conversation. It was Rett's crow in the backyard pen. Danny would not be returning him to freedom. Not until things were settled with Rett.

"You don't think he did it, do you?"

Her father looked away for a moment.

"Do you?"

"What I think does not stand up in a court of law, Virginia. They deal with evidence. And the evidence is pretty strong against Rett. I . . . it's going to be a hard task to defend him. Especially when he cannot defend himself."

"You mean they did find the stuff in his room?"

Her father nodded.

"But that doesn't mean he put it there."

"It seems strange that it would get there another way."

"But it could have happened."

"Anything is possible."

"Maybe his crow?"

"I've thought of that. The landlady has refused to let the crow in the room."

"Maybe Rett sneaked it in—through the open window."

"There's a solid screen on that window."

"Who cleans his room?"

Her father drew a deep breath. "Look, my dear, I know you find all this very upsetting, but it is late, and we are not going to solve this problem tonight. I'm working on it. I'll do all I can."

"Jenny says she hopes they string him up."

"Well, there won't be any lynching. I can promise you that."

"What will they do with him?"

Her father passed his hand through his hair. "They—if he's found guilty—we'll try for the insanity plea."

"Insanity?" Virginia felt outrage. "He's not insane, Papa. Just because he's . . . different. He's not—"

"I know. I know. He's not a danger to society. At least he never has been. But . . . but insanity means—well, it means many things. And if used—successfully—he will be sheltered. Protected. Given help."

"But he will not be given freedom, will he? That's what he needs. What he wants. Freedom."

Her father looked tired, but he managed a smile. "Have you ever thought of being a lawyer, Virginia?" he asked teasingly.

For a moment Virginia stood, staring at the strange question. Then she understood his attempt to lighten the situation and compliment her in his own way. She was able to give him the hint of a smile in return.

"Well, I don't think he did it," she still pronounced.

"You think he was framed?"

"Framed?"

"Set up. Someone else placed the evidence in his room."

Virginia thought about that. "Yes!" she exclaimed, excitement taking hold of her. "Yes. That's it. He was framed."

"Now—who would do that?"

Virginia sobered. She had no idea.

"And why? What would anyone gain by attacking such a harmless man?"

"I don't know," she admitted.

It was all such a puzzle. What if Rett really had done it? What if after all of the years of not even being interested in anything material he had suddenly taken some strange urge to accumulate? What if he was a *little* dangerous to society?

But she couldn't believe it. Couldn't accept it. It was all so totally contradictory.

"I don't know," she said again, sobered by the fact that

it sounded as though Rett did indeed have a strong case against him.

"So what can we do?" she asked her father.

He reached out and took her hand. "Well . . . not much, I fear. On the legal front. But maybe a great deal—on the spiritual front. If Rett is not guilty—and I hope with all my heart that he is not—then we need to pray that God will somehow, in His wonderful and miraculous way, bring the truth to light."

Virginia nodded solemnly.

"You pray. I'll work on the case," said her father.

It sounded simple.

"Trust God, Virginia," her father went on. "He's taken on tougher tasks—and been victorious."

Her father was smiling again. But there was an underlying assurance in his voice as well. She gave him a forced smile in return and withdrew her hand.

She turned to go. Suddenly she felt very tired. Drained of the excitement that had carried her through the wonderful day.

"What happened to your cheek?" her father's voice stopped her.

Virginia turned. What could she say? What should she say? She could not lie.

"Jenny," she said at last.

A frown. Then fatherly concern. "She was *that* angry?"

Virginia nodded, tears welling up in her eyes.

He leaned forward slightly. Virginia had never seen that look in his eyes before.

"Perhaps you need to reconsider that friendship," he said firmly. "Anyone who strikes out in—"

"I'm not sure there is any friendship left to reconsider," Virginia choked out through her tears. "Perhaps becoming friends again—with Jenny—would take an even bigger miracle than getting Rett pardoned."

Virginia found it difficult to start back to school. Her mind was still churning over Rett, trying to come up with some kind of plan, some way to find an explanation for the stolen goods appearing in Rett's room. And then there was the other matter of facing Jenny again. Jenny had not appeared at church on Sunday, and though Virginia had been disappointed, she had not been surprised.

But Jenny would be at school. Virginia was sure of that. They would share a classroom and meet in the halls. There would be no way for them to totally avoid each other.

Jamison would be at school, too. His final year. And even if he followed his past pattern of heading for the ball diamond at every school break, Virginia—and Jenny—would be sure to confront *him* as well. Virginia wondered if he had any idea of the trouble he had made between Jenny and her.

Virginia's feet dragged as she neared the school steps. Francine urged her forward, a switch from the usual when Virginia had to prod the dreamy Francine.

"We'll be late if you don't hurry," the young girl reminded, but Virginia did not hasten her steps. She did not want to arrive at school before the large bell began calling students to the classroom. She did not want to find herself face-to-face with Jenny—with no words to say.

"Go ahead," she said to Francine and received a perplexed look in reply. But Francine did go ahead, breaking into a run after a few steps.

Virginia neared the school just as the bell began to announce its first ringing invitation. She had timed it just right.

Breathlessly she slid into a seat and laid her books on the desk top before her just as the teacher began to address the class. Virginia felt relieved. The first hurdle had been overcome.

But just as she began to relax, the thought came crashing in that there were many even more difficult hurdles that lay ahead.

Jamison did dash out to play ball with the other boys. Jenny seemed as intent on staying away from Virginia as Virginia was in avoiding her. The day passed with no major incident. Virginia, relieved, gathered her books and headed toward the door at the end of the first day. But she was just about to step onto the sidewalk at the front of the school when a movement to her left caught her attention.

There stood Jamison, books tucked under one arm, a smile lighting his face.

"Mind if I walk along?"

What could she say? She did not mind. Not one bit. But Jenny would mind. Terribly.

She gave one nod of her head, and Jamison fell into step beside her.

They walked in silence for half a block before Jamison spoke.

"Noticed you're pretty quiet today."

Her head came up. When had he been noticing her?

"Worried about something?"

Virginia nodded. She was worried. Not just about Jenny. More about Rett.

"I . . . I guess I am," she admitted.

Silence.

"Want to talk about it?"

Virginia debated the answer she should give and decided to be open and truthful—at least in part.

"Rett Marshall. He's been . . . locked up, you know."

Jamison nodded. "I heard." He didn't sound particularly disturbed.

"He didn't do it," said Virginia, agitation coloring the words.

He looked at her then. "I don't know him well. Just seen him wandering around."

"My grandpa has known him since he was a baby. Grandpa doesn't think he did it, either."

Now she seemed to have Jamison's full attention.

"It just doesn't add up," she went on, her disturbed thoughts giving her freedom.

"Yeah? How so?"

"He . . . he's never cared about . . . things. Just birds and animals. He never even gathered pretty rocks—or flowers. And he never builds things. What would he want with a crescent wrench and a lathe?"

"Some people say the crow—"

"How could a crow transport an object that heavy?"

"A crescent wrench, you say? That's true. Crow couldn't haul that. I'd just heard of things like Mrs. Parker's red pin and Mrs. White's necklace. Bright stuff like that. They say crows like shiny things."

Virginia nodded. She had heard that, too.

"Well, it doesn't add up. I'd like to—"

He turned to her, a glint in his eyes. "You wanna play detective?"

"Me?"

"Sure. Somebody's got to get to the bottom of it."

"I couldn't—I wouldn't even know how to go about it."

"But you think he's innocent—you want to help him."

She nodded her yes on both counts.

"Then why don't we see what we can find out?"

She wondered if she understood his question correctly. Was he suggesting that they work on it together? She looked at him. "I'm not sure. My father is trying to help him, and . . . and I don't know if he would appreciate me snooping around."

"Then perhaps I'll have to do the snooping. You sort out whatever I find."

She stopped and turned to him. "You're serious?"

"Totally."

She was still hesitant.

"I . . . I just don't know. Papa said we should pray."

"We can do that, too."

Of course they could.

"It's just that . . ." She began to walk again, and he matched her steps. "I have this strange feeling about all this. I keep thinking that it is somehow tied in with the accident."

"What accident?"

"At the creek."

"The rafting?" He sounded incredulous.

But she held to her opinion. "Ever since then the Crells have vowed to get back at Rett for not saving Freddie."

He nodded slowly. He had heard some of the rumors. "I guess they were pretty angry, all right. But you don't think they would go so far as to do something—unlawful—do you?"

"I don't know. Mr Crell was awfully mad."

He shook his head. "It sounds pretty vicious. Setting up an innocent man just because—"

"Maybe they still don't think he was innocent. Maybe they have convinced themselves that Rett really could have saved Freddie. Papa says that the mind and emotions can play some terrible tricks."

"I can't believe—"

"Look—maybe we'd better just stay out of it. Just pray—like Papa says."

He nodded. "You're right. I'd never make a good detective." He grinned. "Besides, I'd never have the time.

My folks keep me too busy choring."

Virginia managed a smile. She was sure they had made the right decision.

But her mind still could not put the matter to rest. She was sure that something was awfully wrong about this whole theft charge.

CHAPTER 20

"Grandpa, may I join you?"

Virginia stood before her grandfather on the back porch of the farmhouse. The day was warm, but to Virginia it somehow held the promises of a coming fall with its cooler weather. Perhaps it was the colors that made the suggestion. Already the nearby trees were showing some changes from the summer dress of green, and her grandmother's fall flowers were in full bloom in the nearby garden. Her grandfather smiled and patted the seat beside him.

"Where are the other men?" she asked as she lowered herself. It was not often that her grandfather was left alone on a Sunday afternoon.

"Playing horseshoes. I told them I needed a break from all the chatter."

"Then maybe I—"

"No, no. Sit down. I jest meant male chatter."

Her grandfather's words were no longer slurred. Except for the hesitation of his hand to do his bidding, one would have never known that he had suffered a stroke.

"Since the stroke," he confided softly, as though it was their little secret, "I sometimes need me a little alone time. Brain gets tired trying to keep up."

He tapped his forehead and grinned.

Virginia smiled.

"You're doing real well," she said and laid her hand on his arm.

"Something on yer mind?"

She drew in a deep breath and turned to look at him.

"Rett," she said simply.

He nodded. "Yeah, it troubles me somethin' awful, too. I been to see him agin Friday. He looks . . . looks jest . . . jest caged."

She had been to see him, too. She went with Danny, who took the crow over to see his master after school every day. Her father said he thought it was the only thing that kept the man sane.

"I don't think he did it. I . . . I have tried to . . . take him a few things. Just to make him more comfortable. He looks at them and smiles, or looks confused, and then shoves them right back under the bars again. Why would a person like that . . . *steal* something?" asked Virginia.

"I don't know."

"And why would he hide them in among his socks? He wouldn't even open drawers. Mrs. Kruz had to go in and lay out clean clothes and tell him to make a change. She tried and tried to teach him to open the drawer, pull out the clean things, and do the changing on his own. He wouldn't."

"You've talked to Mrs. Kruz?"

"I . . . I—sort of. I know I'm to stay out of it. But Papa let me go over to get Rett some clean things. They had to insist that he change at the jail, too."

They sat silent, sharing deep, troubled thoughts.

"I still think someone else put the things there."

"That would be a terrible thing to do—an' awful hard to prove, I'm thinkin'."

"I tried to talk Papa into speaking to the sheriff. Getting him to release Rett and then watch."

"You mean set a trap."

"Not really a trap, but sort of. I mean, if someone else has done it, it would likely happen again. Especially if they thought that the courts were not convinced it was Rett."

"What did your pa say?"

"He said the court did not believe in playing games."

"I don't s'pose."

"But Papa is filing a petition to get Rett released until the trial date. He says there is no need to hold him in jail until he is proven guilty. If Papa is successful, that would accomplish about the same thing."

"That would be a blessin.' I don't think the boy is even eatin' in there."

Virginia noticed the use of the term "boy." Just like most of the neighborhood, her grandfather still thought of the man as a boy. Virginia guessed that no matter how old Rett became, he would be thought of as a boy right up until the time the grave took him.

"He eats my cookies when I take them," she said.

"A man cannot live on cookies alone," quipped her grandfather.

"I still think it has something to do with that creek accident," Virginia maintained.

"Yer pa and I have talked about thet. I have the same feelin'. He says he has dug into all the past records and can't find any link."

"Perhaps they are not *in* the records."

"Ya mean—maybe there were some facts thet didn't come out."

Virginia nodded.

"Well, it were a bit scrambled, but the courts seemed content thet they had pieced it together pretty good at the time. Most of the stories fit."

"Maybe someone is just using that accident to sort of . . . sort of implicate Rett to cover their own tracks."

Her grandfather looked thoughtful. "You might have

something there. But what could anyone possibly gain by havin' the man put away?"

"I have no idea. I've tried and tried to figure it out."

Her grandfather placed an arm about her shoulders and drew her close. "Yer pa is working on it. I think he stays up nights tryin' to sort it through. Rett couldn't have anybody better on his case."

"I know that." Virginia had confidence in her father. Knew how hard he was working to try to find some way to have the charges dropped. But it seemed as though every new thought led to a stone wall.

Though not exactly friends again, Jenny did start speaking to Virginia now and then. She had found a new friend in Trina Hughes and probably wanted to impress Virginia with that fact. The two tittered and whispered and took to flirting with some of the older boys. Jamison was not in the new little pack. Jenny seemed to have given up, at least momentarily, on Jamison. But he had never given her much encouragement.

"We're going to The Sweet Shop, wanna come?" Jenny surprised Virginia by asking as school was letting out for the day.

Virginia was tempted to give a quick no, but she was still praying for Jenny. Perhaps this would open the door a crack again. There seemed to be no harm in a little trip to The Sweet Shop.

"I'll have to pop into Papa's office to see if it's all right." She thought quickly. "Then I could send a note home with Francine," she answered.

Jenny shrugged. "No problem. We can wait."

"You won't have to wait. You go on ahead, and I'll catch you there."

"Fine." Then Jenny added as though it was an afterthought. "Wanna ask Jamison?"

There it was again. Jenny was using her to get to Jamison.

Virginia opened her mouth to say she'd had a change of plans when she heard another voice.

"Ask Jamison what?" Jamison was beside her.

Jenny gave one of her most fetching smiles.

"We're going to The Sweet Shop. Would you like to join us?"

Virginia could not now change her plans.

"Sure," said Jamison without hesitation. "When?"

"Now." It was Jenny who continued the exchange.

"Can't now. Don't have any money with me."

"I'll lend you—"

But Jamison was shaking his head. " 'Neither a borrower nor a lender be,' " he quoted.

"Join us tomorrow then," decided Jenny.

"We'll do that," replied Jamison and reached for Virginia's books. He was speaking for both of them.

Virginia felt relief. Yet agitation. Now she would be able to ask her mother ahead of time and get her permission. On the other hand, what was Jenny planning now? She knew that the girl had some scheme in mind.

"My pa is gonna scour this whole town to get to the bottom of this Loony Marshall thing," Jenny said the next day after they had all purchased their sodas and gathered around the room's largest table.

Virginia felt her eyes widen. Was that what this was all about?

"So, what's to figure?" asked Sammie. "The guy was caught with the goods."

Jenny nodded. "But some folks"—she said the words with emphasis, giving Virginia a challenging look as she did so—"still think that loony fella is innocent."

All eyes turned to Virginia. Her chin lifted. She was

not going to be pushed into a corner simply to save face in front of her schoolmates.

"I do," she said with conviction.

There were several snickers around the table.

"She even talks with spooky Adamson," put in Trina, giving a nod toward Virginia.

"Mr. Adamson is a fine old man." Virginia could feel the color flushing her cheeks. Had this all been planned? Had Jenny simply brought her here to humiliate her before her school friends? But what of Jamison? Surely Jenny hadn't turned on him, too.

"Pro'bly likes her brother's pet skunk, too." This came from George Booth. A howl of laughter followed. "Virginia the Crusader for the Downtrodden."

Jamison stood to his feet. "I think we should go," he said to Virginia, taking her arm. Now it was Jenny's face that flushed.

"Whoops," she said, casting a look around the little cluster. "Sorry. Finish your soda. We didn't know it was a touchy subject."

Jamison hesitated. "The subject was not touchy," he said in an even voice. "The attack was."

"Sorry," Jenny said again with a light shrug. Her face was pale now. Apparently she realized her mistake. She would not win Jamison by attacking Virginia.

"Sit down, Curtis," said Georgie. "We didn't mean no harm. Just having a little fun."

"I don't care for fun at another's expense."

"We said we're sorry. Sit down."

Jamison sat down. Virginia felt that he knew she wished to let the matter drop.

There was an uneasy quiet at the table. No one looked up from the sodas before them.

"Let's see . . ." Jenny mused. "What can we talk about . . . that's safe?"

She gave Virginia just the hint of a look under her long

lashes. Virginia knew that the girl was attempting to gain control of the group again.

"What did you think of that history exam?" burst out Sammie.

"Oh, not school. That's boring," chided Jenny to squelch any answers that might be forthcoming.

Silence again.

"Hey, I know. We should plan a party." This was Jenny's idea.

"A party?"

"Yeah, a . . . a Harvest Gathering or something."

The idea seemed to be appreciated.

"Where?"

"Well, I'll do it." Jenny sounded all bravado.

Virginia wondered how she planned to pull it off. Parties took a lot of work. It had taken her mother and Clara many days to prepare for her birthday. Jenny had no one to help her.

"What kind of party?" asked Trina, sounding excited about the prospect.

"Maybe a . . . a masquerade party. That would be fun."

Trina beamed. It was clear that she was enthused by the idea.

"When?"

"Hey, how about Halloween?"

Most of the members at the table expressed their agreement.

"You help me with it, Virginia?"

There. That was part of Jenny's unspoken plan. It was she, Virginia, who would be called upon to do the work. Maybe Jenny even expected her mother and Clara to pitch in.

Virginia shook her head. "My parents don't favor Halloween parties."

Jenny looked disappointed.

"When then?" she asked, tipping her head to one side.

Virginia knew that if she named a date, it would mean they would all expect her to be part of the plans. Jenny would put her in charge of the preparations. Jenny's party preparations. She didn't want to be a snob, but she didn't like to be used, either.

"I'm afraid I'm out," she said with finality. "I'm already on the committee for the Youth Group fall party. I don't have time for two."

"Jamison?" asked Jenny coyly.

"Me, too."

Virginia could see the anger rise in Jenny's face.

"So what is your exclusive Youth Group planning?" she asked, making the words a distinct dig.

"A hayride," answered Jamison, pushing back his empty soda glass. "And we are not exclusive. You're all invited. October twenty-fifth. Meet at the church at seven."

And saying the words, he stood and reached for the pile of school books. Since Virginia's books were also in the pile, it seemed her signal that it was time for them to leave. She nodded to the group and rose to join Jamison.

Good news awaited Virginia when she arrived at home. Her father had come home early from the office to report that Rett had been released from his jail cell until the date of his upcoming trial. Virginia gave her father a big hug.

"I'm so proud of you," she told him.

"Now wait a minute. This is a temporary measure. We still need a solution here."

"Well, you'll find one. I just know you will."

He shook his head. "If there is a solution to this one, God will have to find it. I've about exhausted my resources."

Virginia laid aside her books and reached for an apron.

As she tied it about her waist her mother spoke. "How was your soda outing? Jenny make up again?"

Virginia's eyes flashed fire. "You will never believe that girl. First she started out by throwing barbs my way, naming me a . . . a loony lover of . . . of Rett and old Mr. Adamson and . . . even skunks. When that didn't work she changed to asking me to help her with a party. Halloween."

"Halloween? I don't think that's a good idea," her mother said, shaking her head.

"I already told her no. That I will be busy with the Youth Group party. Then she made a remark about the exclusive church group."

"That was unfair."

"That's what Jamison basically told them. He invited them all."

"Good for Jamison," laughed her father.

"They won't come," expressed Virginia. "They all have had any number of invitations in the past."

"You never know," said her father. "Just keep trying. Keep praying. One of these days they might surprise you."

"She keeps bringing up Rett," Virginia said as she placed some potatoes in the pan for peeling.

"She knows it bothers you," replied her father. "Don't let her get to you."

"But sometimes I wonder if it is more than that."

"Meaning?"

"I don't know. I can't put my finger on it. But it's just like . . . like she knows something about it. You don't suppose she would—?"

"Now, Virginia. Let's not jump to any ugly conclusions. Jenny is . . . difficult, but I don't believe she's criminal."

"Well, something is funny. I can just feel it."

"Okay. In the name of justice we must investigate everything. So, let's take a look at Jenny."

Virginia wondered if her father was just humoring her,

but when she looked at his face he seemed serious.

"How could Jenny do it?"

"Well, I don't know."

She turned back to her potatoes. "But I sure would like to do a little digging to try to find out."

"Then, why would she do it?"

"Maybe . . . maybe just to get at me. I still think it might have something to do with that accident."

"Jenny was badly injured. Close to losing her life. She was hardly in condition to do something strange at that time. She wasn't even aware of what happened with the others."

"At least she says she wasn't."

"No, I think the doctor would verify that statement."

Virginia thought of her uncle Luke. She would ask him someday just what shape Jenny was in when he reached her.

"Then the Crells?"

"I will admit that I had my finger pointed at the Crells as well. But the sheriff has done a thorough investigation. They were out of town. Went on back east to visit family. They were gone for a good part of the summer. Certainly at the time that a number of the items were stolen."

Virginia wondered why she had not heard that before. "How come folks don't know that?" Virginia knew that others had pointed fingers at the Crells, as well.

"Now, how can you clear a man who hasn't even been condemned? Take out an advertisement in the paper saying, 'Folks, what you are thinking and gossiping about is not true. Frank Crell did not frame Rett Marshall.' "

Virginia had to smile at the foolishness of it. But she quickly sobered. "Jenny said her father is going to 'scour the town until he gets to the bottom of it.' Guess he thinks there's a news story here."

Her father looked up, concern showing. "He'd be wise to let it alone," he said, stirring slightly. "The sheriff is the one to be doing the scouring."

CHAPTER 21

To Virginia's amazement, Jenny and her little troop did show up for the fall hayride. They came together in a tight little knot, tittering and whispering and, Virginia feared, ready to make trouble. She prayed it wouldn't be so and welcomed them with genuine warmth on behalf of the entire Youth Group.

There was no need for introductions. In the small town in which they lived, they all knew one another and attended the same school. But it was the first time that most of Jenny's crowd had been at one of the church activities.

Jenny, of course, had been with the church group many times. Now she acted as though she was trying to impress her followers that she knew the ropes. She talked louder than necessary and used her hands a lot, explained things that needed no explanation, and insisted on giving instructions and leading the way, even when no leader was required.

But in spite of it all, Virginia felt that the evening began well. Even the visitors seemed to slip into having a good time.

There was a little good-natured roughhousing as the hayride began. But that was always expected. Boys shoved one another off the hayrack or teased girls with handfuls of hay stuffed down coat backs, and girls squealed in pretended alarm as they initiated a chase. But there were no casualties when the ride ended and the young people gathered round the campfire for the evening's refreshments and devotional time.

"Here's where we get preached at," Virginia heard Jenny whisper loudly to her little entourage.

"You're all going straight to hell," intoned Sam, lifting his hands and waving them like some weird monster over the heads of the group members.

There was loud, howling laughter.

Georgie took up the chant in a whispery voice, his hands going up to join Sammie's. "Where the devil will stoke up the fire and throw you in to burn and burn—"

"Stop it," cut in Trina. "It's rude."

Jenny gave her a scowl. She had been enjoying the performance. "What's wrong with you?" she asked with a flip of her hair. "Who put you in charge?"

"Well, it *is* rude," Trina dared to answer back. "They've been nice. The least we can do is be decent."

"And listen to the sermon about hell," snorted Georgie.

They laughed again, but Virginia noticed that Trina did not join in.

There was no sermon about hell, but after they had finished their lunch there was a devotional on heaven.

"God would like to have every single human who has ever lived join Him there," said Troy. "It says so in the Bible. 'God is not willing that *any* should perish but that all should come to repentance.' That's why God did everything in His power to make that possible. He sent His only Son to bring us salvation. But we need to accept that gift. It is His gift of love to us, and if anyone here"—his eyes scanned the entire group—"isn't sure about your standing before a holy God, if there's fear in your heart or doubts in your mind, then I'd love to talk to you—anytime. Or see Pastor Doyle—or one of the other adults who are here with us tonight. Any one of us would love to talk with you."

The evening was over.

Virginia breathed a little sigh of relief. There really had been no problems with the newcomers. Inwardly she breathed a little prayer as she went to invite them back to the next youth function.

Jamison was waiting for Virginia when she arrived at church on Sunday morning.

"Got some good news," he said, nodding with his head for her to step aside. She noticed that his eyes were shining.

When they had retreated a few paces he leaned toward her and spoke softly. "Georgie came to see me yesterday."

She waited for him to go on.

"He wanted to find out how one becomes a Christian."

"Georgie Booth?"

His smile widened. "Georgie Booth," he nodded.

"Well, did he?"

"He did."

"Georgie Booth?"

Virginia could scarcely believe it.

Jamison's eyes turned sober. "Poor guy," he said. "He's been having a real hard time ever since the accident. He feels—well, responsible for Freddie's death. It's really been eating at him. Says he still has trouble sleeping at night and often can't eat."

Virginia's heart constricted. She knew the feeling.

"And now with Rett Marshall charged with this theft thing."

"He thinks it's tied to the accident, too?"

"He . . . he's—well, he can't help but tie the two together, but he can't figure out how they fit."

Virginia nodded. She felt the same way.

"The Crell boy won't even talk to him anymore. He's not welcome anywhere near the Crells. Georgie says the Crell family have become almost—reclusive. Won't let their young people associate with others. Mr. Crell even took the older two out of school. The boy didn't mind. He hated school anyway, but the girl, Tess, really fought against it."

Virginia felt her stomach tighten. What a mean thing for a father to do.

"How does Georgie find out all this?"

"The younger girl still talks to him on the sly. Slips him notes from Tess. He and Tess used to be a little sweet on each other. Maybe in a way, they still are. Tess says that even though folks aren't right out and saying it, she knows there are those who think that they have had something to do with pressing charges—or even worse—of sort of framing Rett for the thefts."

"They didn't," Virginia was quick to say. "They were away when some of the things were stolen. The sheriff checked it out."

Jamison's eyes widened.

"I don't suppose I am to say that," she hastened on. "Papa told it to me in confidence."

He nodded, his promise that he'd hold his tongue.

"Well, even though they are innocent, they feel condemned. That's why Mr. Crell is keeping his family tight to home. He says if the neighbors have no more faith in him than that, then they aren't fit for his family to associate with. Georgie feels responsible for that as well."

"He's really got himself a burden," said Virginia.

"He *had* a burden," corrected Jamison. "Yesterday he asked forgiveness and gave all that over to the Lord."

Virginia smiled. It was good news.

Just as quickly her smile faded. She heaved a deep sigh and looked up at Jamison. "But it doesn't fix everything, does it? I mean, what a mess we can make of things when we disobey. I never thought—I mean I was with them, you know, for part of it. I could have been on the raft. I'm as guilty as any of them. It was just my . . . my anger that sent me on home."

Jamison touched her arm gently in sympathetic understanding. Virginia looked up and said, "We've got to get this thing settled so folks can get on with life. Look what it's done to . . . to so many lives. To the whole town. Freddie's death—so horrible. And his whole family suffering. Accusations and gossip stories, and then Rett, accused for something I'm sure he didn't do. It's a horrible mess."

Jamison nodded, then shrugged. "Don't know what we can do. Your pa is working on it."

"I know. He always tells us to pray."

"Guess that's the best possible advice he can—"

"It's getting us nowhere. I've prayed and prayed. There haven't been any answers. We need—"

"Georgie is an answer," said Jamison softly. "He never would have—" He stopped a moment. "Maybe this whole thing is about Georgie."

Virginia felt chastened. She managed a weak smile. Of course he was right. Who knows, she told herself, perhaps God is working on other hearts—even now. Her thoughts and prayers reached out to embrace Jenny once again.

"Virginia, wait up."

Virginia turned to see Jenny and Trina a few steps behind her. She was surprised at Jenny's call. They had not shared the walk home from school for some time.

She shielded her eyes with a mittened hand from the bright winter sun.

"What's the rush?" Jenny asked as the two girls came even and Virginia fell into step with them.

"Mama is going out to check on Grandpa, and I'm going along."

A strange expression flicked over Jenny's face. Virginia could not be sure of its message. Jenny looked mournful. Sad. Regretful. Maybe even lonely. But she quickly hid any of those emotions that might have been revealed. "How's the old man doing?" she asked flippantly.

"Fine. But Mama still checks on him often."

"Yeah."

They talked of other things then. Eventually Jenny asked a question.

"So how's your . . . pet?"

"Pet?" Virginia was baffled.

"Yeah, that Marshall idiot."

"He's not an idiot," Virginia said, not able to keep the anger from her voice.

"I've never figured out why you are so . . . so touchy about him. All one has to do is mention his name, and you get all riled up."

"I'm not touchy about him. It's just that . . . that when *you* mention him, it's always in a very . . . very disrespectful way."

Jenny poked Trina and grinned.

"Disrespectful? You expect folks to have respect for loonies?"

"Yes," said Virginia before she could even sort out her words. "If you consider him a loony—if by that you mean a person who is . . . different, yes. And I would think that you, Jenny, more than anyone, would realize that. He saved your life."

"Well, that's *your* story," said Jenny, lifting her nose.

"And what's *your* story? He pulled you out of the creek, all bruised and battered. You could not have made it to shore on your own. You know it."

"Maybe he dumped us over in the first place."

"That's not true."

Jenny did not back down.

"Well, it really has nothing to do with me."

"Yes, it does. It has everything to do with you. And with me. If we hadn't gone to the creek when we shouldn't have, this whole thing wouldn't have happened. Freddie would be alive, your hand—" Virginia could not finish the comment about Jenny's hand. "The Crells would still be in school. Rett would not—"

"Wait a minute," said Jenny, coming to a halt. "You're feeling guilty about all this?"

Virginia's cheeks flushed. "Yes, I do. I never should have disobeyed my parents. None of us should have gone to the creek when we had been told not to. Then none of this would have happened."

"Don't be so . . . so thin-skinned, Virginia. Old folks are always saying don't have fun. If we listened to them all the time . . . I don't feel guilty."

"Perhaps you should."

"Don't think that you can hang all this on me, Virginia," Jenny said hotly.

Virginia shook her head slowly. "No . . . no, I'm just as guilty. I've already said that. I . . . I feel terrible that . . . that so many people have suffered because—"

"Hear that, Trina," Jenny said with another poke of her elbow. "Virginia feels guilty. I didn't think church folks were supposed to feel that way. Didn't they say the other night that God takes care of all that stuff?"

Trina, who had been silent through the whole exchange, remained so.

"God has forgiven me, even though I don't deserve it," Virginia went on, her voice now soft and controlled, "but that hasn't eased the hurt of the Crells or the wrongful suffering of Rett Marshall."

"What's the theft got to do with the creek thing?"

"I'm not sure," admitted Virginia, "but I think there's some connection."

Jenny lifted her hands and went through an elaborate washing mime. "Well, I guess no harm has been done to Loony Marshall. Saw him out wandering again the other day."

Virginia said nothing.

"Your pa got him off?"

"He's . . . he's not off, exactly. He's just out until . . . the trial."

"Then he'll be locked up for good," pronounced Jenny, showing no feeling at all for the man.

"Maybe not," said Virginia with more confidence than she felt. "Papa says there really isn't much evidence against him."

"The stolen goodies were found right there in his drawer." Jenny used some of her nasty words. "What more evidence does one need?"

"Anyone could have put them there," said Virginia.

Jenny whirled around. "What do you mean? Anyone? Only the cleaning staff gets to go in there. And then you are given strict orders—just get in and get out."

Virginia turned to Jenny, a frown on her face.

"What do you mean?"

"Just change the bed, sweep up the floor, put the clean clothes in the drawer, and take out the dirty stuff—then get out. At least he doesn't have clutter to make the job tough like old Mrs. Hanson."

Virginia was still frowning.

"How do you know all this?"

Jenny waved an impatient hand in the air and uttered another one of her vulgar words. "I worked there for the whole summer," she exclaimed impatiently. "Guess I oughta know."

"Papa, I need to talk with you."

Virginia had not waited for her father to come home from the office but had gone round to see him after school. All the previous night she had battled with what to do about the conversation with Jenny of the day before. She still wasn't sure how it should be handled, but she knew she had to talk with her father. Leave the decision to him.

"Come in," he welcomed her. "Shut the door."

Virginia stepped into the office and closed the door behind her. At her father's nod she took the chair that faced his desk and knotted trembling hands in her lap.

Her father sat back and waited.

"It's Jenny. Something she said yesterday. I . . . I don't know what it means—if it means anything—but she worked all summer for Mrs. Kruz at the boardinghouse."

Her father still waited quietly, his face showing no change of emotion. Sometimes Virginia felt impatient at his patience.

"Don't you see? She cleaned Rett's room. She was in there."

Her father studied her face intently. He seemed to know just how much those few short words had cost her. To think that Jenny had—perhaps—caused such pain, for whatever reason, was hard to accept.

"Virginia," he said, leaning across the desk toward her. "Thank you for sharing this difficult fact. I know it's been . . . unpleasant for you." He hesitated. "But remember, no one is guilty until proven guilty. Because Jenny had access to Rett's room proves nothing. Now we are working with circumstances. What would be the motive? What could she possibly gain? Why would she do such a thing?"

"She doesn't like him," Virginia said, her chin trembling.

"That's not a very good reason."

"She knows I do."

It was a fact. Virginia had to face it.

"Surely . . . she . . ."

"She might. Jenny is . . . is very mixed-up, I think. Her mother leaving and her father being cruel, I don't think Jenny knows how to love. Just how to . . . to manipulate."

Her father sat quietly, shaking his head. "If—and I say *if*, Virginia—if this proves to be true, then Jenny needs us more than ever."

It was true. But how could one help a person like Jenny? Virginia was wondering.

"We'll just have to keep praying," said her father. "In fact, we'll have to increase our praying."

Virginia nodded silently.

"And, Virginia," his voice went on, "please, don't try to force something here. Please. Be patient. This will be properly investigated. We'll do a thorough check. This could be another dead end. Jenny could be perfectly innocent—I pray she is. But it will be checked. I promise you that. But, Virginia, let God work it out—in His own time. He will. I have every confidence that He will."

Virginia hung her head. She still wasn't quite sure that her father's way worked. At least it didn't seem to work very fast.

CHAPTER 22

It was difficult for Virginia to keep her impatience in check. Her human side insisted that she should be doing something about the situation beyond simply praying. She wasn't sure what that something should be, or she may have yielded to temptation and tried to accomplish it. Every night she asked her father about the progress of the investigation, and every night he gave her an answer that somehow satisfied her without giving her any specific information. He was good at that, she admitted. Perhaps that was one of the characteristics that made him a good attorney.

Jenny did not seem to be aware of the dark cloud that hung over her head. She tossed it in the same fashion, flipping her mane of gold-red tresses. She continued the friendship with Trina, but Trina did not seem quite as spellbound as she once had.

Whether Jenny felt threatened by that or not, Virginia could not tell. She did seem upset that Georgie was now making friends with some of the boys from the church. Virginia heard whispers of "traitor" and "turncoat," but there seemed to be no open declaration of war on him.

One had only to look at Georgie to know there had been a change in his life. He looked so much more at peace with himself now that he had found peace with his God. He settled down, not feeling the need to be the constant class clown, putting down others in order to get a laugh. The change was so dramatic that even the schoolteachers noticed it.

The trial for Rett Marshall had been set for the first week in December. Virginia fidgeted and fumed as she saw the date draw closer and closer. For now, the man was enjoying his freedom. Each morning he pulled on his warm jacket against the chill of the winter wind to strike off into the forest of bare-limbed trees, seeking solace in the only way that he knew how—communing with nature. Whenever Virginia saw him she waved to him, and he responded with a jerky wave of his own and a broad, acknowledging smile. It tore at her heart to think that these might be the last days of freedom for this man who would never knowingly harm anyone or anything.

"We've come up empty," her father admitted as he lowered himself onto a kitchen chair. Virginia saw his hand rub the back of his neck, as though the tension had built there over the difficult days of searching for answers.

She tried to keep her voice patient and even, so as not to bring further agitation to her father, but her emotion was evident in each word that spilled out.

"What do you mean? Empty? Surely you have found something . . . something to indicate . . . she was there."

What was worse? Virginia heard her heart cry. *To condemn Rett—or Jenny?*

But she pressed on. "Did the sheriff talk to the landlady?"

"Yes, of course."

"And what did she say? Didn't she tell him that Jenny worked for her over the summer?"

"She did. Each Monday washday and some Wednesdays and Saturday afternoons."

"So—?"

"So that proves nothing. She said Jenny seemed very reliable and honest."

But she can't be, Virginia wanted to cry. *It had to be her who set up Rett*.

"We asked if anyone else had access to the rooms. She said no."

"See!" said Virginia.

"Virginia—just because one had access to the room does not make one guilty of a crime."

"I . . . I know that. But if it wasn't Jenny, who was it?"

"Maybe it *was* Rett."

"Papa!"

"Maybe he doesn't realize the consequences of what he's doing." Her father's voice sounded very tired. "There have been another three items reported missing."

"When?"

"Within the last week." He smiled. "You'll never believe this, but one of them was a checkerboard."

"A checkerboard? Now that should prove it. What ever would Rett do with the checkerboard?"

The smile disappeared. "Maybe the same thing he'd do with a crescent wrench. Look, Virginia, the stolen things do not make sense. There is no logical pattern. They seem—well, random. A few pieces of jewelry, some tools, a kitchen gadget or two, the checkerboard, a jackknife, even a child's toy. It doesn't make much sense. That's why the sheriff thinks that Rett really did do it."

"The sheriff thinks that?"

"Well, if one is honest, there hasn't really been any good reason to think otherwise."

Virginia felt a sadness fill her heart. Her father was right, of course. Even though she had fought against it, it seemed that it was so. Rett had been pilfering throughout the entire town.

"He's going to hate it—prison," said Virginia forlornly.

"We'll just have to pray. . . ."

But Virginia did not hear the rest of her father's statement. She had heard it often enough—she had been praying. And it had really done little good.

Virginia had never gone to a court session before, even though her father was the one defending most of the local clients. Usually his practice consisted of out-of-court claims. Little land disputes. Arranging of legal titles. Drawing up wills or settling family estates. But this was to be a full-blown court hearing. A man came from the city to act as judge. All of the evidence was to be placed before the court. Virginia, though she was reluctant to see poor Rett in such circumstances, could not keep herself away.

The case seemed to draw the interest of the entire town. Even though Virginia arrived early, she had a hard time finding a place to sit. Two of the town's merchants moved over, and she wedged herself on the bench between them. She felt hardly able to breathe, but it was the only spot she could find.

Rett Marshall sat beside her father, head down and hands twisting nervously. Virginia was sure he had no idea what was going on around him. At the front of the room, at a simple borrowed table, a black-robed man with a stern face and white chin whiskers sat, a strange-looking hammer in his hand.

To the side sat the town sheriff, sweating profusely in spite of the wind-chilled day, his hankie continually in use to wipe at his brow. For the first time, Virginia felt sorry for the man. He was only trying to do his job. He took no pleasure in condemning a local citizen to be locked away—whether in a jail cell or an asylum room.

Across the table in front of the judge was a line-up of

items. Virginia knew without asking that these were the things Rett Marshall was accused of stealing from neighbors.

The judge smacked his hammer, and the people stood. Virginia stood with them and wondered fleetingly if there would still be room on the bench when she went to sit back down.

After the judge had made his charge before those in attendance, they were allowed to reclaim their seats. Virginia pushed herself in again, an elbow nearly in her face.

At last the proceedings began.

The sheriff was the first to speak. He laid before the people the charges against the defendant, naming item by item on the table and telling the court where they had been found.

"The pin," cut in Mrs. Parker, unaware that observers are to be quiet in court. "I don't see my red pin."

The sheriff mopped his brow again and admitted that the pin in question had not as yet been found.

Mrs. Parker began to mumble in protest, but the judge whacked his hammer on the table and called for silence.

The sheriff went on. "There isn't much more I can say," he said, "except the law has done all it could to make sure that the accused is not presented erroneously. I have followed every lead given in the case and have found no evidence to the contrary."

He sat down and rubbed the sodden hankie over his flushed face.

The judge called on the defense.

"Your Honor," began Virginia's father as he rose to face the judge. "We wish to beg the court's indulgence as we present to the people the evidence in this case." He turned toward the sheriff. "Our good sheriff has done his job thoroughly, having few leads to follow. But we wish to submit that, contrary to the accusations against my client, the stealing of property is not in keeping with the character of the defendant."

Character witnesses were called, Pastor Doyle being the first of them.

"Do you know the defendant?"

"I do."

"How long have you known him?"

"Twelve years."

"Have you ever known him to be guilty of an offense against another?"

"Never."

"What kind of person would you describe him to be?"

Hesitation followed as the question was carefully considered.

"He is a free spirit—a soul who wanders the out-of-doors and lives there with the creatures that inhabit it. His one and only love is all things that have been made by the Creator. Material possessions seem of little worth to him."

"Knowing the man as you do, do you think him capable of committing this deed? Theft?"

A long, aching silence. Pastor Doyle raised his head. His eyes were clear, but filled with compassion. "Sir," he said, his voice ringing over the packed assembly, "I have lived and ministered for many years. Long enough to know that I cannot judge what is in the heart of another. Men have let me down. Brought deep disappointment and sorrow to my soul. Others have amazed and thrilled me with the depth of their valor and unselfishness. Only God can truly know the heart of a man. But with God as my witness, if this man has done as charged, I will be shocked and deeply saddened. I would not have thought him capable of such a deed."

Virginia felt the tears forming in her eyes and brushed at them with her sleeve. She was packed in too tightly to be able to reach her pocket handkerchief.

The pastor was allowed to step down, and other witnesses were called. They all expressed the same sentiments, though not as eloquently as the pastor.

"I call Clark Davis to the stand," announced her father, and Virginia heard the familiar uneven step as her grandfather moved forward. She wanted to turn her head to look at him, but she could not see past the jacket of Mr. Lougin.

The same procedure was followed, and her grandfather took the chair beside the wooden table.

"Do you know the defendant?"

"I do."

"How long have you known him?"

"Since his birth—and his parents before him."

"So you would say that you know him well?"

"'Bout as good as one man can know another."

"We have heard that the defendant is a lover of the outdoors."

"Thet's true."

"So true that he rarely spends time in his room at the boardinghouse."

"Correct."

"In fact, he rarely spends time in town at all."

"Correct agin."

"Have you ever seen him loitering about the streets?"

"No. He lives in the boardin' house right at the edge of town. He strikes out right from there, gittin' away from buildin's as quick-like as he can."

"If he doesn't care for town, why is he living in town?"

"He was born and raised on the farm. Lived there most his life. His mama died several years back, but his pa and him still kept to the farm.

"But his pa learned thet he was sick—heart trouble. My son, Dr. Luke Davis, told him he didn't have long to live. He came to us then. Told us his story. He was right broken up over it. Wondered what he'd ever do with his boy."

"Go on."

"Well, my wife and me we talked and prayed about it and went over to see Cam—thet's his pa—and told him we'd keep the boy fer as long as we'd be able.

"But he already had another plan. He said he was sellin' the farm and movin' to the boardin' house. Then when he was gone, Rett would still be cared for. Have his meals and git his clothes washed and all."

"And they did that?"

"They did."

"How did Rett Marshall adjust to town life?"

"First it troubled him. He was agitated 'bout it. So his pa made arrangements for the lady of the boardin' house to fix his lunch and send him off. He was better then. Long as he can roam about freely he's happy enough."

"So the boardinghouse is where Rett has lived ever since he lost his father?"

"It is. Least he spends the nights there. He don't stay around in the daytime. Summer or winter, spring or fall, he takes his lunch and goes off."

"When he leaves in the morning he heads straight out of town?"

"He does. Anyone can tell you thet. We've all seed it."

"What about when he comes in at night? Does he go through the streets of town then?"

"No sir. He heads straight to his room agin—after putting his friend in the cage in the backyard."

"His friend?"

"The crow. Rett never goes anyplace without his crow."

A ripple of quiet laughter spread through the filled room.

"Thank you, Mr. Davis. You may step down."

Virginia managed to catch her grandfather's eye. He

had done a good job on behalf of Rett. She prayed it might be good enough to convince the judge.

"I call Sheriff Brown to the stand."

Virginia blinked. What was her father doing? The sheriff had already as good as said that he believed Rett Marshall was guilty as charged. After the taking of the oath again, the sheriff lowered himself to the chair and began mopping in earnest.

"Sheriff Brown, you have been in charge of this case from the beginning, have you not?"

"I have." The sheriff's voice was so husky he could hardly be heard.

"And after investigating all of the evidence, you have charged the defendant with possession of stolen property. Is that right?"

The sheriff nodded, then was asked by the judge to give an oral response.

"I did." He nearly choked on the words.

"On what did you base your decision?"

The sheriff fidgeted nervously. The handkerchief was far too wet to do much good. "The evidence."

"And the evidence was?"

"The stolen goods. We found all of it—" He cast a quick glance in Mrs. Parker's direction. "Almost all of it," he amended, "in Rett's—the defendant's possession."

"On his person?"

"No. In his room."

"Where in his room?"

The sheriff looked even more agitated.

"Confound it, Drew—"

The judge's hammer rapped sharply, and the sheriff squirmed on his seat.

He mopped his brow again and spoke slowly. "Like I told you before, we found the stolen property in the room of Rett Marshall, in his top drawer, under a pile of socks and underwear."

"Thank you. Were there any other personal items in the drawer?"

"What do you mean?"

"Any razor or pictures or mementoes of any kind?"

"No."

"You're sure?"

"I'm sure. Nothing else. Just the clothing items and the stolen goods."

"Did you happen to notice if there were any such personal items anywhere else in the room?"

"I didn't see any."

"Nothing? No books or games or tools or souvenirs?"

"I didn't see any."

"Did you check the room thoroughly?"

"Of course."

"And you didn't see any?"

"No."

"Might that indicate that the defendant, Rett Marshall, is not interested in such items?"

"It could."

Virginia's father stopped and allowed the sheriff time to pass the limp piece of cloth over his cheeks and jowls.

"Was there anyone else who had access to the defendant's room?"

"Like—?"

"Anyone? Could anyone have entered through a window, for instance?"

"No, I checked the window. The screen was nailed firm and it hadn't been tampered with."

"What about the door? Could anyone have come through the door?"

The sheriff hesitated. "Could have," he admitted at last.

"So all you really know for sure, Sheriff Brown, is that the stolen items were found in Rett Marshall's room. You agree that other people had access to that room. Rett Marshall was gone from that room, day after day, from early morning to late at night. Correct?"

The sheriff nodded, then quickly caught himself and answered aloud, "That's correct."

"Did anyone—anyone at all, during your careful and thorough investigation—say that they had seen Rett Marshall place those stolen items in that top drawer?"

Weakly, "No."

"Did anyone say that they had ever seen Rett Marshall with those items on his person or in his hand?"

"No."

"Did anyone say that they had ever seen Rett Marshall around those houses from which the items disappeared?"

The sheriff blew out puffed cheeks as though trying to cool himself.

"No."

"Then how do we know, Sheriff Brown, that it was Rett Marshall who placed the stolen items in that drawer?"

There was no answer. Virginia held her breath.

CHAPTER 23

"You were wonderful, Papa," Virginia exclaimed as soon as her father came in the door.

He placed a leather satchel on the table and sank to a chair. "I don't feel wonderful."

Virginia's eyes widened.

"You've won the case—I'm sure you have. The judge—"

"The judge is known to be a man who sees things his own way. He does not like defense lawyers, and he does not bring in his verdict until tomorrow. No one knows how he will rule."

"But you showed—"

"I also put a very good friend in a difficult position. Ross Brown and I have worked together ever since I came to town."

He sounded very tired. Very distraught.

Virginia had only thought of winning.

"Well, Sheriff Brown will not be called on to go to jail," she reminded her father. "That's what would happen to Rett had you not defended him so expertly."

She thought the words would make him feel better. Less guilty. But he seemed not to hear them.

"Folks in this town have had high regard for Sheriff

Brown because he has earned it through the years. If what I have done today destroys any of that, then we are all losers."

"But surely folks—"

"People can be strange, Virginia. Fickle. They too easily forget all the good one has done if they think you have made a mistake. Ross didn't make any mistakes, but I can't stand up and tell folks that. He was thorough and careful, and he hated this whole process just as much as I did."

Some of the excitement drained from Virginia. Perhaps they had not won a victory, after all.

Virginia made sure she was at the school building, converted to courtroom, early the next day. The crowd would be back. Everyone was buzzing about the verdict. People were taking sides. For and against. Trying to outguess one another as to the judge's decision. Virginia prayed it would be in Rett's favor, then realized that if so, their dilemma would not have been solved. If Rett had not committed the crimes, then who had? Were they right back to Jenny again?

"All rise."

The judge entered and set his sheaf of notes on the desk in front of him. He cleared his throat and paused. Virginia thought he enjoyed having the whole, tense group in his full control.

"Well, this has been a . . . a difficult case. I have pondered it carefully . . . for half the night."

Virginia cringed. Local gossip had it that the judge had spent the entire evening playing poker at the town's only saloon.

"It seems like Sheriff Brown has done a commendable

job in his pursuit of justice. He has investigated carefully all aspects of this case and would not have had this matter brought to trial had he not felt that it was warranted.

"The defendant, Mr. Rett Marshall, is not able to speak for himself. The character witnesses have brought a good report—perhaps too good—making me ask the question, 'Can anyone really be that sure of another?' Like the parson said, 'We cannot know another man's heart.'

"The defense council—" the judge stopped and fixed Virginia's father with a cold stare, "is skilled with words. But is that what this trial is all about? Who is the best orator? I think not.

"As I said, my evening—and yes, well into the night—was devoted to working though this case, and I am prepared to hand down my decision."

He cleared his throat again.

"In the case of the State versus Mr. Rett Marshall—"

"Wait!"

It was more a screech than a call. It made Virginia's spine tingle. Who had been so bold as to interrupt such a solemn occasion? But she could not see for the press of bodies.

She could hear the commotion. Someone was moving forward, loud sobs coming from the very depths of an anguished soul.

"I can't stand it anymore. I can't," the person was crying. Virginia shifted in her seat and saw Mrs. Kruz, the landlady, as she turned to face the crowd, her hat askew, her face crumpled in torment as the tears streamed down her face. "I did it. I did it. I had to. He made me."

Virginia took one look at the distraught woman and felt a little shiver pass through her entire body. It was one of both sorrow for what she saw and relief for what she instantly understood. It wasn't Rett. And it wasn't Jenny. Thank God.

"Then what happened?"

Virginia was reliving the entire trial for Jamison on the way home from school. At times she was so animated she had to stop and look up at him, her eyes, her face, her hands all beseeching him to see and feel what she had seen and felt in the makeshift courtroom.

"Everyone was stunned. Just stunned. There she stood—shaking—sobbing—crying out that she was the one who had stolen the items. Placed the things in Rett's room. I think most folks would have dismissed her even at that point. Silly, isn't it, but there was this feeling that no, it can't be you, you must be mistaken.

"And then she slowly lifted up her shaking hand and gradually uncurled her fingers and there—right in the palm—was Mrs. Parker's pin. Well, that set Mrs. Parker off, you can be sure of that. I heard her all the way to the front of the room. Then I . . . I just felt a tremble go through the whole gathering.

"Someone asked for a glass of water to be brought. The woman was so beside herself that folks feared she might faint. My papa brought her a chair, and they sat her down—told her that she didn't have to say any more, but she almost pushed them away—sort of flayed out at them.

" 'I want to say it all,' she cried. 'I can't live with it anymore.'

"The room quieted down and folks sort of leaned forward to listen.

" 'He made me do it,' she said again, and no one understood who *he* was.

"The judge looked over and nodded to my father and said in a funny-sounding voice, as though he was totally thrown off by it all and calling for help, 'Counselor?'

"My father stepped forward. He first tried to calm her

some. Then he slowly began to question her. And she poured out the whole story.

"There is this man—Jenks is his name. Maybe you've seen him around town. He's . . . rather . . . greasy looking and has these strange, shifty eyes. He lives at the boardinghouse and some way or another Mrs. Kruz owes him a large sum of money. Some old debt of her husband's—from the past. She didn't reveal all that, and my papa didn't ask her to.

"Well, he—this Jenks—was pushing pretty hard for payment—and the poor woman had no way to get the money. She was desperate. Then—when the accident happened, she got to thinking about Rett. Folks were already talking. Blaming him for things he didn't do.

"She let it go for quite a while, pushing the idea away, but then the man kept on tormenting her, and she kept mulling it over and over. Finally she decided to do it. She stole the first thing and hid it in Rett's drawer. But the sheriff didn't look for it there. He never really thought that Rett had done it. At least, at first.

"So she had to keep on and on. Taking little things. Pushing them in among Rett's clothing. Rett never found them. He never even bothered to open the drawer himself. But when she took the pin—intending to do the same with it—she thought it so pretty that she couldn't give it up. She hid it in her own drawer and just went in and admired it from time to time. She didn't use it as part of her trap to catch Rett."

"But *why*?" Jamison could not resist interrupting, his voice incredulous. "How could framing an innocent man help the woman with her debt?"

"That was what we were all asking ourselves. Why? What possible good for her could come from framing Rett? My papa asked her. What was her purpose? How would this act help her cause? And then it came out. Before his death, Rett's father, Cam Marshall, had set up a trust. Mrs. Kruz was to take out the monthly funds for caring for Rett as long as he lived with her. When those funds were no longer needed, she was to have whatever remained."

Jamison stopped dead still, his eyes on Virginia's face. "No!"

"Yes," she replied, her body trembling with intensity. "She said with Rett sent away to an asylum—that's what she figured would happen with him—that Rett would be given proper care, and she would have full and rightful—in her mind, at any rate—access to all of the remaining funds. She could pay the man off and still have money left for herself."

"It's unbelievable!" said Jamison.

"I think that's the way we all felt. She was going to move away. Take the rest of the money and move away somewhere and start over, she said. Just . . . just put the whole thing behind her."

They began walking again, their footsteps slowly leading them toward the Simpson household.

"Well, it nearly worked."

Virginia shivered. "It would have, had she not had a conscience."

"A conscience? I bet God just kept hammering away at her, didn't He?"

Virginia had not thought to bring God into the picture. But it was true. Her father had been right all along. Prayer had worked.

Virginia nodded slowly. "But I feel so, so sorry for the poor thing. You should have seen her. It was . . . was heartbreaking."

"Will she be sentenced?"

"I'm sure she will, though Papa will plead for leniency."

"What about the—this other fellow? Was he in on it?"

"Oh, yes. He knew of the trust. He was the one who

pushed Mrs. Kruz to take advantage of it. The sheriff has already gone to bring him in for questioning."

A silence hung between them, relaxing the excited tension of a moment before.

"You know . . ." admitted Virginia with a self-condemning tone. "I had convinced myself that it was Jenny."

"Jenny?" He waited for her to go on.

"She . . . she was always so—I don't know—anxious to heckle me about Rett. To insist . . . And she did work for Mrs. Kruz over the summer."

"She just likes to torment you. See the fire in your eyes."

"Do you think so?"

He nodded. "I don't think that Jenny understands—really understands—any other emotion than . . . than frustration and . . . and anger. That's the only way she knows how to . . . to relate to people. It's all she has ever learned."

Was it true? Yes—perhaps it was. If so, she had truly failed her friend. She had never succeeded in showing Jenny anything else. She had always been on the defensive. Fighting back. Holding herself apart. No wonder Jenny had found her Christian faith confusing. No wonder she had wanted no part of it.

Virginia felt tears sting her eyes. Her thoughts went back to the scene in the courtroom. Her father had extended a hand and, by the look on his face, an unspoken apology to the local sheriff. The man had taken the outstretched hand, and the two had stood, actions and eyes expressing to the entire gathering that there were no hard feelings between them.

"I've got to try again," Virginia said, and the words were spoken softly, more to herself than to Jamison.

"We will."

Virginia blinked away the tears and looked up at him.

It was so nice to have Jamison as a friend. Sort of like a team. She managed a smile, the tears still glistening on her lashes.

"We'll start by praying," Jamison said. "That seems to get the most done." He grinned at her, and she chuckled softly. It was a bit of shared humor, but a reality all the same.

Jamison shifted the books he was carrying to the other arm. She felt fingers reach—rather tentatively—for her own. She did not pull away. Shyly—yet with certainty—she curled her hand about his and felt his grip tighten in response. Perhaps it wouldn't hurt to be—*special* friends.

They were almost home when Virginia saw Mr. Adamson lift his head above the wooden pickets of his fence and squint to look down the sidewalk. When he saw Virginia, his wrinkled face lit with a broad smile.

He seemed to take in the situation with one sweeping glance, then lifted his hat and scratched his graying hair with fingers dirtied with garden soil. The gap-toothed smile on his face widened, but he said not a word. Just watched Virginia and her friend walk dreamily down the sidewalk toward her home.

His eyes twinkled.